Kristine, Finding Home

Norway to America

Aleta Chossek

www.ten16press.com - Waukesha, WI

Kristine, Finding Home: Norway to America
Copyrighted © 2019 Aleta Chossek
ISBN 978-1-64538-096-2
First Edition

Kristine, Finding Home: Norway to America
by Aleta Chossek

For information, please contact:

www.ten16press.com
Waukesha, WI

Cover design by Tom Heffron

"Chapter 6: New Life" was previously published in *Family Stories from the Attic*, edited by Christi Craig and Lisa Rivero (Hidden Timber Books, 2017).

Praise for *Kristine, Finding Home*

"There are books you can nestle into and feel like part of the family. *Kristine, Finding Home* is one of those. From beginning to end, I was Kristine's little sister, listening to her, admiring her, sticking up for her at each turn of her fascinating life. From Norway to Illinois, Kristine's story captivates. It is a pleasure to read."

– Judy Bridges, author of *Shut Up & Write!*

"*Kristine, Finding Home* is a story about resilience and dignity in the face of monumental life challenges. Immigration, the Great Depression, and assimilation compelled Kristine and Fredrik to cherish Norwegian culture while ultimately embracing American citizenship and all that it offered. An entertaining and inspiring read."

– Richard Staff, RN, MSW, Norwegian American Musician

"I have heard stories about Kristine and her journey to the United States since I was a child, and my grandmother told me stories of her aunt who had left Førde to join Fredrik in the U.S. Human migration is not a new thing. This story that started more than 100 years ago in Norway might not be that different from the stories we see on the news every night."

– Olaug Marie Reiakvam, MD, Oslo, Norway

The stories in *Kristine, Finding Home* are dedicated to Kristine's descendants, especially the fourth generation, including Samantha, Emilia, Riley, and Garrett. May you be inspired by these stories to be people of courage, strength and love.

Acknowledgements

This book gets its life from the translated letters collected from trunks and boxes of the sons and daughters of Kristine and Fredrik Hjelmeland's family in Norway, and from papers and photos of the family of Odny Hjelmeland Reckling and Ruth Hjelmeland Monson. Ruth Monson is particularly important for her meticulous and loving treatment of these materials. She had two volumes of letters translated and has organized and documented thousands of photos.

Thank you to John Monson, Kristine Monson Wilkie, Martha Monson Lowe and Thomas Monson for full access to and release of Ruth's private collection.

Thank you to the family of Odny Hjelmeland Reckling for permission to use her writings and photos from the family archives of Aleta Reckling Chossek, Fredrik W. Reckling, Kristine Reckling Clemens, Mark R. Reckling and Petrina Reckling Gillman.

Norwegian family including but not limited to the family of Olav Reiakvam, Svein Kristiansen, Signe Bruland, Kirsten Rygg, Gerd Buhaug and Ragnhild Bustnes participated in asking questions, sharing letters, pictures and memories.

Without the encouragement of Judy Bridges of Redbird Studio and Kim Suhr of Red Oak Writing and the marvelous writers they assemble, my humble stories would not be the narrative it is.

I would like to acknowledge by name, all the people who have helped and encouraged me along the way, but that could become its own book length manuscript. If you are reading this, know that I am grateful and do not take any of your interest or support for granted.

My most profound thanks and deepest love goes to my family especially to my husband Walt Chossek for believing in me and encouraging me when I was in front of my computer instead of with them or off to find one more letter, fact or picture.

Finally, to Kristine Kristiansen Hjelmeland and her sisters in courage who leave one homeland in search of a better life and make the new homeland their home.

For all your life lessons, Grandmother, thank you.

Table of Contents

Foreword

As told at family gatherings, Kristine Kristiansen was eighteen years old in 1910 when Fredrik Olav Hjelmeland asked her to marry him and she accepted over the objections of her parents. Before they could marry, Fredrik had some business to do in America. He anticipated being gone two years. Kristine waited.

The story in this book begins in Førde, Norway, with a letter to Kristine from Fredrik. She's now twenty-six and he hasn't returned for her yet. What has she been up to? What happens between 1918 and 1940 in Waukegan, Illinois? Read and find out.

Joan Didion wrote, "We tell ourselves stories in order to live." My hope is that in reading this book, you will recognize in Kristine´s courage, her grace, her kind sense of humor, her loving spirit, your own unique personhood, shaped not just by DNA but by story.

Kristiansen family in front of home, Førde, Norway, 1907.

Kristine with baby Anna and nephew Alf, Førde, Norway, 1908.

Chapter One

Everyday Dreams

Norway, 1918

Kristine Kristiansen Hjelmeland, St. Olaf College report, as told to her daughter, Odny, 1943:

In the same year that I was confirmed (1907), Fredrik Hjelmeland came to work in a store for Nicolai Andersen. It was at this time I became well acquainted with him. Three years later just before he left for America, we were engaged. He planned to come back in two years but time went on and it was thirteen years before he returned to Norway. Fredrik wanted me to come to America and get married, but my parents wanted the marriage to take place in Norway."

Kristine stood in the parlor after lunch, waiting for *Far* (father) and her brother Karl to settle themselves in their chairs. Her father had said they needed to have a conversation, but she could not think of anything they couldn't have talked over during *middag*, dinner. *Far* was too kind to allow any talk that would upset her delicate mother, but what would that be? It had been months since her sister-in-law had died giving birth to baby Anna. There had been many sad, private conversations then, but not recently. Their pipes lit, *Far* and Karl seemed relaxed. Looking down, she laced and unlaced her fingers. She did not know why, but she felt like crying.

As if from a distance, she heard her father clear his throat. "Kristine, Karl and I have been discussing the situation here. You have been very good with his children. Sometimes Alf and baby Anna almost seem to think you are their mother." He paused and waited.

Kristine remained silent. Smoothing back a wave of brown hair that had escaped her hairpins, she felt the warmth creep up the back of her neck.

Karl filled the silence with his deep voice. "Yes, you have done a good job with my motherless children. I can see that our mother is too old to take care of them by herself." He went on detailing how much their mother depended on Kristine, his children's need for her, the flaws in her plans to leave for a seamstress job in Bergen.

Anxiety turned to anger as her cheeks grew red. Still, she did not look at the men. Why was he talking about her job, her chance for a different life? On one level she knew Karl was right. Why did she want to leave? She was needed, loved and comfortable. And yet, she was twenty-six years old and had never been on her own, had lived her entire life with her parents. Was it so wrong to want something more? Her feelings swirled around.

"So, we have made a decision," Karl said and looked toward their father as if to say it was his turn to speak.

Her father delivered their news. She would not take the seamstress job in Bergen and move in with cousins there. She was to stay home and help. They had already written her cousins that she would not be coming. She must write to *Fru* (Mrs.) Severson that she would not be sewing for them.

At that, she raised her head and locked eyes with her father. The terrible decision, made without her, blotted out the sadness she saw on his face. Feeling as if she would cry or explode, she pivoted, turning her back to her father and brother. Striding from the parlor, she headed out, grabbing her shawl as she let the door bang shut behind her.

Once out on the dirt lane in front of their home, she walked to the right and soon was on the bridge over the river that flowed into the Førdefjord. The river divided the town between the older settlement and newer shops. Many businesses, including her brother Alfred's new dry goods shop, were on the south side of the river right along the road that led to the ferry. Travelers used this road if they were headed all the way to Bergen. At the middle of the bridge she paused, shaking so hard she felt weak and unsteady. Listening to the water tumble toward the ocean steadied her enough to figure out where to go.

She did not even pause outside Alfred's shop. He, like their father, lived with his family adjacent to the business. If her problem had not been the men in the family, she would have stopped to talk with Alfred's Anna, her sister-in-law, who had been her friend longer than she had been her brother's wife. In *husmorskole* (homemakers school) together they had competed for honors and speculated about who would become a housekeeper in a rich person's home and who would marry well. Anna lived the expected life: confirmation, homemaker's school, marriage, and motherhood. She had gone directly from *husmorskole* into marriage with Alfred. She might not understand.

Kristine kept walking. She pulled her shawl closer around her shoulders. A light mist had begun to fall. When she arrived at Kvål Bakery, she peered through the steam-covered window to see if Astrid was working the counter. Spying an angular figure bending over the bread case, Kristine opened the door and stepped into the warm, moist air of the town bakery. The sweet smell of almond cake layered with yeasty breads enveloped and comforted her.

"*God dag* (Good day). Oh, it is you, Kristine," Astrid said with a smile as she straightened and saw her friend.

Kristine tried to smile but felt her upper lip quiver. She did not trust herself to say anything in front of the single customer who was waiting for a loaf of *rugbrød* (rye bread) to be wrapped. Instead, she nodded and stepped to the side, hoping she looked like she was just waiting her turn.

As soon as the customer left, Astrid hurried around the counter, locked the door, and flipped over the Closed sign.

"Astrid, are you sure you can do that? I didn't think what time it was before I came."

"Ja, Kristine, you know that we close about now anyway. It's only old bachelors and lonely ladies who come after *middag* for bread."

Kristine began to cry in earnest. "Now I will be one of those lonely ladies."

Handing her a hankie, Astrid put an arm around Kristine's shaking shoulders and said as if to a child, "There, there, Kristine."

Then she went over to the counter and put some *boller* (golden rolls) on a small plate and said, "Take these upstairs. You can put on the water for tea and I'll join you after I finish closing up.

Kristine went up to the apartment that Astrid and her husband, the baker, shared. Still wiping her eyes and sighing, Kristine set the teakettle on the wood stove and began to put out cups, plates, sugar, and spoons. It was early in the afternoon for tea, but the familiar tasks calmed her. Astrid joined her, and soon they were settled at the small tea table in the sitting room.

"Now, what is this all about?" Astrid asked. "Is it your mother? Must she go to hospital?"

Kristine sat hunched over, folding Astrid's handkerchief into smaller and smaller squares.

"I think that it would be easier for me if I had to stay home because *Mor* (Mother) was that sick," Kristine nearly whispered, still not looking at Astrid.

"Stay at home? Aren't you going to Bergen?" Astrid asked.

"No, *Far* and Karl have decided. They even wrote our cousins." Kristine's voice shook.

"Decided? Decided what?" Astrid asked.

While she listened to Kristine tell of her meeting in the parlor with *Far* and Karl, Astrid sipped her tea, her brow furrowed.

"I'm so sorry, Kristine, you are such a good seamstress and you have dreamt of this chance to move to the city," Astrid said with a sympathetic note. "Do you think your mother will get strong enough by spring for you to leave?"

"*Nei*. I don't really believe that it is *Mor* who needs me. It's Karl. Since his Anna died, he doesn't do anything but work in the shop and go to church. He never pays any attention to the children. That's my job. He wouldn't know what to do if I wasn't there to take care of them."

Astrid poured fresh tea into the delicate cups. "And your father agrees with Karl?"

Kristine studied the pale amber tea. "He was just looking for a reason to keep me at home. I was surprised when he let me talk to the Seversons about being a seamstress. He probably never thought they would want a country girl sewing for their fashionable city shop. Now, that I was actually going to leave, Karl gave him the perfect plan."

"Kristine, you do work hard with the children and sewing for Karl's shop. What would they do without you?" Astrid asked.

"They would manage. Probably work my poor, weak mother to death. If I got married, they would have to figure something out." She was sarcastic with her childhood friend, more than she could ever be with her father. Kristine was realizing that the only way he would ever let her leave home was to get married. Right now that seemed to be as likely as moving to Bergen. She reached for a *boller* and broke off a bite of the buttery anise roll.

"Oh, have you heard from Fredrik? Is he coming home?" Astrid asked. She and Kristine entertained themselves speculating about her distant fiancé.

Kristine gulped, the bite of *boller* stuck in her throat. How to answer that? Her friend knew so much about her dreams for the future. She coughed, not sure if it was the words or the roll that choked her.

"*Ja,* I did get a letter from Fredrik last week. He didn't say anything about coming home. You know how it has been. Always next year. This time he did say if the war ends, his brother, Mikal, will come home and take over the family farm before Christmas."

Mikal, Fredrik's oldest brother, was in line to inherit the family farm, but he had been in America even longer than Fredrik.

"Did you hear that Martha Andersdotter got married?" Astrid giggled. "She didn't wait for Mikal."

"No, really? How did you hear that?" Kristine asked even though she knew the people talked all about their friends and neighbors when they waited their turn in the bakery. It was better than the post office for getting news.

Astrid laughed, relieved for the moment that Kristine had something else to think about. While the two friends finished their tea, they gossiped about unimportant things until Kristine was calm enough to go home. Astrid loaded Kristine with comforting hugs and extra *boller* for the children.

On the walk home, Kristine dawdled. She was thinking about Fredrik and his recent letter. Too proud, she had not told Astrid that the letters came less and less often. He wrote mostly about what he was doing and nothing about missing her or coming home. More and more he seemed like a dream. A dream she could pull out when she was frustrated or disappointed. She wasn't even sure that she could remember exactly what he looked like. Eight years was a long time. She had changed since she was eighteen. All his travel and work had probably changed him, too. The letters came from such strange-sounding places, Whitefish and Swift Current, sometimes a place she had heard of, Chicago. Still, at the end of this letter like all the rest, he said he would send a ticket if she would come and marry him there in America. Wouldn't he be surprised if she did?

Where was Saskatchewan? It seemed even farther away than Minnesota, where so many Norwegians now lived. Then there was Fredrik's work with electricity. No one in Førde had electricity. In Bergen she had seen electric lamps shining out of the lobbies of big hotels but not in people's houses. Did America really need something so new and so expensive? How would they live? The whole idea seemed impossible.

If her father couldn't even let her live in Bergen, how would he ever allow her to go to America? To marry a man who didn't own a farm or a shop and did work that was so risky? Since her sister Pauline died, *Far* hardly let Kristine leave home alone in town, as if she wasn't a grown woman. She wondered if he believed that by keeping her at home, he wouldn't lose another daughter.

When she reached home, she stood at the gate a moment and took a deep breath. *Dreams change before they die*, she thought. For now, Fredrik was too far away, and she had too many people to take care of to daydream about being a seamstress in Bergen or a wife in Saskatchewan. Opening the door, she heard baby Anna, awake from her nap and crying.

"*Tante* (Aunt), *Tante*, where were you?" Called Alf as he toddled toward her open arms.

Chapter Two

Ekte Norsk Wife

Førde, Norway, 1922

Fredrik Olaf Hjelmeland, Moose Jaw, Saskatchewan, Canada, letter to Kristine, December 10, 1922:

> *I have applied for a passport and hope to receive it sometime during the winter. I will come as soon as it arrives. When I am able to come, Kristine, will you marry me? I had hoped to be home for Christmas and ask you in person, but it has not been easy to break away. It has been many Christmases since I was home. We are not children anymore. It is not good for me to live alone, and they are treating you like a slave at home. You must decide soon, because I am coming as soon as I get my passport.*

Kristine touched the letter in her skirt pocket like a good luck charm. It was postmarked Moose Jaw, Canada. Fredrik must be working there again. She was glad that she had picked up the mail today instead of Father. When he picked up a letter from Fredrik, he always had something discouraging to say.

"*Tante, Tante,* are we going to Leidulf's today?" Little Anna asked. Kristine looked down at the four-year-old. Daydreaming about Fredrik, she had forgotten her companion and missed the path to her brother Alfred's house.

"Not today little one. Your grandmother needs us at home."

Kristine's mother had not recovered her strength since a bad cold had kept her in bed most of October. In addition to working in the shoe store and doing her seamstress work, Kristine now did all the cleaning and laundry at home. When her mother was well enough to cook, she still asked for help cooking *middag,* the hot meal of the day. Kristine spent any extra time working on the needlework and dress orders she had for Christmas. It would be hours before Kristine could go to her room to savor her letter from Fredrik in private.

Kristine had little Anna carry the kindling while she refilled the stove wood box. If it weren't for Elise sending cheese and eggs from the farm, she wouldn't have much to cook with. Karl had brought home fish from the fjord, so that and a few potatoes would have to be *middag* today.

Since it was December and rainy, the few hours of daylight they had were cloudy and dark. Her mood matched. After the bad harvest no one had money for Christmas gifts, which meant no one was buying new, handcrafted shoes. Even the factory-made shoes that Karl had introduced to the shop were not selling. What little business there was came from the brooms, paper, needles, and fabrics that Karl had added to the shop's stock. *Far* kept himself busy with cobbler repair work. She wondered if Fredrik had more bad news.

Hours later, after putting the children to bed and helping her mother upstairs, Kristine could finally read her letter. The thin blue paper shook in her hand as she read it again. Not believing her eyes, she studied the unromantic proposal. Would he really come? How many times had he said that he was coming only to disappoint her? He had actually applied for a Canadian passport. He must be a citizen there now. What should she write back? Alone in her room, she cried and laughed as excitement, fear, disbelief, and desire tangled in her heart. After she wrote Fredrik about her parents' ultimatum that they must marry in Norway, he had not written about marriage. Until now. Did he plan to marry and stay in Førde or go back to Canada? How confusing. Maybe she would have a home of her own one day. The hope that she had tamped down for so long now flamed. She took out her fountain pen and checked that it was filled with ink. She wanted to write while she had courage; besides, sleep would not come for some time yet.

"*Kjaere Fredrik, Gladelig Jul* (Dear Fredrik, Merry Christmas)…" Her pen flew across the page. "You have given me a wonderful Christmas gift to even think that you'll be home soon. Will you be staying? How are things in America? We are having hard times here. You may have heard from your family of the short summer and the poor potato and carrot crops. You must write more about your plans so that I can answer from my heart. If we marry, where will we live?" She would think about what to say to her father later.

Kristine Kristiansen, 1923.

On the third Christmas Day, December 27 in Norway, Karl took his children to their brother Alfred's, so Kristine was alone with her mother and father. The days between Christmas and New Year's were relaxed. People were trying out new Christmas skis and gathering with family and friends to eat Christmas cookies. She knew there was not a better time to tell her parents of the plans she and Fredrik were making.

"*Far*, I have had a letter from Fredrik. He is coming home in March for a visit. I am so happy I will see him again."

"Humph, he's coming back? Probably failed. You must not encourage him, Kristine, we cannot feed any more people in this family."

"I don't think he has failed at all. He is coming for a visit now because it is too cold for him to do construction or farm. His homestead in Canada is his now and he is a Canadian citizen."

"Kristine," *Far* chewed on his pipe before continuing, "He has been gone years and years. You were just a girl when he left. What interest does he have in you?"

She put down her knitting, picked up her mother's hand, and looked steadily at her father. "Fredrik has written to ask me to marry him while he is home. I told him I would but that I must first talk with you." Kristine's voice wavered. As much as she tried to sound firm, she only managed to plead. She rarely stood up to her father, even if she was thirty-one years old.

"You what? Have you no thought for your poor sick mother, or your niece and nephew? You've cared for them since they were born." Her father's genial blue eyes glinted with a steely anger.

Kristine's mother gasped and withdrew her hand to her lap.

Kristine felt her tremble at this anger-laden exchange between her youngest child and her husband.

"*Far,* Fredrik will not wait any longer. If I don't marry him now, when he is in Førde, I will live here, in this house, the rest of my life." Kristine choked out the words from her tears.

"Kristine, what nonsense are you talking? This is your home. Are you so unhappy? You don't really know Fredrik anymore. Where does he propose to live? Let him come buy a farm and then he can talk to me."

She took a deep breath. This part of the plan was the hardest for her but even harder to tell her father. *Far* didn't really know the Hjelmelands but had heard enough rumors about their farms and road building that he did not believe they should be trusted.

"Fredrik is not yet ready to stay here. He is coming so that we can get married and both go back to America, to his good-paying electrical work. He plans to start a business of his own instead of work for others. When we have saved enough, then we will return to Førde and buy a farm or set up a shop."

"No, those Hjelmelands are all good-for-nothings. I should never have let him even talk to you when you were so young and put these crazy ideas in your head. If you go there will be no one from your family to help you. You know that, don't you?"

"I am thirty-one years old and Fredrik is thirty-six. We cannot put this off any longer," she argued.

"What kind of man is he if he wasn't interested enough to come back for thirteen years?"

"*Far,* I am a grown woman. Don't you want me to have a chance at something better than just scraping by?" she said.

"No, you are still my daughter. I do not give my permission. He's not welcome in this house, and I will not talk of this anymore," he said turning his back to the women.

With a sob, Kristine ran from the room while her mother wept softly in her chair. Christmas was over for them.

In the months since then, true to his word, her father had not talked of the future with her. When she and her mother talked, it was more open, without rancor. Her mother acknowledged that Kristine deserved a home of her own but couldn't think of Karl's children if Kristine left. How would they manage without her to run the household? She, too, wondered what kind of man would keep Kristine waiting for so long.

Karl told her that neither mother nor father really believed that Fredrik would do as he had promised. Day after day they went about their lives as before. Mother seemed to grow weaker rather than stronger during the dark winter days.

Kristine could find no one among her family or friends who would encourage her hopes. Perversely, their fears made her more determined to accept Fredrik's proposals and plans. She carried her secret hope for a different life like an emergency satchel, there if she needed it, with light to find her way through the dark winter months.

The weeks passed until March when the sun finally came over the mountain for the first time in 1923. Maybe the bright day would help with *Far* and *Mor*. Today she had to tell them that Fredrik was actually in Norway. He would be in Førde by Sunday. He'd written that he had also sent a letter to her father, but her father had said nothing.

Once again, she confronted her father in the parlor after *middag*. His pipe smoke was so thick that she was breathing in little gasps. *"Far,* Fredrik has written," she paused for emphasis, "from Bergen."

"Ja, I am aware." Her father did not look up from his newspaper or say any more.

In a flare of anger, Kristine raised her voice, "Fine, then you need to know I am preparing to see him."

Her father considered her as if she were a stranger, holding her gaze for a moment before nodding and returning to his paper.

Dismissed, Kristine retreated to the kitchen, where she nursed her hurt feelings and cleaned up from *middag*.

On Sunday, when Fredrik arrived in time to walk her to church. Kristine's father met him at the door. Waiting upstairs, Kristine listened in suspense. Would *Far* send Fredrik away?

"God dag, Herr Kristiansen, takk for sist (Hello, Mr. Kristiansen, good to see you again). How are you and your family?" She heard Fredrik say, thinking he would be reaching out to shake hands.

"Ja, we are fine and you, Fredrik? It has been many years." To Kristine, her father sounded wary of the man in his doorway.

"May I walk with you and Kristine to church?"

"Of course, of course. Then we will have Sunday dinner and talk about your letter."

From the top of the stairs, Kristine could hear her father's grudging respect as he continued to question Fredrik. What had changed *Far's* mind? He seemed to be welcoming Fredrik. Was it the offer to attend church? Was it the man who greeted him rather than the boy he remembered?

She smoothed her hair and straightened her collar before calling to little Anna that it was time to leave for church. After waiting so long for this moment, she was so nervous she felt a little sick. Taking hold of the five-year-old's hand steadied her.

Before Fredrik turned to look up the stairs, she glimpsed a medium-height man with thick brown hair. When he looked up at her, the light in his deep-set eyes, took her breath away. He seemed equally stunned. For a moment, there was silence as they gazed at each other. Little Anna broke the silence.

"*God morgen* (good morning). Who are you? We're going to church. Are you?" she said with a curtsy. Other than her grandpa and uncles, she had not seen men in her front hall.

"*God morgen,* pretty lady, I would like to walk with you and your aunt Kristine to church. May I?"

A perceptive child, Anna saw that he was really asking *Tante.* But *Tante* had still not said anything.

Finally Kristine managed to say, "*Velkommen, Fredrik, takk for sist.*"

"*Kristine,* is it really you, all grown up?" he said with a smile.

"It is so good to see you, Fredrik. Thank you for coming." Kristine felt her father's eyes on her as well as Fredrik's.

"Time to go," said *Far.* "Take my hand, Anna. Your father and Alf have already left."

"Shall we?" Fredrik said to Kristine as he held out his arm and tucked in her hand.

Self-conscious but proud, she walked into the familiar church with a handsome man in a tailored suit made from a finer wool than anyone in Førde could afford. Together they held her hymn book and sang. She stood and sat at all the correct times and appeared to be paying attention, but her mind was on Fredrik's rough, calloused hands and the smile that made his bright eyes dance. His hair was longer and darker than she remembered. Her family was right. She really did not know this man, whose deep voice stirred something in her. On the walk to church, he had told her how beautiful she had become, but the compliment sounded rehearsed to her. Kristine was surprised to realize that the *presten* (minister) was saying the final blessing.

Once they were down the steps and in the churchyard, her friends and brothers crowded around.

"*Velkommen hjem* (welcome home), Fredrik, how are you doing?" The usual greetings flew around, but the curiosity was genuine. What they were really asking was "How much easier is life for you in America?"

An informal parade formed for the walk back to the Kristiansen house. Talk went to Canada—what it was like to farm so many acres and the price of rye and oats. Kristine's women friends raised their eyebrows and smiled but were too polite to ask what had brought Fredrik to church with her.

At the house, Kristine joined her mother in the kitchen to finish the midday meal preparations, leaving Fredrik to talk with her father. Her mother seemed livelier, even pleased to have Fredrik. By the time they said "*Vær så god,* (Welcome to dinner)," her father was smiling. Fredrik was smiling, too. What did that mean? Kristine clenched her fists under the table as they bowed their heads for the prayer. After the meatballs, potatoes, and carrots had been served and the homemade *flatbrød* (very thin, cracker-like bread) passed around, her father spoke.

"*Ja,* Kristine, we are thinking that the end of May, when Lent is over and the first hay crop is in, will be a good time for a wedding. What do you think?"

Kristine flushed a rosy red to the roots of her brown hair. She could not catch her breath. She opened her mouth but no words came out. The men laughed. *Mor* cried but smiled. Fredrik reached for her hand when she gasped out, "May? This May?"

She turned and stared at Fredrik, wondering how he had brought about this miracle? What promises had he made to her father?

"Does this mean you will be going to America, Kristine?" asked her brother Karl in his forbidding way.

"We will marry, and I will return to the United States to start a business." Fredrik answered. "I need to save some more money for a proper home for us, while Kristine applies for immigration papers."

"Kristine will go to Chicago when Fredrik has his Delco electric generator business set up," *Far* said.

"Yes, the money for generators is much better than farming, and there is so much more building there than in Saskatchewan."

Kristine looked from her father to Fredrik. *Far* talked as if he was an expert. Was this all decided? Where were these places? How was she to manage there? Immigration papers, how complicated was that? Was she to travel alone? When? Would she even be asked if she wanted to be married and go to America? She and Fredrik needed to talk, but right now she had a more basic question.

"*Far,* have you really given your permission for us to marry?"

"*Ja,* I plan to talk to the *presten* tomorrow. But we should eat before the meatballs get cold."

The rest of the meal passed in a blur for Kristine. Fredrik entertained her father and Karl with tales of life as a homesteader. In order to take full title of the land in Canada, he had become a Canadian citizen. This allowed him to go more freely to wherever there was electrical work in the U.S.A. or Canada. The homestead only required six weeks in the spring and six at harvest time. The rest of the time he moved around installing electricity in homes and barns.

Kristine's mother wanted to know who took care of him when he worked in so many places? Fredrik charmed her with his modest grin.

"*Ja,* I manage with rooming houses and my own poor cooking at the homestead. But that is why I have come all the way to Førde for Kristine. She will be my *ekte Norsk* (true Norwegian) wife."

* * * *

When the peach preserves in cream dessert had been cleared away and *takk for maten* (thank you for the food) had been said, Kristine and Fredrik went for a walk alone before the next meal, *kaffe,* (coffee) and cakes. A salty damp wind blew off the fjord as they walked the lane out of Førde toward Bergum. Not knowing where to start, neither one said anything.

"I have missed this," Fredrik mused as he took Kristine's hand.

Kristine smiled, wanting to tease him about what it was he had missed, walking the lane or holding her hand.

Instead she asked, "How did you find things at Hjelmeland? Has your father changed since you last saw him?"

"He has. He's so bent over that he can no longer help with the haying. He tends some animals, but Mikal's wife, Maria, tends the cows. She milks fourteen cows with baby Gunnar on her back. What a worker!"

Once begun, Fredrik chattered on about his sisters and brothers and their families, none of whom was even married when he had left in 1910. She tried to keep track of who lived at *på Hjelmeland* (neighboring farms known as Hjelmeland) and who had moved away. Among his two brothers and four sisters, she had only met his sister Petrina, to whom he was closest in age.

Her reply was not about family, "Fredrik, do you have cows on your homestead? I've only milked once or twice, ever."

"Ach, nei da (Oh, no indeed), the homestead is not a farm like here. I grow only grain to sell. Besides, did you think we would live there? We can't live in a shack, a day's ride by horse from Moose Jaw."

"I heard you say Chicago and Moose Jaw and talk about the homestead. I'm confused. I don't know where all these places are or how far they are one from another," she said in a shaky voice.

"We'll live near the city of Chicago in the state of Illinois. It's not on the ocean, but it's near a very big lake, Lake Michigan. I will be working full time on installing generators in new buildings and farms."

"Chicago? That's where the Moen girl died isn't it?" Kristine's voice filled with fear.

"Ja, your father asked about her, too. I heard that Guri Moen

got TB. Working in a factory with other poor girls from Poland
and Ireland is dirty, hard work. That *tante* she was sent to live with
made her cook before and after her factory work in a boarding
house. She got sick before she found a husband."

Kristine didn't respond. Her eyes widened, and she chewed
her lower lip, thinking.

Fredrik realized she knew nothing of immigrant life and less
about America. He pulled her to the side of the road, took both
her hands in his, and leaned against a tree.

"Your life will be nothing like Guri Moen's," he pledged.
"We'll live outside the city, away from the crowded tenements
where most people start out. That's why I didn't come back
sooner. I knew that moving from place to place following the
work is no life for a wife and family."

He went on to tell of installing electricity all over the upper
Midwest states but also logging and homesteading, staying in
boarding houses wherever the work took him. He did not tell of
the smelly rooms or the terrible food. He told her of the good
money to be made in construction but not the drinking and
gambling that went with the hard work and money. He told of the
excitement as he met other settlers who claimed Western Canada
for their own, but not of the loneliness in the shacks that the settlers
built on those prairies. He painted a picture of opportunities
for those who would work hard. He left out the disease, the
homesickness, and the obstacles that so many had faced.

Almost all unmarried Norwegian women who emigrated
to the United States worked either as domestic servants or in
factories in Brooklyn, Chicago, or Minneapolis-St. Paul. Once

they married, they generally did not work outside the home unless they were in partnership with their husbands in a business. When they could, they would take in other new immigrants as boarders to supplement the family income. Most women continued to do what they had done in Norway—make a home and make it as Norwegian as possible. While the husband adapted to working with many kinds of people in the course of his work, his wife maintained the best of Norwegian traditions within the home.

This is what had brought Fredrik home for Kristine. In all his years in America, he had courted some women or they had pursued him, but he kept going back to his vision of the home the young and refined Kristine would make for him.

"Are there other Norwegians in this place outside the city?" Kristine asked, not reassured yet.

"Not so many, but I know a lot of *Norsk* farmers. With my car we can visit them whenever you get homesick."

"But I don't speak English. How will I go to the market? Or talk to neighbors?

"Kristine, you worry too much. You will learn quickly, and I will be there to help you," he said, growing impatient with her fears. "We'll be married you know."

Kristine thought she wanted to get married, but she knew from her friends that being married brought its own set of problems.

"What did you tell *Far?*"

"I told him that we would have a fine apartment and a car of our own."

"Is that why he gave permission for us to marry?"

"I don't think so. I think, partly, it was that you will not leave before Christmas. Hopefully everything will be arranged next spring."

"Did you promise anything else?" She looked directly into his deep-set eyes, searching for a hint of what it was he had really promised her father.

"I promised that I would take very good care of you," he said with a chuckle. "Your father and I have agreed this is the best plan." He pulled her closer in a loose embrace, avoiding her serious stare.

Kristine suspected they had also talked about money. Not until she was in America, years later, did she learn that he was sending money for the housekeeper who was hired to help in her absence.

"Who do you think will come to the wedding?" Fredrik asked, changing the subject.

Kristine's eyes lost their anxious look. She had dreamed of this question for a long time. The guest list and hopes for their wedding day spilled out of her. Before they turned back to join the others for *kaffe*, Fredrik hugged her closer and kissed her lightly. Kristine savored the quick kiss she had only imagined for so long. At *kaffe*, she was once again blushing.

From that day the wedding was less than three months later, so Kristine added visiting Fredrik's family, introducing him to her friends, and traveling to Bergen for dress fittings and meetings with emigration officials to her busy days. In her few quiet moments, she thought about how much her life had changed since Fredrik had reappeared. Whenever they were together, she felt that marrying him was the right thing, but much of the time they were apart. While he was home at Hjelmeland, she was in Førde preparing for the wedding. Every few days he would take the bus to Førde, but usually it was for a visit to some friends or to work on some aspect of the wedding. On the few occasions when she took the bus to Hjelmeland, Fredrik was only present for *middag,* since there was so much to do to help Mikal around the farm. The weeks leading up to the wedding passed in a flurry of activity, but without Kristine and Fredrik getting to know one another much better than they had through years of letters.

Chapter Three

From This Day Forward

May 31, 1923

Kristine Kristiansen Hjelmeland, St. Olaf College report, as told to her daughter, Odny, 1943:

We were married on May 31, 1923, in Førde church. Many, many people attended the wedding. We had eighty guests at our home. Wedding dinner and supper were held in the Bedehuset, (parish house) and coffee and cakes were served at home. We received many gifts, much of which was silverware because they knew we were going to America. We also received forty-one telegrams.

At the Kristiansen home and shop, Kristine's sister Elise had come to help. She was Kristine's attendant and would assist their mother in hosting and feeding the wedding guests. Up under the slanting ceiling of their childhood bedroom, Kristine sat on a stool so that Elise could reach to pin a floor-length veil on her sister's thick brown hair pulled back in a loose, low bun.

"There! Does it feel secure? That blue brings out the color of your eyes." Elise stepped back and fluffed out the veil around Kristine's shoulders. "The headband is especially fine with both silk and lace."

"*Ja*, it is not easy to work with lace. Can you see the stitches?" Kristine asked.

"No one will be looking at your stitching. They will look at you!" Elise kissed Kristine quickly on her cheek. "Now, I must go. Karl is waiting to walk Mother and me to church!" With a final squeeze to Kristine's hand, she ran down the stairs and out the front door.

Kristine followed Elise down the stairs and went into the parlor, where their father was waiting. The last two to leave the house, they heard the bells ring from the steeple of the white frame Førde *kyrke* (church). She reached for her father's hand and looked into his face.

"Kristine, are you ready to become *Fru*, Mrs. Hjelmeland?"

"Ja, *Far*, I think I am, but this will always be home for me," she said, looking around her.

"*Nei*, Kristine, you and Fredrik will make your own home. I pray that one day it will be here in Førde."

"It has to be. Fredrik promised me that." Kristine flushed, rocketing between excitement and tears.

"Oh, yes, Fredrik." He paused and, with a twinkle, said, "I believe those bells mean that he and eighty of our friends and family are waiting, Kristine." With that, he tucked her hand under his arm and led her up the path she had walked every Sunday since she was a toddler.

Among the eighty guests were most of Fredrik's family, his father Gunder Michael Hjelmeland, and, of course, his brother, Mikal. Bonded by their years together in America, they had become even closer since the unexpected death of their middle brother Marthinn earlier that winter. Three of his sisters had left their farms, too, for their younger brother's wedding. They had tended the cows before they drove over Langeland from Bygstad to Førde in horse-drawn wagons. Neighbors all over the district were enlisted to help with feeding and milking the animals, since most people attending the wedding would miss both the evening and the morning chores. Førde was not close enough to get home easily by wagon. Only Fredrik's sister Petrina was unable to come all the way from her home in Brekstad, outside of Trondheim.

Inside the white frame church, the organist began to pump out the hymn "Love Divine, All Loves Excelling." All the guests stood. Heads turned as Andreas Kristiansen ushered his youngest daughter up the aisle to where Fredrik and the severe *presten* waited in front of a lavishly carved Baroque era altar. Kristine's mother turned with a small smile that did not reach her eyes. Maternal pride for her youngest daughter mixed with fear over what marriage to an adventurer like Fredrik would mean.

Many, including the bride and groom, had not really believed this day would come. Despite the doubters, Kristine and Fredrik radiated confidence born of patience and faith. Neither wore *bunads,* the traditional country apparel that was coming into favor again. Their wedding clothes were formal and modern, as suited a couple bound for America. Kristine's navy-blue, ankle-length dress was both stylish and practical. She planned to wear it again, many times, to attend other weddings and formal events. Blue silk hung in ribbons from a bouquet of white and pink roses. Fredrik was resplendent in a white tie and finely tailored suit. The wedding photo showed a handsome but solemn couple.

Despite the *presten's* ominous homily about the evils of life in America, Kristine and Fredrik exchanged their vows with firm conviction. Kristine promised to obey her husband. Together they promised to love and honor each other until death.

When the *presten* finally pronounced them man and wife, the organist pumped out Bach. The bells pealed again as the guests cheered the couple exiting the church.

The fiddler stood ready in the hard-packed dirt lane. As soon as the couple emerged, he struck up "Bruremarsj," a traditional Norwegian wedding march. Jubilant, Fredrik and Kristine led a parade of guests to the *bedehuset* where the wedding *middag* feast was waiting.

The celebration consisted of traditional foods, speeches, and music. Teetotaling pietists, the Kristiansens did not allow the homemade beer there would have been on the Hjelmeland farm. Beginning with dumpling-meatball soup and continuing through roasted beef and lamb with vegetables, potatoes, and brown *saus* (gravy), the meal celebrated the marriage with abundance. Each course was served twice before the dessert of *rysngrot* (rice porridge) with berry sauce was offered to complete the meal.

Andreas began the toasts and speeches. "Today we celebrate the wedding of my beloved daughter Kristine to Fredrik Hjelmeland. Welcome to all of you who have made arrangements for your farms so that you can celebrate with us. We pray that you are satisfied with the meal and that you will pray for this couple. Oliane and I are praying that having been married here, they will one day return to home in Førde. Now, I invite Gunder Hjelmeland to say a few words about his son, Fredrik."

Fredrik's father was followed by Kristine's brothers, who had written a song for the couple. Fredrik's brother, Mikal, followed with a long speech recalling their years together in America. He predicted exciting and prosperous times for the couple in Chicago.

As the speeches, singing, and jokes about "running away to America," became louder and sillier, Kristine began to wonder if the outhouse was the only reason so many were making frequent visits outside. Her smile grew into a grin as she realized she did not need to worry about that, someone else could. It was her wedding. After more celebration, including the reading of the many telegrams and the opening of gifts, Elise whispered in Kristine's ear.

"Tell Fredrik *kaffe* is ready. It is time for him to invite people to move." Aside from *takk, tusen takk, mange tusen takk* (thank you, a thousand thanks, many thousand thanks), Kristine was not expected to make speeches or issue general invitations. She passed the message to Fredrik who invited everyone to move to *kaffe* next door at the Kristiansens' home and garden.

Kristine, Elise, her mother, and Kristine's friend Astrid Kvall had baked for three days straight to offer the seven kinds of cake, including *kransekake, mandelkake,* and *blotkake,* and dozens of cookies, which marked good hospitality. During coffee, Kristine's father played the organ while her brother Alfred and his wife accompanied with guitar and fiddle.

Kristine and Fredrik Hjelmeland, Wedding
Photograph, May 31, 1923.

At 10:00 p.m., amidst raucous cries of "Good luck!" and laughing encouragement, Kristine and Fredrik departed for the Førde hotel on the other side of the river from the Kristiansen home. Because it was used mostly by business travelers, Kristine had never been inside. The dark wood floors of the reception area gleamed in the late evening sun. A golden light shone through the lace curtains. Since May 31 is so close to the summer solstice, they would have only a few hours of darkness in Førde.

The proprietor welcomed them and led them up a finely carved open staircase to their room. He asked Fredrik if his father was still building roads and told him of the increased traffic they got as the roads improved. Kristine looked around, nervously grateful that she did not need to make conversation. They were shown the indoor toilet and sink that the six rooms on the second floor shared. Such convenience. After assuring them a girl would bring a pitcher of warm water soon, the proprietor grinned, and with a wink to Fredrik, wished them a good night's sleep. The door closed behind them, and for the first time since the wedding ceremony, Kristine and Fredrik were alone as husband and wife.

"Are you…?"

"Do you…?" Both spoke at once, stopped, smiled.

"This is beautiful, Fredrik," Kristine started again. "Such fine things here." Waving her hand to the single chair, the Tiffany lamp and washstand, she avoided the bed.

"Uh, yes. Are you tired, Kristine?" he responded, not quite looking at her.

His shyness helped her relax. Fredrik seemed almost as nervous as she. They had only been alone as a couple a few times before. Now they were alone in a hotel room. She assumed he had much more experience than she. Oddly, his shyness helped her to think about pleasing him.

"*Nei*, Fredrik, it has been such a wonderful day, how could I be tired? I am so happy we are married." Her voice fell to a soft whisper. She reached for his hand and looked directly into his eyes.

Standing, face-to-face, holding hands by the side of the bed, they drew together in their first real married kiss. When someone knocked on the door, they jumped apart like guilty teenagers. A young girl entered carrying towels and a water pitcher.

When the girl left, Fredrik told Kristine that he would go downstairs for a smoke while she prepared for bed.

Glad for the privacy, Kristine took off her new traveling dress and put on the cream-colored nightgown embroidered with tiny blue flowers that she had made for this very night. As she brushed her hair out from its bun, she wondered how it could be that she was alone in a hotel room with a man and that man was her husband. Her brush tugged at a snarl. Her thoughts tugged at how inexperienced she was.

When Fredrik returned, she was sitting straight up on the edge of the bed. "Fredrik, I don't know how this goes," she whispered. "You must be my teacher."

"*Ja*, Kristine, I will be gentle," he said, his voice softening to match hers, "but you must tell me if I hurt you."

Desire for one another, for a life companion and a family, for someone to share new experiences with, had brought them together. That night, love for one another began to grow.

* * * *

In the morning, they did not get to linger in their private getaway. It was their responsibility to serve the overnight guests coffee, cakes, and a bride's porridge. The bride's porridge was generally *rømmegrøt*, a sour cream porridge. Served with cured mutton leg, *spekekjøtt*, and fruit juice, *saft*. The porridge sustained the guests for their travels home. When Kristine and Fredrik arrived back at Kristainsens' to serve the wedding breakfast, they were greeted with more good-natured cheering. They circulated, shaking hands, pouring coffee, ladling out porridge. Kristine needed only to catch Fredrik's eye and tilt her head when she saw his father arrive. When her *tante* needed more juice, Fredrik's light touch on her arm and a nod in *Tante* Lena's direction took care of it. By the time the meal was completed and the last guests were sent off with a "*Takk saa meget, god tur* (Thanks so much, good travel well)." Kristine and Fredrik were acting like a couple.

It was midafternoon before the borrowed dishes were returned and the helpers were sent on their way. Only the wedding couple and immediate family remained at the Kristiansens'. Exhausted, Kristine's mother needed help with the simple family supper that concluded their day.

Miraculously, it was Kristine's father who acknowledged the change in life for them all. He welcomed Fredrik to the dinner table, having him sit in the place normally reserved for Karl, his oldest son. Miffed at being displaced, Karl sat with his children at the foot of the table.

In evening devotions that he led for the entire family, Andreas prayed for Fredrik, the marriage, and life together with Kristine. Not only had he accepted Fredrik despite his reservations, he treated Fredrik as a full member of the family. Kristine's anxiety over defying the family's wishes lessened.

Karl and his children had no such sensibilities. Alfred and Anna continued to look to Kristine to take care of them. She had given them the love of a mother since Anna was born. They knew that she had not cared for them after the party but did not know how much this marriage would change their lives.

* * * *

Married Life

Having no place of their own, the newlyweds lived some weeks in Førde, some weeks on the farm in Bygstad, and some weeks separately from one another. When they were in Førde, Fredrik did not have anything to do. Kristine continued to care for her niece and nephew, do her household chores, and help in the shop. The only visible change was that Kristine's small maiden aunt bedroom had been fitted with a double bed.

When Fredrik was in Bygstad helping his brother Mikal, he returned to Kristine in Førde every few days. When she joined him there, Kristine tried to help with cooking and the children but didn't really know how to milk or do farm chores, and had no real interest in learning. After a few weeks, they began to spend as much time separately as they did together.

One cool night in late July, Kristine and Fredrik walked hand in hand down from *Hafstadfjell,* where they had gone to enjoy the summer evening sunshine and to get some privacy from both their families.

In a clearing they sat on some large, flat boulders. Fredrik put his arm around Kristine. She nestled her head on his shoulder.

"Kristine, I bought my ticket today. I leave on August 15th, sailing from Bergen."

"So soon? You promised it would be fall before you left." Kristine sat straight up and pulled away. Did Fredrik think of her when he bought this ticket? She was dismayed to learn that the ticket was bought. The decision made. She did not know that it would become a familiar pattern in their marriage. Fredrik decided. She made the best of his decisions.

"I had hoped to stay until then, but I've heard from the farmer who's taking care of my homestead in Canada. My wheat crop was harvested. It's time to plant the winter crop."

"If someone else harvested, can't they plant, too? Why must you be there?"

"I didn't think it would be so important for me to be there, but I didn't know how much money I'd be leaving here." Fredrik took his arm from around her.

"What do you mean?"

"*Ja,* you shouldn't worry about this. It's just that both our fathers need help. My father is not as strong as before. I gave him and Mikal some money to buy more cows and hire the neighbor boy to help at Hjelmeland." He clasped his hands between his knees and looked down at the rocky path. "And I gave your father money to build up his business."

"What does that have to do with winter wheat?" Kristine's questions became more plaintive as she grasped that he would be leaving very soon.

"It's not just the wheat, but I do need to make sure they plant more than we planned. Don't you understand? I can make more money faster in America, but I have to be there to do that."

"But what about us? When do you think I will join you?" Kristine tried to keep the panic from her voice.

"I hope by spring, maybe as early as February. We need to get top dollar for the wheat and actually begin the job with Delco in Illinois. If that all goes well, I can send money for your passage before Christmas."

"It seems too soon to say goodbye again. Is there no way for me to come with you now?" It dawned on her that Fredrik expected her to travel to America alone.

"*Nei*, there's not enough money, but I opened a bank account for you. It's the beginning of what you'll need to apply for your passport and emigration papers. Your father said he'll go with you to Bergen to apply."

"So, you've already talked to *Far.*" She paused for a long moment and gulped. "Fredrik, what if your plans don't go well? What if I never see you again?" She began to cry.

"Kristine, what are you afraid of? We're married. Of course we will be together again, very soon. Don't you believe me?" he asked.

"I do, Fredrik, but you were gone so long the last time. You've only been back a few months and you're leaving again?"

Fredrik, not having much experience with crying women, held her hand and looked directly into her eyes. He brushed a tear from her cheek and kissed her tenderly on her forehead, her cheeks, and finally her lips.

"I'm afraid that nothing will change. You will be in America and I will be here in Førde taking care of mother and Karl's children until we are both old." She cried harder.

"Kristine, that is nonsense. Please believe me. I'll work as hard as I can so that you can come. If I could, I would stay here, but there's no money in farming and no need for electricians in Førde. We can do so much better in America."

"If I go to America, will we ever come back?"

"We will, as soon as possible. Together in America, with you encouraging me, I'll be able to sell even more generators." His voice changed as he talked of a world unknown to Kristine. "You'll see, there's so much building there. The railroads all go through Chicago. They're making bicycles, radios, electrical supplies, transformers in big factories. Chicago is growing faster than any other city, and every newcomer needs a place to live, with electricity. Everything there is very modern!"

"So, modern is good, Fredrik?" she asked. To her, modern was another word for different from what she was used to. She had heard of radios and electricity in homes but had no experience with it.

Not hearing her concern, Fredrik continued to tell of all the opportunities they would have, the money they would make, and his plans for coming back to Norway one day as a successful electrician. "There's a club in Chicago called the *Norske Klub*. Lots of fellows like me, who went to technical school, go there. It's a good place to meet people who are in business."

"Are there any women there?"

Kristine noticed that Fredrik replaced his arm around her shoulders before he answered. She wondered why he hesitated. Did the women at that club dance, play cards, or drink alcohol? In her world, only loose women did that. Maybe that was modern? She became more suspicious when he changed the subject.

"As soon as I get to Waukegan, I'm buying a car. I'll be able to take generators to so many more places with my own car. I've heard farmers are putting electricity in their barns before their houses. Just think, Kristine, how nice it will be to take a ride in the evenings when I am done working."

"Do you know how to drive? Is it safe?"

"*Ja, ja,* I had a truck for the homestead, but I sold it when I came here."

As Fredrik went on spinning his plans for buying land and building a house, maybe even a store, Kristine listened and tried to make sense of these ideas and places. Her head swirled with images she couldn't imagine. Was it his imminent departure that was making her feel lonely, or an element of foreboding? She had thought about them together, but now she pictured herself alone in a house not knowing anyone. He had a different way about him when he talked about America, talking louder and faster than usual as if giving a speech to a crowd.

Kristine fell quiet. Leaning into Fredrik, she was lost in her own thoughts of the future. It was after ten, when darkness fell. Hand in hand, they picked their way down the rocky path back to Førde. That path was clear to them even in the dark. The path to their future was not.

At the Kristiansens', they crept through the sleeping household to Kristine's small bedroom, where Fredrik undressed his wife with deliberation but not a sound. As they lay in her childhood room, their lovemaking began tenderly, each touch growing in urgency with thoughts of their imminent separation. First Fredrik, then Kristine cried out, heedless of who in the house would hear them.

Just three weeks later they said good-bye, not knowing when they would be husband and wife together again. For days, Kristine could not sleep or eat. Dreaming of possibilities was no longer good enough. She'd had a taste of life beyond her former daily routine. Their weeks together had fueled her dreams of a life outside her parents' home, with her husband. But America was far away. Now that he was gone, would it be another thirteen years before she saw her husband again?

Chapter Four

Home Birth

Fredrik Olaf Hjelmeland, letter to his father, Gunder Mikalsen Hjelmeland, June 24, 1924:

Have you been over to see my daughter, Father? It will be some time yet before I can see her. But I have thought of bringing Kristine over here this summer, if she can find good company and if things are such that she can leave her home. But I'm a little afraid it will be difficult to get her into the States as I'm not a citizen here. I could have her come to Canada, but this will not help if she cannot proceed to the States... They mustn't leave before they apply for immigration papers.

After his sailing, Kristine dragged through her chores. She could not regain her spirits or her energy. Then one morning, serving the usual herring for breakfast, she ran from the room. Her mother heard her retching in the kitchen.

"*Mor*, I am so sick, it is the smell that makes me vomit," she said unsteadily.

"Kristine, how long have smells made you sick?" her mother asked.

"Since just after Fredrik left. But it's getting worse, I thought I was just so sad from missing him."

"I think you are sad, but I do not think you are sick. I think you are quite well," her mother replied.

Kristine thought back to the tender night when they walked, talked of their future, and sealed it with their love. Pregnant. How could it be with all the talk of the future, they had not talked of a child? As soon as she was certain, she wrote to tell Fredrik that sometime in the New Year of 1924, she would have their baby. She did not wait long for a reply.

He telegraphed back. "Come now, money to follow."

She wrote, "I will not have my baby among strangers. Who will help me? I'm old to give birth for the first time." She was thirty-two.

Back and forth, the letters and telegrams seesawed, writing of immigration papers, money, who was caring for whom, where this baby was to be born. Fredrik's replies slowed as he grew busy starting his business. Often one letter crossed the other in the two-week journey from Førde to Waukegan.

Kristine was embraced by her family and community: the baby would keep her with them for a little longer. Distance, time, and stress took away from the bond of their brief time together as a married couple.

Christmas 1923 came and went. Last year she'd dreamed that this Christmas they would be together. She had not dreamed that she would be pregnant and still living in her family home, caring for the same people. She struggled to keep up the household as her mother wanted it. She sewed diapers and baby buntings, knit socks and caps. She helped her niece and nephew with their lessons. She greeted friends as they joined her on the Sunday walk to church with their husbands and toddlers. But in the evenings when she sat knitting in the quiet living room, after her mother and father had gone to bed, she allowed herself to think of Fredrik and ponder their future with a baby. On those evenings, her doubts crept in. Would she ever go to America? Would this child be *Norsk* or American? What kind of father would Fredrik be? Would she live through the childbirth? Too many did not.

Weeks later, after settling mother in the parlor with a shawl for her shoulders and a cup of tea, Kristine stretched her aching back, changed into her Sunday shoes, and walked up the lane to church. She joined her brother Karl and her father Andreas in the second pew from the front where they always sat. Usually the organ music could take her mind off her worries. Mr. Stram was playing today. He had taught her to play.

She rubbed her growing belly and thought about her husband in America. She wondered if there were organs to play in America. Just as quickly her mind went to her mother. *Mor* wasn't getting better. Her labored breathing often kept her in bed. It had taken a long time to get her downstairs to the parlor today. Maybe when the days got longer and she was able to be out in the sun, her terrible cough would stop.

That night, April 15, 1924, Karl was sent to get the midwife. Kristine's sister, Elise, came in from the farm to attend her. In the same room where she'd grown up and made love above the shoe shop, Kristine gave birth to a healthy baby girl whom she named Odny.

Kristine had had an uneventful home birth, and soon she was able to resume her role in the household plus caring for Odny. Anna and Alf felt they had a new sister. Her mother took particular pleasure in holding Odny throughout her naps while Kristine tended to the cooking and cleaning. Bringing her girls, Elise visited more often. As spring became summer, Kristine took Odny with Anna and Alf on outings to her sister's farm, to the Hjelmeland farm and to the mountains.

Fredrik wrote of his joy but could not quite believe that he was in fact a father. He had not seen his daughter's round face, watched her as she nursed or heard her cry. His letters focused on immigration and money for tickets. He began to write hoping Kristine would set a date to depart.

Kristine arranged for Odny to be baptized at Førde church where she had been baptized, confirmed, and married. At that time, baptism was still the way births were registered in the public record, but more important to Kristine were the warnings from the minister of dire consequences for unbaptized infants. Fredrik's father came over the mountain from Hjelmeland to stand in for Fredrik. Baptisms without the father present were not common, and there was some uncertainty about the irregularity of it. Once the baptism was completed, though, she was able to apply for a passport and immigration papers for both her and the baby.

* * * *

Fredrik to his brother, Mikal, August 1924:

Did Kristine ask Father for money? She must get money for herself, for the tickets, and for everything that she needs. I, for my part, will send her $100, which she can show for herself when she comes ashore here. You don't think she needs to wait in turn for her going, do you? I want her over here now so very much. You know it is no way to live, staying apart for a lifetime. She sent me a picture of herself and Odny, if there is anything you can do…do it for my sake. I know I have a pretty good wife. The only trouble with her is she does not know her own good.

Now it was Kristine who was slow to respond. Day-to-day life was better with a child of her own, and she got so much support from family and friends that she began to think of going to America as giving all that up. And then there was the matter of her mother's declining health. How could she leave her?

First, she told Fredrik that she couldn't travel by herself with a baby. He wrote that his nephew Alf would wait to come to America and travel with her. His papers were complete.

Then she said the immigration papers were taking too long. She wouldn't set a date until they came through. He responded that the U.S. government would not approve immigration without an arrival date.

Finally, she said she did not think she could leave her mother at such a time.

As another Christmas approached and Fredrik was still alone, he lost his patience and issued an ultimatum. Kristine had to set a date and come or they were finished. He would not stay married to her and see her only every few years. He promised her again that they would return to Norway but that right now he needed her in America. As soon as she had her passport, he would arrange for a ticket that would include a baby, but only until her first birthday. It would cost hundreds of dollars more to buy another ticket if the baby girl turned one

His letter crossed in the mail with Kristine's letter that her mother had declined to the point that she rarely left her bed. When she received Fredrik's stern letter, Kristine looked at her growing daughter and her dying mother and began to pray. Kristine believed that prayer is answered in one's own heart, so she consulted no one, but wrote another letter to Fredrik. She would come on the first passage he could arrange in the New Year. She missed him so much and wanted him to meet their daughter. There was too much sadness, too much loss, and not enough hope in the Kristiansen home. Karl and father were far too content with her taking care of them and the children. Her mother at least understood that Kristine should be free to have her own family. While Kristine knew that her mother did not want to keep her from her husband, she held her decision secret until she received Fredrik's response.

Kristine and Baby Odny in Førde, Norway, 1924.

Chapter Five

For Everything There is a Season!

Fredrik Olaf Hjelmeland in Waukegan, Illinois, letter to his father, Gunder Mikalsen Hjelmeland, on Hjelmeland Bygstad, Norway, January 7, 1925:

Had a letter from Alf Solemslid; he said he would wait until Kristine left. The Bergensfjord departs from Bergen February, 11. I feel it would be best if they would come with that ship. But she has to make that decision herself. I am so looking forward to Kristine and my little daughter's coming and we can start a home. I still haven't given up Norway, and if it is God's will, I would like to go back one day. You know I am on my own here, and Kristine has all her folks back in Norway, too. You know it won't be the same over here as it would be in Førde together with you. But hopefully it will work.

Kristine had delayed as long as she could. Fredrik had booked first class passage to make sure Kristine had help with baby

Odny. Odny's first birthday was April 15. That meant that the March 18, 1925, sailing of the *Bergensfjord, NAL* was Kristine's last chance to join her husband. After months of indecision, she decided. She could not stay any longer. Life with Fredrik and their child was the future for her.

But the leave-taking nearly made her change her mind. She told her father first; he was little comfort.

"*Ja*, Kristine, I had hoped Fredrik would find a way to come here to be with his family." His voice trailed off, and he looked into the distance.

"I, too, kept hoping for a way to stay," Kristine choked out. "Maybe I should not go?"

Far's head came up and he looked directly at her. "What? No, Fredrik is your husband. Odny is his daughter. It is not right to be apart. You must go."

Kristine gulped. She wondered if *Far* was telling her this or himself. He was such an honorable man that he would urge her to do the right thing, no matter what.

"You must find someone to help you here with the children and with *Mor*. Shall I start to ask around?"

"You can, but Karl must take care of this. Anna and Alf are his children."

"I will tell Karl that I am leaving on the next sailing, but I cannot tell *Mor*."

Her father took a deep breath before saying quietly. "Kristine, I think we will let the Lord take care of that. If *Mor* does not ask, do not tell her. She asks less and less these days."

Kristine buried her head in her hands and could not speak.

Saying good-bye to Anna and Karl was not any easier. When the black trunk in which Kristine stored many of her wedding gifts was brought out to pack, she sat with Anna and Alf on the floor in front of it.

"*Tante*, do you have a present for us?" Anna, six years old, had peeked at all the packages inside the trunk.

"Those are presents I got at our wedding. Do you remember *Onkel* (Uncle) Fredrik?"

"The one you have a picture of next to the bed?" Anna was observant.

"Yes. Odny and I are going to live with him."

"But you live here. Where does he live?"

"He lives in America, and he misses us."

Alf spoke up. "I think America is far away."

"You are right, Alf. How clever you are." Kristine said. "We are taking a boat that goes from Bergen to a city across the ocean called New York."

"I like to take boats." Alf had not outgrown his mental slowness. At nine years old, his thinking was not developed and kept him focused on a single concept. Anna was not so limited.

"Can we go, too?" Anna said. "How long will we be gone? Why are you crying?"

Kristine could barely breathe, much less tell these children who had only known her as a mother that they were not going with, that someone else would be taking care of them, that she didn't know when or if she would see them again. As much as she knew she must go now or risk her marriage, which had barely had a chance to be, she could only say, "*Onkel* Fredrik has promised that we will come back to Norway to live, but I don't know when."

Anna and Alf accepted this simple answer.

Then her mother died. How could she go now? How could she not?

Kristine stood in the parlor, next to the casket. "*Farvel mama, takk for alt* (thank you for everything, rest in peace)," she whispered. She was alone for the first time in two days. Just twelve hours before, she and her sister Elise had bathed and dressed their mother's body in a final act of caring for her. Yesterday, while her father, five brothers, her sister, their spouses, and children sat with the *presten* to arrange the funeral, Kristine had finished preparations to emigrate to Waukegan, Illinois. Today she was leaving. Tomorrow there would be the funeral.

A tear rolled down her cheek as she lifted her mother's hand one last time. "*Mama,* I know you knew I was leaving sometime soon. Thank you for leaving before me.*"

Taking a fresh, embroidered handkerchief from the sleeve of her gabardine traveling suit, she wiped her tears and pinned on the tan, felt hat she had just finished making. Trimmed with a pheasant feather, the hat was molded closely to her head with a turned-up brim. Hats were her specialty. Putting it on gave her more confidence. Her millinery teacher at school had recommended her to many customers. After making hats for the town's wealthiest women, she knew what she wanted for her long trip.

She stepped into the narrow hallway where Elise was stooped down buttoning Odny's coat. Her face filled with sorrow, Elise stood and handed Odny to her sister. Odny wore a navy blue wool coat over her dress, hand knit stockings, and the small white shoes made of glove leather that her grandfather had made for her baptism. The sturdy brown shoes that helped her take her first wobbly steps a few days before were in Kristine's suitcase. Maybe the weather on the ship would be fine enough for Odny to practice walking on deck.

All her siblings had been at breakfast today. She had said her good-byes and tried one more time to explain to Anna and Alf that they must be good and helpful while she was gone. She sat between them at the table but would not talk about when she would see them again.

Kristine's mother Olianne's funeral, March 1925.

"The others are waiting for you outside. Are you ready?" Elise asked as she gripped Kristine in a hug until the baby sandwiched between them began to howl.

Arm in arm, they went out the door into the muddy roadway. The March sun had just reached over the mountain, weakly brightening the gray day.

A horse-drawn wagon parked next door to their home in front of the *bedehuset* was loaded with her trunk filled with dishes and tablecloths, clothes for her baby, work dresses and church clothes, hand stitched shirts for her husband, and shoes her father had made for Fredrik and her.

Her father reached out his hand to his youngest daughter. Her brothers and spouses, a few friends, even the children, in somber mourning clothes, stood waiting and talking.

"Hold Odny one more minute while I pray with *Far*," she said to Elise. The good-byes had all been said, but her pious father Andreas held her hand and prayed a blessing on her journey. When he finished, Elise and Kristine both held in the tears that overwhelmed any more talking.

"Kristine, *du må reise, n*å, *Alt er ferdig* (You must leave now, everything is ready)," her brother Karl told her as he gave her a hand into the waiting wagon. Amidst shouts of "*God tur* (Safe travels)" from brothers, spouses, nieces, and nephews, Elise handed up Odny and they left. Kristine waved and waved, twisting around in her seat. Excitement mixed with her sadness, but she needed to keep her wits about her if she was to manage this long journey. She could think more about her mother, her grief, and the mystery of what she was going to on the transatlantic crossing from Bergen to New York City. Eight days on a ship would provide plenty of time for thinking.

The band of mourners stood in the road until the wagon clattered over the bridge and turned up the dirt road toward the ferry landing. Most believed they would never see their sister again. Once people went to America, few returned.

"Might as well be three deaths: yesterday mother, today my sister and her baby," Elise sobbed.

On the ferry to Bergen, Kristine held Odny in her arms in the rough seas off the Western coast of Norway. She comforted her daughter from the rolling pitches of the ferry while the little girl's warmth comforted Kristine. Her husband's nephew, Alf Solemslid, was traveling with her. Fredrik had promised Alf work if he accompanied his wife and baby girl. It was good to have company, but she found she had little to say to the nineteen-year-old.

In Bergen, they were met by cousins who took them home for the night. Kristine felt almost detached as she received their condolences for her mother and praise of her baby. They were to board early the next morning, so all the departure rituals were included with *kaffe* Despite the long, emotional day, *kaffe* was extended with gifts: a doll, a ball and toy boat for Odny, a scarf for Kristine, and tobacco for Alf to enjoy on their journey. Migration to the U.S. had slowed after World War I, which made this departure more exciting for her father's nieces and nephews.

"Kristine, do you know anyone in this place near Chicago that you are going?" Her hostess Mari asked her.

Alf spoke up before Kristine could respond, "No, *Onkel*

Fredrik says that is why it is such a good place to do business, not much competition."

"Isn´t Fredrik farming?" Jens asked. "Is he working for someone else? I don't know if I could take orders from an American. It´s hard enough here." Jens worked as a processor for a herring fishing operation.

"No, Fredrik has his own electrical business. He says that with Alf and my help, he will be able to make enough money for us to move back to Norway and start another business or buy a farm in a few years." Kristine could not keep the doubt from her voice. "He thinks it will help him work harder and save more if we are there to come home to. Alf will work for him."

"Sounds like he is taking on more, not getting money-making help," Jens muttered.

Mari scowled at her husband and turned to Kristine. "Do you know any English? I suppose that Fredrik does."

With a weak smile, Kristine tried to sound hopeful. "I don't, but Fredrik is quite fluent. He tells me it will not take long to learn."

"I have been studying and will help Kristine translate on the voyage," Alf said.

"Oh, I hope you can find someone to talk to there." Mari understood it would be difficult for Kristine to not know anyone or the language. "You say it's a big place, surely there will be someone."

Kristine kept her smile pasted on and nodded, but wondered. Once she had committed to going, she had tried not to think too much about the difficulties of daily life in a strange place

"*Ja*, we shall see. For now, I must say *tusen takk for matten* (many thanks for the meal). Since Odny has fallen asleep, I think I will go to bed too."

Anxious to board the ship that would take her to her new life. Kristine insisted on getting to the dock very early the next morning. At the dock, a small band played, and smartly uniformed Norwegian attendants greeted the first-class passengers at their exclusive gangplank. Alf, as Kristine's helper, was able to board with her and wave from the first-class deck before finding his way to his tourist-class quarters. They waved and smiled as the cousins shouted, "*God tur, farvel* (farewell), write us soon!"

* * * *

Kristine Hjelmeland, St. Olaf College report, as told to her daughter, Odny, 1943:

Two ladies from the Norwegian American Line, who were hired to assist foreign travelers, assisted Mother and me to New York. There were very few children on the boat; therefore I became the center of attention. Everyone had to dress up for dinner on the boat, and no children were allowed in the dining room, therefore a girl had to take care of me at every meal.

Kristine discovered she was a good traveler. She enjoyed Inge, her tablemate at dinner, who was returning to Brooklyn after a long visit with family in Bergen. She had lived in America for fifteen years. She told Kristine of the bustling city and the large Norwegian-American community living in Brooklyn, working in the shipyards. She began to teach Kristine some simple English words. Kristine contributed to the social life by playing the small piano in the first-class lounge after the elegant, four-course dinners. Having help with her baby, no meals to cook, and no nursing or cleaning to do, Kristine almost believed she was on a pleasure cruise.

But when the spring North Atlantic winds blew so hard the big ship rocked, Kristine left Odny with an assistant and walked the deck alone, thinking of her mother's funeral held without her, *Far* and Karl as they took care of her niece and nephew. When she turned her back to the sea spray and tasted the saltwater hitting her face, she tried to picture Fredrik, the apartment he had rented in Waukegan, the people she would meet there. Then her father's prayer echoed in her mind, "*Gud bevare deg*" (God protect you).

60

Chapter Six

A New Life

Fredrik Hjelmeland, Waukegan, Illinois, letter to his brother, Mikal Hjelmeland, in Norway, April 15, 1925:

And now I have started a new life, quite different from what I had before. All of a sudden I have a large family! April 1, Kristine, Odny and Alf came to Chicago. We stayed there for a night at a hotel, and we came to Waukegan, April 2. I guess they were pretty happy when they saw us and the long journey was finally over. Do you remember, Mikal, the first day we arrived in Chicago?

* * * *

New York to Chicago

On the morning of the eighth day, they woke to quiet. The ship was not rocking.

Faintly Kristine could hear some shouting and banging but no engines clanking or roaring.

They had docked.

America, New York. Now she would see what she had only heard about. Relief mingled with excitement and fear. Everything that could be done was done. Kristine had laid out their traveling clothes the night before. She peeked out of the stateroom to see that the big suitcase she set out last night was already gone. As she bustled around getting herself ready, she worried about how she would manage getting from the boat to the train with only Fredrik's nineteen-year-old nephew Alf to help her. They would carry a travel basket and small valise. Fearing she would miss their train and be alone in the big city of New York, she paced in the tiny room.

When she finished washing herself and brushing her hair, she woke Odny to feed her before dressing them both. Odny wore a plain smock, fresh-knit stockings, sturdy shoes, and a coat and hat. Kristine's own traveling outfit was similar, brown and practical. She knew that they would be in these clothes at least two days. Since she didn't know if it would be mild and spring-like or still wintry, she hoped their Norwegian woolens would be warm enough. After processing through immigration, they were to get a bus to Grand Central Station for the twenty-hour train trip to Chicago.

At breakfast, she sipped her coffee and pushed around a piece of bread and cheese, too excited to eat anything more. Her shipboard friend Inge tried to reassure her.

"Kristine, once you are settled, you must bring your husband back to New York, to Brooklyn. I'll bet he knows some of the Norwegians in our neighborhood," she said.

"I wish you could go with us, Inge. You've been such a help to me. Is Chicago far from here?"

"Oh, it's many miles, but the NAL, Norwegian American Line, has you booked all the way through. I'll make sure that you and your nephew get in the immigration line before I say good-bye. Then once you are processed, just look for the NAL bus to Grand Central Station."

After they got in the line and Inge hugged her farewell, Kristine clutched her daughter in her arms and her paperwork in her bag.

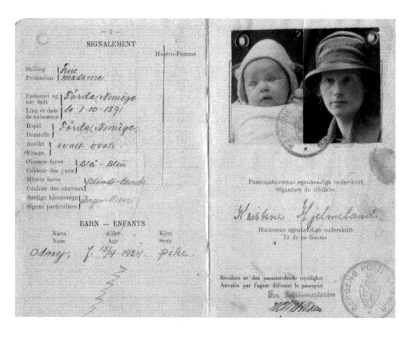

Kristine and Odny`s passport, Norway to America, 1925.

* * * *

Kristine Kristiansen Hjelmeland, St. Olaf College report, as told to her daughter, Odny, 1943:

Before we could leave the boat in New York, we were to have a physical examination. However, my mother and I only had our eyes examined.

The first step was to fall into two lines, men in one and women and children in another, for a physical by American officials, all men. When it was their turn, Kristine stepped up to a rough-looking man with a white coat. He took hold of her chin, jerked her head side to side, looked in her eyes and then into Odny's. After he wrote on her papers, he thrust them at her and said something she didn't understand. "You're okay, lucky to be here. Next!" Not until the woman behind her pushed her away did she understand that not only were her papers in order, but that they had passed the "physical exam." People talked so loud and so fast, she couldn't understand a word.

Alf had been taken out of the men's line and had gone behind a screen to be examined more thoroughly. As she moved to the departure deck, she worried that he would be detained. How would she ever find her way without him to help? She looked for another passenger who might help her locate Alf, but saw no one she knew. She chose a place to wait near the rail where she thought he would see her. Despite her layers of wool clothing, she shivered in the raw wind from the harbor. As the minutes stretched on, Odny began to squirm in her arms. She tried to distract her by looking to the pier at carriages, horse drawn and motor, and the stevedores unloading the ship. After what seemed to be a very long time, Alf found them.

"Thank goodness you have come." Kristine was relieved to have Alf's solid presence next to her. He took Odny from her arms and spun her around.

"Look at all the people little one. We are in America!" Alf was jubilant, not overwhelmed at all by the people and bustle on the dock. His excitement reminded Kristine that this was what they were traveling for, a new place, not Norway.

Soon, they too made their way in the steadily moving line down the gangplank and onto American soil. The clamor and surge of so many people kept them moving through the processing hall and on to find their baggage, but as much as Kristine had dreamt about this moment, she couldn't really take it all in. Once they were on the NAL bus that took them from the docks to the train station, the driver told Alf where to look for the train to Chicago. Kristine hoped that Alf understood enough English to lead them through even more crowds with their trunks and baggage to the right place.

From the open windows of the motorbus, she took in the muddy streets and breathed in the stench of open sewers running alongside the roadway. Ragged children held the hands of tired-looking women outside shops below the many-storied buildings of the Bowery. Kristine pulled Odny even closer on her lap. Alf told her the tall, dingy buildings were apartments for the poor called tenements.

By contrast, Grand Central Station seemed luxurious and enormous. From the gilded entrance at the carriage drive where the bus dropped them off, to the echoing Great Hall, Kristine looked for the tracks that would take them away. Important-looking men in dark suits and overcoats hurried as they crisscrossed from one side of the arching hallway to the other. While uniformed workers behind wrought iron ticket windows called out departing trains, porters vied to help with their trunks.

"We do not have much time until the train, *Tante*. I will get the trunk and suitcases checked in, and you must take Odny to the platform of the New York Central to Chicago." Alf shouted over the din. "Kristine, can you do that?"

"I think so. How will you know which car we are in? What if you don't get on the right one?"

"I will be able to run if I have to, but you cannot with the baby. Just get on the train. Find our compartment and I'll find you."

* * * *

Kristine Kristiansen Hjelmeland, St. Olaf College report, as told to her daughter, Odny, 1943:

While we were on the train, carrying us to Chicago, we were supposed to have a sleeper. It was all paid for, but we never got it, and we couldn't do any complaining because Mother couldn't talk English and neither could I. My mother tells me that she literally carried me from Norway to Chicago.

Getting to the right track for the train to Chicago didn't seem so simple. Kristine checked the numbers on the tickets and studied the signs. Not knowing English, she ignored the remarks from passersby swirling around her as she stood still in the midst of so much activity. At the New York Central Platform #12, she found a stocky man in a navy blue uniform directing people. She showed him her tickets. Odny wiggled in her arms. When the man waved her toward seats in a car, she tried to ask about a *seng* (bed). No one understood her, so she found two seats together and let Odny stand until the train began to move. Alf found her only after the train had left the big station.

"Alf, you're here! It did not go well without your English. I tried to make them understand we are to have a bed. I showed two different men my ticket, but I think they told me to sit here," she said. "What should I have done?

"I don't know. My little English is not enough for all these questions. Maybe when they collect the tickets later, we can move. At least I think we are on the right train," Alf said and sat down next to her.

Side by side on little more than a bench with a wooden back, they sat looking out the window at tall buildings, railroads and shipyards, factories and warehouses. They crossed bridges and slowed for some crossings. Dirty puddles and patches of ice littered the muddy roads that crossed the tracks. Lost in a muddle of dark thoughts, neither Kristine nor Alf had anything to talk about.

After a half hour, a conductor came by and punched their tickets. They tried to ask about a sleeper compartment, but the only English word they could come up with was "bed." The conductor hardly slowed down, shaking his head as he moved to the next passenger.

Alf looked at Kristine and saw her that eyes were squeezed shut. "Are you all right?" he asked.

"I'm very tired. Will you take a walk with Odny? Just the length of the car?" Her voice quavered, but she did not allow the tears to fall.

"Sure, I can use a stretch. You rest for a few minutes." Alf carried the little girl up and down the aisle of the railroad car until she fell asleep against his shoulder. He sat down and gently shifted her to Kristine's arms. They settled in, gazing out the window, not talking, trying to rest like the napping Odny.

Once they left the buildings behind, the land was flat and not green; no fjords or mountains broke up the late March landscape. The steam and soot from the locomotive gave a gray cast to the windows they peered through. The cloudy afternoon turned to an early dusk. Kristine had not expected it to be so dismal. Throughout the night, Kristine's head fell forward onto her chest and jerked back as the train steamed its way through town after town. Odny whimpered even as she slept in her arms. How she wished she had known enough English to get the sleeper car that Fredrik had said was included in her passage.

A man in front of them had been smoking a cigar since he got on at a stop during the night in a place called Pittsburgh. Kristine stirred from her fitful sleep when the woman across from her pulled a jar of something that smelled of onions and cabbage from a yellow tapestry bag. She watched in dismay as the woman dug into the jar with her fingers for her breakfast. Kristine rubbed her forehead and breathed into her fine white handkerchief. Her head ached from the sour smell, the smoke, and too many bodies on the noisy train. For reprieve, she, Odny, and Alf went to the dining car, where their tickets got them a breakfast of dry white bread and coffee. There was no milk or *farina* for a baby. How good it was that Odny was still nursing.

After twenty hours of sitting in this stiff, upright seat, she was tired, dusty, and a little nauseated. Odny needed a bath. In the washroom, she had tried to rinse out diapers but there was not much she could do with so little water, not even heated. Their bundle of soiled diapers and clothes was growing in the bottom of Kristine's travel valise. What would Fredrik think when they got to Chicago? She had so wanted his first meeting with his daughter to be perfect. She'd never imagined America was so dirty, gray, gritty. She'd begun to feel as if she'd made a terrible mistake.

After the ship, where everyone had some connection with Norway, she longed for someone other than Alf to talk to, but all the people on the train spoke English or another language. Alf had gone quiet, too. She wondered if he was just tired or nervous.

The man in the blue uniform came through shouting something she didn't understand until he said, "Chicago." Dozing in his seat next to hers, Alf shook himself awake. In his broken English, he asked the gruff man across the aisle what the conductor had announced. An hour to Chicago! This town with the ugly smoke stacks and sulfur smells was someplace called Gary.

Kristine was wide awake now. She handed the baby to Alf, who held her in front of him, like a bag of oats, gripping her little shoulders. Digging in their belongings, Kristine found a clean dress and hand-knitted stockings for Odny and a fresh collar for her own blouse that she had put on before leaving the ship yesterday morning. She took Odny from Alf and stood in line for the washroom.

Twenty minutes later, feeling refreshed, she settled back on the wooden bench, peering out the window at fences and the back of passing warehouses. Then they plunged into darkness. It seemed as if they were underground: no sky, no trees, no town visible. The brakes screamed as the train slowed. Where were they? They had been told they were coming into Union Station, brand new and the biggest in the United States. To Kristine, it looked like a giant steel cave. Just as suddenly, they emerged into a pale light and could see ropes of tracks winding past the stopping train.

A new building for trains was not on Kristine's mind for long as she leaned forward in her seat, peering out the grimy windows. Finally, she spotted Fredrik before the train fully stopped. She exhaled a breath she did not know she had been holding. He really was here. He would take care of them in this strange place. Who was that fellow standing next to him?

* * * *

Kristine Kristiansen Hjelmeland, St. Olaf College report, as told to her daughter, Odny, 1943:

My father and Ben Hjelmeland, a boyhood chum of my father who also lived on the Hjelmeland farm, met us at the station in Chicago on April 1, 1925.

"Union Station, Chicago, Illinois!" the conductor bellowed. Alf stood up and pushed his way to make a path among all the other passengers. He carried the two suitcases while Kristine followed with Odny and her travel basket.

As she took the porter's hand to step over the tracks onto the train platform, she felt Fredrik reach for Odny. She tumbled into him, handing him their daughter.

"You're really here!" Kristine cried.

"Finally, you have come," Fredrik answered.

"This is Odny. Odny, this is your daddy."

"She's beautiful, you're beautiful."

"Can you smile for your daddy?"

Two years since they had married, nearly that long since they had been together. They clung to one another as a family, laughing and crying at the same time, an island among the bustling hubbub of travelers being met, taxis being arranged, and luggage handled.

Fredrik introduced his friend Ben, who happened to be working in Chicago.

Kristine barely looked at the neat short man who looked like so many other young Norwegians, with brown hair and blue eyes. She did take in his uncalloused hands when he shook hands in greeting and wondered what he did if he wasn't a laborer. She knew he wasn't related, but he did look as if he could be Fredrik`s younger brother: same straight nose, wavy brown hair, and medium height. Alf shook Ben's hand while asking question after question about work, women, and life in Chicago, thrilled to meet another Norwegian man who was young and single. The younger men took charge of getting the trunks while Fredrik led his little family to a shiny sedan. Kristine was awestruck.

"Fredrik, whose car is this?" she asked.

"It is mine, Kristine. It was new when I came to Waukegan two years ago. Do you like it?"

"Yes, of course, but you own it? You can go wherever you want?" she asked, stunned at the idea of ordinary people owning a car.

"Well, there are not so many good roads. I can't take it on some of these farm paths, but most places, yes, I can go where I want when I want," Fredrik said with a proud smile

Kristine had never ridden in a privately owned automobile, only taxis in Bergen. No one in Førde had a car yet. Before they even left the train station, she was learning how different life would be in America.

From Union Station, Fredrik first drove them to a hotel where they could clean up and be alone as a family. The sixty miles to Waukegan on unpaved roads was too far to go before dark. Having finally gotten his wife and baby daughter to Chicago, he wouldn't risk spending their first night stuck in a rut on the muddy road to Waukegan.

As tired as Kristine was, the energy of Chicago thrilled her. While Odny napped, she bathed and changed into clean clothes from the skin out. When she emerged from the bathroom, Fredrik took her in his arms.

"Kristine, I have dreamt of this day, but holding you is so much better than my dreams. Thank you for coming. I prayed you would."

"You are my husband. Odny is our daughter. We should be together. We are a family," she whispered, shy with this man with whom she had spent so little time.

* * * *

Kristine Kristiansen Hjelmeland, St. Olaf College report, as told to her daughter, Odny, 1943:

They took us to a café and mother thought the cups were much too big and clumsy. She was used to the fine China ware in Norway.

Odny woke, and it was time to go to a neighborhood café for supper. As they walked a few blocks to the café, Kristine and Alf peppered Fredrik with questions.

"Are the gas street lights on all night?"

"Where are all these people going?"

"How many streetcars are there? Where do they all go?"

"How many stories are these buildings?"

"What kind of work is done there?"

So much to look at, to ask about. Fredrik carried Odny while he answered their questions. She clung to his neck, fascinated by the lights and noise. Kristine teared up, so relieved that her baby and handsome husband liked each other. Doubts about leaving her friends in Norway, being in America, learning a new language faded as she felt Fredrik's hand on her back, guiding her, cherishing his baby, speaking lovingly in Norwegian. They walked for two blocks along a brick sidewalk with cars and streetcars passing by. Fredrik stopped where storefront windows shone with the glow from hanging electric bulbs.

"This is the café where we will have some *kveldsmat* (evening food)," he announced.

As they opened the glass doors, Kristine took in the long, narrow room, the assortment of painted tables, and the bare wooden floor. Rugged-looking men sat one or two to a table, bent over plates of food.

"Fredrik," she whispered. "I don't know if we should be here. There are no women."

He looked around, seeming surprised that she was right. He had eaten here before and had bid on installing the electric lights. It was a workingman's place for those not living at a boarding house with meals. Fredrik had expected to see these ruddy-faced fellows in dungarees with rolled up shirtsleeves bent over their plates, shoveling in food without much chatter. He hadn't realized that Kristine had never really seen laborers indoors, in a café.

As their little group stood trying to decide what to do, a round, cushiony woman with a full white apron over her flowered dress bustled out of a back room.

"Hello, welcome. Are you here for supper? We have ham tonight on our blue plate special," she said.

"*Ja*, that sounds good," Fredrik told her and introduced Kristine, Alf, and Odny.

The proprietress seated them at one of the painted wooden tables, all the while chattering away about how nice it was to have a family come in from time to time. One bold fellow asked Fredrik how he had gotten so lucky. Others broke out laughing. Kristine shrank from the attention. The bright light, the bare tables, and snickers from the men made her feel conspicuous, not knowing what was funny. Kristine examined the heavy knife, fork, and soupspoon laid out on the table. Their hostess returned with three mugs of coffee and a piece of soft bread for Odny to chew on.

"Shall I bring the baby some mashed potatoes?" she asked.

Kristine didn't understand the question and Fredrik didn't know what babies ate, so they all looked politely at one another until he nodded. By the time he'd translated for Kristine, the woman had returned to the kitchen.

When the food came, they all got the same thing: a good-sized piece of dry-looking ham with a roll perched on it, mashed potatoes, and waxed beans served on one plate with a blue stripe around the edge. Sipping her coffee from the mug made of the same heavy ceramic as the plate, Kristine thought of supper in her cramped childhood home, where she would have served smoked fish, *flatbrød*, cheese, and fruit. Where *kaffe* did not come with the meal and men did not sit in their shirtsleeves. Suddenly, she felt very far away from Norway. Her new life—creating a family, being a wife, making a home—was beginning.

Fredrik to Mikal Hjelmeland, April 1925.

And now I have a new life, quite different from what I [they] had before.

Chapter Seven

First Impressions

710 County Street

Fredrik Olaf Hjelmeland, Waukegan, Illinois, letter to his brother, Mikal Hjelmeland, in Norway, 1925:

I had already gotten an apartment before they arrived, so that had been well taken care of. We have two bedrooms, a dining room and a living room, kitchen and bathroom. We do not have electric light yet, but that I'm going to install. If everything goes well this summer, I may build my own house before next winter, but it is rather expensive to build these days.

The family set off from the hotel early the next morning, Kristine seated in the front of the shiny Model A. In the second seat, Alf sat swiveling his head from side to side at all the amazing sights Chicago had to offer. Odny was wrapped as warmly as possible, for Fredrik had warned Kristine that the wind off Lake

Michigan was cold on the first day of April even though the sun glinted off the gray water.

When they reached the outskirts of the city on Sheridan Road, they could see glimpses of the lake.

"It looks like the sea," Kristine shouted over the car noise.

"No, it is not a fjord or an inlet from the ocean. It's a very large freshwater lake. They call it a Great Lake." He pointed out of the car at all the homes and offices under construction. "The area is growing because of the railroads and the shipping on the lake."

"So many buildings and houses. Who lives here?" Kristine was curious.

"You can't see it from here, but a lot of factories are being built. Mostly it's the bosses who live along this road, but everyone needs someplace to live. The whole area is filled with new houses being built. I told you I have been very busy installing electricity. It's the building boom that made me choose here to live," Fredrik explained over the wind in the windowless car.

After three hours of driving, Fredrik announced they were almost there. Kristine shifted in her seat. The damp wind blowing in from what still seemed to her like the sea had given her a chill. She loosened her hold on Odny, who had awakened from a nap in her arms. Kristine longed to be wherever it was that he was taking them. Fredrik seemed proud that he had gotten them a flat with two bedrooms, a living room, dining room, and kitchen—plenty of room for their little family and for Alf.

Finally they came to a paved road where the buildings were closer together; they passed a big, fenced-in area with guards.

"What is that?" Kristine asked. "Is it Waukegan?"

"No, it is a base for the U.S. Navy. It's the Great Lakes Naval Station. It's been pretty quiet since the war ended. We're a few miles from Waukegan now, but first we must go through North Chicago."

Kristine merely nodded. It had become such an effort to try to take in all the names and information that Fredrik was telling her. She was ready to be in just one place for a while. When they turned off the paved road onto a dirt street, she sat straighter and turned Odny to look at the duplexes and wooden houses that lined the street, some with two entrances side by side and others with only a single front door. This early in the spring there was no green grass or flowers to brighten the muddy street.

With one more turn onto another residential street, they arrived in front of a two-story house with two doorways. Kristine smiled in relief. They had arrived at their new home, 710 County Street, Waukegan, Illinois.

"Which door is ours, Fredrik?"

"Welcome home. Ours is the doorway to the left. We are on the second floor."

He hurried before her and unlocked the door with a flourish. Carrying Odny, Kristine climbed the stairs to her home as if she were entering a new shop, not certain of what she would find, but interested. She scanned the room that the small hallway opened into for something comfortable or familiar. To her dismay, she had to swallow down her sudden tears. There was hardly any furniture. A stack of newspapers covered a low table next to the single sturdy horsehair chair. Where would they all sit?

Through an archway, she caught a glimpse of a square oak

table with four chairs. Aha, at least they'd all be able to sit and eat together. No candles or houseplants adorned the bare table, only some wires and small metal pieces she assumed to be part of Fredrik's work. Burning coal mixed with the smell of fried onions and garlic in the stale air. A giggle bubbled up—this was home? She needed to compose herself. Thank goodness Fredrik was still bringing in the luggage.

She was tired. Everything she saw looked unfinished, too new. The furniture was too sparse, no curtains or rugs. The grimy windows faced dingy siding on another two-flat, just a few feet away. For this brusque man and this meager flat, she'd left behind everything and everyone she knew and loved?

Fredrik and Alf interrupted her brief reverie. "Kristine, should we put this trunk in the kitchen or one of the bedrooms?" Fredrik asked.

"The bedroom, I guess. I haven't seen it yet."

She put Odny down. The baby took wide steps staggering after the men, hanging onto Kristine's hand. Trying to take in all she had expected to see but didn't, Kristine watched them put the trunk next to a bed covered with rumpled sheets and a scratchy-looking blanket. A chest of drawers and an oval wicker basket in a corner completed the furnishings.

"Fredrik, where is a bed for Odny? I need to feed her and see if she will take a nap."

He looked from the toddler to the basket in the corner, "*Ja,* I thought maybe here?"

"In the basket?" Kristine laughed.

"What's so funny?" Fredrik scowled.

Kristine tried to swallow her growing panic over what she had hoped for but was now seeing. She turned to him. "Look at her. She's taller than the basket is long."

Odny took a few steps, fell to her pudgy knees, and crawled to the basket. She grabbed the side of the basket so hard it tipped over her head like an oversized hat.

Kristine could not contain herself. Her laughter tinged with hysteria got Fredrik to laughing. When Alf brought in another suitcase, he found Kristine and Fredrik sitting on the edge of the bed, giggling with their little girl. They looked like a family.

Sometime later they managed a simple supper of porridge and some smoked meat Kristine was able to find from the specialties she had packed in her trunk. They had arrived in the place that would one day be home, but for now it was enough to be together.

Kristine and Odny, 710 County St., Waukegan, IL, 1925

Chapter Eight

Making a Home. Day to Day.

Fredrik Olaf Hjelmeland, Waukegan, Illinois, letter to Mikal Hjelmeland, April 15, 1925:

Times are good. Much construction work is going on in Chicago as well as here in Waukegan. I work mostly out on the countryside and in small towns. I have plenty to do and am very busy. Kristine is happy to have me at home [today], you see, as I have been away almost every day since she arrived. We [he and Alf] drive in the country every morning and return home around six or seven in the evening.

* * * *

Kristine opened her eyes to bright light coming through curtain-less windows. She didn't recognize the room, the rumpled bedclothes next to her. Maybe she was still dreaming. Seeing Odny asleep on a makeshift pallet on the floor, Kristine sat up, trying to piece together where she was. *Fredrik's voice from another room, apartment in America.* She jumped out of bed and pulled on her dressing gown. After the long journey, she had overslept, but that was not how she wanted her first day to begin. Hurrying to stoke the stove, she charged into Fredrik coming out of the indoor bathroom.

"*Uff a meg* (oh, no), I can't believe I slept so long. It won't take long to make some breakfast," she said, trying to pass him to get into the kitchen.

Fredrik grabbed her arms and spun her around as if to dance, exuberant to wake to an apartment filled with people, and not just any people—his wife, daughter, and nephew.

"Kristine, it is done! The coffee is cooking and the hard tack is out. I keep things very simple, you know."

"What I know is that I'm supposed to make breakfast. Do you have eggs? Herring? Bread? Cheese?"

He dropped his hold of her.

"Nothing so fancy as that, just coffee and some bread," he said.

She bustled over to the stove and checked for coffee in the pot. It was, in fact, brewed. After she found a towel to use as a hot pad, she poured Fredrik a cup, and looked around. She'd forgotten that the stove was gas like the lights, so she didn't have to stoke it.

"*Ja,* I suppose you have been making your own breakfast for a while," Kristine said. The newness of it all was fresh on her first morning of her new life. "Where is Alf? Getting dressed?"

"He is. I'd like to get going soon. Today's job is out in Grayslake, an hour's drive from here, and I have a lot to teach him."

"You're leaving me here alone?" Kristine asked in disbelief.

Alf Solemslid with Fredrik and Kristine, 1925.

Fredrik paused in spreading butter across his piece of rye bread, as dry as a thick cracker. In his excitement to see Kristine and Odny, he hadn't thought about changing his routine.

"I have taken two days off from work already. The rent here is $40 a month," he said, his voice rising. "We can't pay that if I don't work. I only get paid if I work."

Getting paid only for working made sense to Kristine, but she didn't really know what he meant. Not since she was a girl had she had a job other than mother's helper. She'd never had money of her own to spend, but she'd never paid rent either. Money was something men handled. She could tell from the way he'd changed when she asked if he was going to leave today, she had asked something she shouldn't. There always was something that shouldn't be asked about. She took another approach.

"When will you be back?"

Before he could answer her, she heard Odny awake and crying. Fredrik heard her, too. The baby reminded them both that living as a family was new. Kristine left Fredrik in the kitchen with some cheese to go with his coffee and bread. By the time she got back, carrying Odny, she was calmer and Fredrik was standing at the sink.

"I think I will spend the day unpacking and make a list," she said. "Can you get eggs and some more milk?"

"That I can do. I know all the farms around here. We will pass the best place for eggs on our way to the job," he said. "Is your list all food? We have a good market just down the street."

"Oh, no, we will need to buy some food, but right now I have many things to do to make this house a home," she said.

She could see that he was not thinking of what could be needed other than food, but she hoped to surprise him by cleaning and getting out some of the linens and dishes she had brought in her trunks.

"Okay, then, we will try to get back by 5:00 p.m. I don't like driving these country roads after dark."

After pouring more coffee into a thermos and packing enough bread and cheese for both Alf and Fredrik's lunch, she was startled when Fredrik leaned over for a good-bye kiss. No time to ask about the neighbors, the market, what she should do if she got cold or heard strange noises. Just "good-bye, see you later." She turned to Odny who was busy pulling herself from the floor to a standing position.

"Well, little one, what shall we do with today? Shall I start unpacking in the bedroom?"

Odny's only reply was a happy gurgle.

After weeks of caregiving, grief, preparing to leave, and traveling, she was alone in a strange apartment, knew no one, and could not speak English if she did venture out of the apartment. Kristine stared into her coffee cup as if it could make sense of how this had come to be. With a shake of her head, she straightened her shoulders and began to dig in one of her trunks. She knew she needed to be busy, not dwell on what she was missing. Her mother had always said you could not be sad if you kept your hands busy. She threw herself into setting up the apartment, befit for a refined Norwegian merchant. Just as she had been trained to do in *husmorskole*, fifteen years before.

* * * *

Each day the first week, when Fredrik and Alf returned from their day of installing generators and wiring in barns and homes, she greeted them with a hot meal and another room that had been scrubbed and rearranged. Room by room, the lists took shape for additional chairs, end tables, and lamps. She made simple but tasty meals of omelets flavored with the dried mutton leg, *spekekjøttt,* that she had brought packed deep in a trunk, making do with what she had or could get Fredrik to stop and buy. By the end of the week, she was baking bread.

"Fredrik, what kind of flour is this?" Kristine asked as she sliced into a freshly baked loaf of bread.

"What do you mean? It's flour. I asked for flour at the market, and that's what they gave me."

"The bread looks different from what I made at home. Is it rye or barley or wheat?" Kristine sighed. She was trying so hard to do at least one thing that looked or tasted just like home. Bread should have been so simple.

"For heaven sake, it's flour. You made bread. It's good." He took a big bite of the warm bread slathered with butter.

"It doesn't taste right to me. Next time you must ask for both wheat and barley flour. Bread is best if those flours are mixed." She bit off a small piece of bread. "It's just not as good as it should be."

"Next time I go to the market, you must come along. I will translate so you can get what you want. Not tomorrow, but maybe next week, when we finish the job we are on," he said.

"I would like that. I have begun a list," she said and handed Fredrik the envelope that she had written her list on.

She watched his face close in on itself as he scanned the list: fresh meat, milk, fish, potatoes, farina, a porridge pan, mixing bowls, muslin, and a sewing machine.

"We cannot get everything on this list. There's no herring in Lake Michigan, and I don't really like freshwater fish. What is a porridge pan, and why do you need a sewing machine?" he asked with a frown.

"No fish? I guess it is better than bad fish, but what do people eat?" She wished she knew him well enough to know what was upsetting him. "A porridge pan is round and deep. It is hard to cook porridge in a skillet. And I need a sewing machine to finish the curtains and make clothes for Odny, she is growing so fast."

"Don't count on the sewing machine. I don't think we have the money for that. Is it really necessary?"

"Fredrik, I am a seamstress. How will I work without a sewing machine?" she asked, near tears. This was bad news for her. She loved to sew, and it would help pass the long hours alone with Odny.

"For now you will just have to make do," Fredrik said and pulled out the papers to roll a cigarette. "Let's talk about this later."

* * * *

Indoor plumbing and running water. The gas stove that burned clean and did not need to be stoked. These were conveniences that Kristine was happy to have. Even the many-armed coal furnace in the dark basement seemed like a better idea than individual room heaters or fireplaces. Her first English lessons were how to greet and pay the ice man and the coal man. They became her contact with the outside world, as Fredrik had not been home long enough to introduce her to neighbors.

Proud of herself for learning new ways of doing her chores, she nonetheless found that the days passed slowly. Cleaning and cooking did not take as long as it had in the crowded house in Førde. Having only Odny to care for and only one hot meal a day to prepare left many hours to fill. Despite plenty of hand hemming and knitting projects, she was soon itching to stitch up more work shirts for Alf and Fredrik and start on dresses and a coat for Odny. She'd brought enough fabric for curtains in one bedroom and the front room, but she really wanted a sewing machine to give them a nice finished look.

* * * *

Fredrik Olaf Hjelmeland, Waukegan, Illinois, letter to Mikal Hjelmeland, April 1925:

Today I have been at home installing the lights. I will stay at home tomorrow as well to finish it. Kristine is happy to have me at home; she and Odny are alone every day. But Kristine has been so busy since she arrived getting everything in order and has not had time to become homesick. I believe she had thought America to be much worse than it really is. I was so worried that she would be homesick, but now I don't think she will be.

One evening while Alf looked after Odny, Fredrik took Kristine for a ride to show her the town where she was living. A private car ride with her husband was a treat. It was almost as if they were courting, since she and Fredrik had had precious little time alone as a couple. Driving up Sheridan Road past Bowen Park, Fredrik announced that he would be taking the next day off to install electricity in their apartment and their neighbor's apartment.

"Wonderful! Shall we go first thing in the morning to get a sewing machine?" she asked, sneaking a sidelong glance at him. She saw his clenched jaw as he stared straight out at the deserted roadway. What was his temper like? She had heard stories of other husbands lashing out in anger, but this was her husband, and she was entirely dependent on him in this new place. She felt a ripple of fear.

"Did you not hear me? I'm staying home to install electricity. Won't it be great to have lights that don't flicker around? Then we can get an electric icebox, too. No more melting ice." He sounded annoyed, but not truly angry.

"Yes, Fredrik, those things will be nice, but I need a sewing machine." Kristine tried to mollify him, but also saw this time at home during the days that shops were open as an opportunity, even while she wondered how far to push for the sewing machine.

"Kristine, we will not have money to buy a sewing machine if I spend my work day shopping." he said impatiently. "The landlady is taking my labor off our rent and paying me good money for materials."

"So this is how it will be. You leave me alone all day with

your daughter, and the neighbor ladies start to talk because she has outgrown her clothes. They will know that because there is electric light in the house to see with no curtains to block them from looking in." She tried to tease, but it came out more sarcastic than she wanted.

"What are you talking about?" Fredrik asked, exasperated, not amused.

"Well, you know that Norwegian fellow, he was so busy making everything light up, he forgot about his wife and daughter. That's what they will say if I don't get a sewing machine to make some new clothes for Odny and finish the curtains for the windows." She tried to make her tone light.

After a long pause in which nothing was said and Kristine became convinced that she had crossed some unknown line, Fredrik asked, "How much does a sewing machine cost?"

"I don't know in America. In Norway, it costs many kroner. Usually women get one for a wedding present. At home I used mother's." Sensing he was considering buying, Kristine dropped her teasing. "If we get one, it would be the only one I would ever need."

Talking about home and the things people got there as part of getting married made Kristine think about how different her life was from her friends and how far away from home that she was. She longed for a friend to talk with about the trip, the apartment, the new places she'd been. Writing letters wasn't the same as sharing a cup of tea and chatting. She fell quiet. It was better to be busy and not compare what was to what is.

Fredrik turned the car off the main road to a path on the

bluff and parked, pulling up on the hand brake. Facing Lake Michigan, the breeze carried a damp, fishy smell. In the April dusk, no ship lights shone on the dark waters.

After a few moments of listening to the strong rhythm of the waves on the shore, Kristine said," I understand, Fredrik, if I cannot have a sewing machine yet, but I hope someday I can."

"Are you homesick, Kristine?"

"A bit perhaps, mostly lonely, I think. I have no one except Odny to talk to, and she doesn't answer back." She tried to laugh, but it came out more like clearing her throat.

Fredrik reached out and put his arm around Kristine. She slid across the bench seat. "*Ja*, Kristine, I am a bit out of practice telling anyone what my plans are. I have been alone all these years."

Savoring the weight of his arm pulling her close, she didn't speak but lay her head on his shoulder and stared into the darkness

He broke the silence, "Tomorrow I must work, but perhaps we can take an hour to find out how much a sewing machine costs."

"Oh, thank you, Fredrik." She lifted her head and kissed him. "We could be quick, not take too much time from your day. Do you know where to go?"

"No, but we will find out." He breathed as he lowered his head for a longer, deeper kiss.

She turned into his kiss, and thoughts of work and sewing machines were forgotten for the night.

Sometime later, when they left their spot on the bluff, Kristine said, "I won't be lonely tomorrow." Her natural good spirits had returned. "Do you remember what day tomorrow is?"

"April 15, why?"

"It is your daughter's first birthday, Papa! We will celebrate being together!"

* * * *

Fredrik to Mikal Hjelmeland, April, 1925

And so we have little Odny. She was one year yesterday. She is big and healthy for her age and so good. She sleeps the whole night through which is very nice…when I come home in the evening she calls me daddy. It's nice to get them as big as this from the start! She is fat, like a butterball, rolling and crawling on the floor…Her daddy loves her very much.

Kristine straightened her newly hung curtains. She wanted Fredrik to see something from the sewing machine as soon as he walked through the front door in the evening. She had been sewing and arranging furniture to make the apartment as fine as possible. The two days Fredrik had spent installing electricity had been wonderful for her. Not only had they bought a fine sewing machine, but she had seen Odny capture Fredrik's heart.

Since they had stepped down from the train, Odny had been delighted with her father. Even though he was a stranger to her, she had held out her arms and smiled. If he was home, she only wanted her "Daddy." She was trying to talk, and Kristine thought that even before Odny learned to say "no," she learned "Daddy" in English. He seemed equally entranced. Every morning before he left, he woke her up and held her while he had his coffee. It was as if he couldn't quite believe she wasn't just visiting.

"Hello, ladies. Are you at home for some hungry workmen?" Fredrik burst through the door and swooped Odny from the floor where she had been playing.

"Daddy, daddy…" she chortled.

Energy swirled around Fredrik, a man of medium height and quick, efficient movements. His brown head bent toward her light brown curls as he tickled the baby wriggling in his arms. Alf dragged his steps as he came in, looking like he'd been working hard.

"What have you and mommy been up to today while daddy was working?" Fredrik snuggled her next to him in his horsehair armchair, but Odny wiggled around and dropped herself onto the floor. Perhaps that was why they got along so well, they were both always on the move.

"I could answer for her," Kristine said with a smile. "What do you think of the curtains in this room?"

"I thought it looked especially nice in here. I like them, they look like quality."

Kristine beamed with a satisfied smile. "Quality" was a high compliment from Fredrik.

"The new machine is working out for you?" he asked, opening his Norwegian language paper, *Decorah Posten*.

"Oh, yes, it is nicer than the one I used at home. I also finished the bedroom curtains," she said.

When they were shopping for the sewing machine, she had learned about Fredrik's pride. The least expensive model would have been fine for her, but Fredrik said no. If she needed a sewing machine, he wanted the best. It was to last a long time. When he found out that there was an option for adding an electric motor to the machine, he seemed to get more interested. The motor was more money than Fredrik could afford, but he bought the more expensive model to which a motor could be added later.

While Fredrik and the salesman talked about the mechanics of the machine, Kristine tested the treadle and flywheel. In a beautiful mahogany cabinet, this sewing machine could be used as a side table when she wasn't sewing. She felt excluded from the decisions, but in the end, they were both pleased. She got a sewing machine and Fredrik learned of yet another household item that was being electrified.

* * * *

Fredrik was still doing all the food shopping, but on nice days she and Odny got out for walks. They had walked to the grocer's, past the butcher's, and looked in the window of the hardware store along County Street. One especially nice day they walked all the way to a beautiful stone building with a curved stone front that said "Public Library." When she asked Fredrik whether this fine building was a castle, he said, "No it is a *bibliotek* (library) for everyone." Kristine was astonished by that and didn't really believe that someone like her could go into that fine building. Still, no one seemed to mind if she stood outside and looked at the big lake, which seemed like the ocean. She had stood there a while imagining that she could see all the way home to Norway.

Everything seemed fairly new—the houses, the streets. Many streets seemed to have been paved recently, including Sheridan Road, the main road south to Chicago and north to Milwaukee. Fredrik told her that there were many new people in Waukegan, not just them. After World War I, the factories in Chicago had expanded and built farther and farther north. Railroad traffic and shipping on the Great Lakes made this area a hub for all of the Midwest.

She could see that Waukegan had a raw edge to it, bustling with so many different people from so many places. She was curious about where people came from and how they got to Waukegan. Even though she was interested, she took comfort in Fredrik talking about going home to Norway.

Most evenings they went for a drive. As long as Alf stayed with them, they had a built-in babysitter. When the temperatures got hot and sticky, Kristine appreciated driving along Sheridan Road, where she could catch some lake breezes.

Fredrik drove and talked. "Today I sold three more generators to fellows in Gurnee. If I sell three every day, I will have to hire more help."

"So much business?" Kristine said. "That is good, isn't it?"

"Yes and no." He paused as if he was working out something in his mind. "More help means I might need an office and a place to ship things. Employees and stores are expensive to maintain. On the other hand, the more jobs I get, the sooner we will have enough to buy something in Førde."

That was the magic phrase for Kristine. To her, buying something in Førde meant going home, to her family and friends.

"If you keep getting jobs, when will you buy something in Førde? Next year?"

Hearing the longing in her voice, Fredrik's answer was gentle but more realistic. "No, not next year. It will take a few years. With expenses, the generators alone will not be enough. I will need to buy and sell property here before I can buy in Førde."

"A few years?" Kristine hadn't really thought in terms of more than one or two. "Then I must learn English. I cannot make a good home here if I cannot talk to the grocer or my neighbors."

"Alf is going to take English at the new YMCA at night. Do you want to go with him? It's a short walk from the apartment." Fredrik said.

"Yes, maybe then I can shop by myself and get to know Maggie downstairs," Kristine said. "But who will take care of Odny while we are gone?"

"I will, if you have her fed and ready for bed before you leave for class."

Kristine liked everything about this plan. It would give her someplace to go, and it seemed very modern to her for the father to take care of the baby

For Kristine, YMCA English classes opened a door to making Waukegan a home. Days passed into months.

Kristine became more comfortable in her marriage and in the upper duplex apartment she called home. Only when a letter came from her father or one of her siblings did Kristine long for home, family, and friends.

Chapter Nine

Poot Rohst

Fredrik Olaf Hjelmeland, Waukegan, Illinois, to his brother, F. Mikal Hjelmeland, in Norway, April 1925:

You had to wait a long time for this letter, but you know, I have been so busy, and the time ran short. You see, I have to do the shopping as well. The days pass too quickly, and I feel I get too little done now that I have my family here and a home of our own.

* * * *

Kristine lifted her face to the afternoon sun and breathed in the humid breeze from Lake Michigan while she waited for her neighbor Maggie. On the patch of grass in front of their flat, thirteen-month-old Odny toddled, young blades of grass tickling her bare knees, on this late spring day.

A month ago Maggie was one of the first people to come to meet Kristine. Maggie was new to Waukegan, too, from

Wisconsin. Maggie, her husband, and their toddler son had moved into the downstairs flat six months before when her husband got a job at the new Chain Link factory up the road. Maggie was taking Kristine for her first trip to the butcher shop without Fredrik.

Fitting it in around his work schedule, Fredrik had been doing most of the grocery shopping. When Kristine was able to shop with him, he was too impatient to teach her much. He was away working so much that she was anxious to be able to get meat and groceries by herself, but that also seemed complicated to her. First, she had to know where the shops were that she could walk to. Then, she needed to be able to ask for what she wanted in English. Finally, she needed to understand the money so she didn't pay more than she should for groceries.

"A-piece-of-meat-please." Kristine practiced exactly what Fredrik had written down for her.

When she heard a door open, Kristine stuffed the practice note in her pocket as Maggie and her little boy, Kevin, clattered down the front porch steps. Younger than Kristine, the slight woman with curly black hair waved a hand as she hurried to join Kristine and Odny.

"You look so nice for a trip to the meat market." Maggie pointed at Kristine's neat white blouse and brown skirt and then at her own faded housedress.

"*Ja, takk*, thanks," Kristine smiled, not really knowing what all Maggie's English words meant, but they sounded pleasant. She liked Maggie, who was energetic and talkative even when Kristine couldn't answer her.

Even though she didn't speak Norwegian, Maggie was helping her learn the names of foods. Last week before they went to the grocer's, she had pointed to foods in Maggie's pantry and Maggie had told her what the English word was. Some were very like Norwegian names: potatoes, carrots, but not *lokken,* onions. *Farina* was very difficult, cream of wheat. When Fredrik wrote it down for her at home, she practiced so that one day soon she could shop by herself. She didn't quite understand the money yet, but he had given her some today. Maggie was to help her if she needed it, but she'd asked to try to do it by herself. While they walked down County Street to the shops, Kristine listened to Maggie talk, trying to pick out words she could understand.

In just four blocks, they arrived. The sign painted on the window said Cribbs Meat Market. As they walked in, Kristine was relieved to see there were no other customers in the clean shop that smelled a bit of bleach and blood.

Wiping the curved glass of the long meat case, a man straightened up and said, "Good afternoon ladies, nice to finally get some sun." This must be the butcher. Fredrik had told her his name was Lou Cribbs.

He looked like a butcher should, sturdy with a clean white apron tied securely across his belly. "What can I get for you?"

Maggie called the butcher Mr. Lou. "What's good today?"

After some discussion, Maggie decided on two pounds round steak, four pork chops, and a pot roast.

Kristine listened carefully. What were round steak, pork chops, pot roast? Among all these different names, she didn't hear the word meat. What were pounds? Fredrik did not tell her about this. Her nervousness grew as Mr. Lou wrapped Maggie's order into neat brown papers and took her money.

"What can I get for you?" Mr. Lou turned to her.

Kristine cleared her throat, Maggie nodded to encourage her. Now Kristine wished she had not decided to try this by herself, but they both were waiting for her to say something.

Softly, wrapping her tongue around each word, Kristine said, "Please may I have a poot rohst?"

She saw Mr. Lou dip his head, trying to hide his smile, as he reached into the display case. She wondered if he knew that she was Fredrik's wife. Fredrik had wired the shop for the new cooler case.

"How does this pot roast look to you?" Mr. Lou placed it on a waxy paper square on the scale. "Is three pounds good?"

Kristine blushed, "Poot rohst?"

"Yes, very good, pot roast."

Finally, Maggie spoke up, "Good for you, Kristine. You will like pot roast. You cook it with onions, celery, carrots, and potatoes. I'll show you."

Mr. Lou and Maggie looked at her expectantly. She needed to say something more…

Kristine took a deep breath, "How much?"

"Twenty-five cents a pound, seventy-five cents, it's a nice piece of meat."

Suddenly Kristine smiled. Nice "piece of meat." That was what Fredrik had taught her.

"*Ja,* okay, I will take it." She showed Maggie her money while Lou wrapped the meat.

"Oh, yes, you have plenty of money, two dollars. Do you want to get something else?" Maggie asked.

"Sumting elz?" Kristine didn't understand.

"More meat?"

"*Nei, nei*, no more meat." Kristine didn't know if she could find the words to pay for what she had.

Strolling home, Kristine nodded and smiled as Maggie talked. Odny and two-year-old Kevin toddled along, slowing their progress. Kristine clutched her package, proud that she'd bought meat all by herself.

"You did really well, Kristine. So many English words and you have been here only a month! Did Fredrik help you?" Maggie asked.

Kristine looked at her blankly. She could hear there had been a question, but she had no idea what was said. It was so tiring listening for words she understood. The sounds all were strung together into one long word.

"Fredrik?"

"Um, yes, Fredrik. Will you make the pot roast today?" Maggie shouted each word slowly as if Kristine were a dim, hard-of-hearing child.

"*Ja, toodah*," Kristine answered.

"Okay, good, I will help you. Just let me put my meat in the ice box and we'll come over."

"I don't understand." Kristine tried another phrase Fredrik had taught her.

Through gestures, pointing, and more shouting, Maggie helped Kristine understand that she would lend her a cooking pot and come over to help cook the pot roast.

Later Kristine checked the *saus* (sauce) for the roast and added a little more water to the borrowed pot. If Fredrik didn't come home soon, her surprise would be ruined. Already the carrots were looking dried out. She wanted a pot like this one so she could put the onions, celery, and carrots in with the meat. Maggie said she needed one. She'd called it a "Dutch oven." Another name for Kristine to learn.

"Kristine, what smells so good? Did you make it to the butcher today?" Fredrik was asking even before he came into the kitchen.

"*Tante*, I am so hungry, how long until we eat?" Alf followed Fredrik, shedding his jacket and hat in the front hall.

"As soon as you two can clean up. Odny is already fed and in bed. You are late tonight."

"*Ja*, we were so close that we stayed until we finished. But we're here now."

Minutes later Kristine stood next to the table, holding the Dutch oven.

"The poot rohst is ready," she said in English, just as Maggie had taught her.

"So American, pot roast, Sunday dinner on a Thursday," Fredrik said.

Kristine dished up the meat and vegetables, and the men dug into their meals, hungry after a long day of work. Sometime later, when they had helped themselves to more and complimented Kristine on her cooking and her English, she told Fredrik about her trip to the butcher and that now she needed a Dutch oven.

Kristine had barely begun English classes at night school, but she was learning just the same.

After that first visit to Cribbs', when Kristine made beef, she always cooked pot roasts. Finally, Fredrik asked if they could have beef ribs, a steak, or maybe a pork roast, but Kristine didn't know what those were exactly. She knew how to ask for a pot roast, what it should cost, and how to make the butcher smile, so pot roast became her specialty. If Kristine was making beef, you could be sure it was poot rohst in the Dutch oven with celery, carrots, onions, and potatoes.

Chapter Ten

Christmas in America

Fredrik Olaf Hjelmeland, Waukegan, Illinois, writing to his father, Gunder (Gunnar) Hjelmeland, December 5, 1925:

We are all well. We are healthy and Odny is soon a big girl. She is so busy with toys, and she puts the house upside down. Kristine and Alf have been to evening school this fall and now know a lot of English, but it doesn't go so fast either…I work for myself; I like that best, and have quite a lot of work right now…I shall be here for another year, but then I have to go up to Canada again to take care of my land there.

Kristine rubbed her lower back as she lowered the eggs into the boiling water. One more egg today for Fredrik's nephew, Gudmund, who had arrived in Chicago yesterday. A plume of steam from the boiling eggs made her queasy. With only three more months to go, she'd thought she was past that part of pregnancy. Last summer when it grew so hot, Fredrik had blamed the heat for her fatigue and nausea, but she knew right away it wasn't the heat. He hadn't been with her in Norway when she was pregnant with Odny. Once he was convinced it was a baby, he treated her as if she would break if she picked up Odny or carried the wash out to the line by herself. He so wanted a son. Such a fuss.

Once the worst of the morning sickness had passed, she felt good, and Fredrik relaxed. Now, though, her ankles were swelling more than she remembered with Odny. Every now and then a wave of queasiness reminded her that this pregnancy was different from the first. Fortunately, Fredrik was working harder than ever, away long hours every day. He did not see her crying when she wrote her letters home. If only her sister were nearby to tell her that this swelling and sleeplessness were normal.

Now Gudmund Osen, son of Fredrik's sister, Kristine, had arrived and would be staying with them for the winter until she had the baby or he had made enough money to get a place of his own. Whichever came first. As she set out the bread, butter, cheese, and boiled eggs, she thought back to her first days in America. Gudmund would be worn out from all the newness, especially if he went to work right away with Fredrik. He seemed a nice enough young fellow, but two bedrooms were not enough for two children, two single men, Fredrik, and her.

"*God morgen,* I just woke Gudmund. We'll leave for work as soon as he has had some breakfast." Fredrik sat down next to a plate and cup at the small square table covered with a crisp white cloth.

"I'm glad he is here. I will write to your sister today that we will take care of her boy, especially at Christmas."

"*Ja*, I don't think he's missing much. He told me that his father is struggling to keep the farm. The hay crop failed, so no one had cash for the milk and cheese. Sounds like the whole area is struggling." He laid out his tobacco and rolled a cigarette.

Kristine frowned. She didn't like cigarette smoke in the house but she had something important to ask. She didn't mention the smoke.

"Before Christmas, do you think we could buy that table we saw in the window of Blumberg's? With Gudmund here, we have run out of places for people to sit at dinner," she said, leaning against the sink.

Fredrik put the cigarette away and cracked his egg.

"I can buy another chair and Odny can sit in my lap to make room. She doesn't usually eat with us any way. I want to wait for a new place to get a new table," he said.

"But Fredrik, what will we do if we have Ben or someone for Christmas *middag?*"

"*Ja*, we don't all have to eat at the same time."

Hands on her hips, she peered over her glasses. He didn't look up from his breakfast.

Kristine picked up a dishcloth and swiped at an already spotless countertop. "It has been a long time since you had an *ekte Norsk Jul*, authentic Norwegian Christmas," she said, struggling to keep her voice even. "We *must* all come to the table together."

"We've talked about this already. We will get a bigger table when we get a bigger place." He raised his gaze, blue eyes icy.

She rested her arms on her pregnant middle and didn't say anything.

After some mutual staring, Fredrik's words tumbled out in a rush, "I'm talking today with a fellow about a nice plot of land in Waukegan. You might like that better than moving to Libertyville. Although I already own that piece of land. Libertyville is perfect for a new house. It's growing so fast I could sell whatever I build for a big profit. And then we would have enough money to celebrate Christmas in Norway." With a smug smile, he stood up. "I'll be right back. Tell Gudmund we need to leave for work soon."

Listening to him clatter down the stairs and out to his car, Kristine tried to make sense of what he'd said. For some reason, Fredrik didn't want to buy a proper dining table. In the eight months since she had arrived, she'd learned a lot about living in America, but also about Fredrik. More than having the Norwegian workers stay, more than she and Odny and the coming baby, she was beginning to understand that what kind of house they had was mixed up with how long they would live here. One moment Fredrik told her a new table would wait for a bigger place, the next moment he talked about going back to Norway in a year or two, and the next he was talking about building houses. She was barely oriented to this place, much less talk about another town.

She cut some more slices of bread and turned her thoughts to Christmas preparations. The packages for her father and Fredrik's, and her nieces and nephews, had gone off last week. Hopefully three weeks was enough time to get to Norway. The direct ships didn't sail so often in the wintertime.

"*God morgen, Tante,*" Gudmund greeted her. "Am I too early?"

"No, no. Fredrik will be back in a moment. He went to put

all the supplies you will need into the car. Just sit down, *vaer så god*," she said as she poured the coffee and turned to finish packing lunches and a thermos.

Gudmund was not the first young man she had made breakfast for and would help along, but he was the first close relative other than Alf. In her role as mistress of the household, she'd come to expect that someone might show up with little notice, looking for a place to stay, a Norwegian meal, or tips on who was hiring. Waukegan was a small place but close enough to Chicago that immigrants found their way to Fredrik and Kristine. Somehow, when she was helping others find their way, she felt a little less lonely. Even if he was Fredrik's family, Gudmund being here would make Christmas feel more like home.

Odny toddled in from her bed, still flushed from sleep.

"Say good morning to Gudmund," Kristine said.

"Up, up." Odny held out her arms.

When Kristine bent to pick her up, Odny said with perfect pronunciation, "Good morning, sir."

"*God morgen.*" Gudmund smiled. "Do you speak Norwegian?"

Odny considered the stranger and kept gnawing on a piece of rusk.

"Of course she does, but Fredrik speaks English to her and to me when I am practicing, so I think Odny is a bit confused," said Kristine. Hearing steps on the stairs, she poured a fresh cup of coffee.

"Ah, Gudmund, *god morgen*, are you ready to work?" Fredrik asked as he came through the door, grabbing coffee and Odny in the same quick reach.

"Of course, if you will be along to translate and direct me. I'm not familiar with Delco equipment."

"*Ja*, they didn't teach you everything in that technical school?" Fredrik clapped him on the shoulder, smiling. He had gone to the same school and was proud to be apprenticing Gudmund.

Kristine set the packed lunches and thermos on the table. "You will think about what I said Fredrik? Your first family Christmas in more than fifteen years? What do you want Odny to remember?"

He looked from the toddler in his arms to her and saw that she had not been diverted by his real estate talk. "I am thinking about it, Kristine. I'll see what I can do, but do not get your hopes up. You will make it special with or without a new table."

With a hug, he put Odny down and shrugged on his jacket. Gudmund took his cue from Fredrik, pulled on a coat and hat, and they were down the stairs to the job on a farm.

Kristine in a postscript to a letter from Fredrik to his father, December 5, 1925:

> *Now it is soon Christmas. Would that we remember Him who came to earth to save we who are lost. I am so happy that my mother will be celebrating Christmas in her right home where there is no more sorrow or sin anymore.*
>
> *Now, Grandfather, I want to wish you a blessed Christmas. We often talk about you. Also, you must have a very good New Year. Give my greetings to Mikal and Marie and little Gunnar. Give them our dearest thanks for what we received. It was delicious to have Norwegian meat.*

Live well,
Warmest greetings from Kristine

In a short while, the men left. Kristine hummed the hymn *Deilig er Jorden,* Beautiful Savior, while she put water on to boil for washing underwear. The hymn fit her pietistic, homesick mood. Looking ahead had brought thoughts of her mother, who had died since last Christmas, and all the people she wouldn't be with in Norway. "Bright the flowers of blooming spring…" She imagined her mother among flowers in heaven, how her mother had loved roses.

She was trying to do a little something each day to prepare. It would be strange with just this small family, but it helped her homesickness to make it as much a *Norske Jul,* Norwegian Christmas, as she could. That day she hoped to bake *sandbakkels,* a formed butter cookie, and finish knitting a few ornaments to add to the embroidered miniature baskets she had ready to hang on the tree. She'd had a letter from her sister-in-law, Alfred's wife, saying that *Far* and Karl and the children would spend the holiday with them. Last year Kristine had baked and cleaned for weeks, as mother had been too sick to help with preparations. In a melancholy way, it comforted her to think of her mother. Even if she had stayed in Førde, Christmas would have been lonely with every decoration and traditional meal reminding them of Mother, who was no longer with them.

* * * *

Christmas in Waukegan, Fredrik and Kristine.

"*Tusen takk for fine Julemat*, Kristine (Thank you so much for the wonderful Christmas food)," Alf said as he pushed himself away from the remains of *spekekjøtt, cured mutton, flatbrød,* and, best of all, *rømmegrøt,* sour cream porridge.

This started a chorus of thanks from all the men around the new, bigger table that sat eight comfortably. In the end, Kristine had her way. Despite Fredrik's initial objections, the new table was now in their apartment. In addition to the two cousins, Alf and Gudmund, they had been joined by two young Norwegian men, Ben Hjelmeland and Hagbart Yndestad, who had taken the train from Chicago to spend Christmas Day with Kristine and Fredrik. When Fredrik stood, bent over, kissed her, and said a tender "*Gladelig Jul* (Merry Christmas)," Kristine began to cry.

"And *Hjertelig Gratulerer med dagen,* Fredrik (Happy Birthday from my heart)," Kristine whispered as she wiped her eyes. For Fredrik, not only was it Christmas, but December 25 was his birthday.

"Ah, Kristine. I can hardly believe what a lucky man I am to have you here, a family, and such a beautiful Christmas." He pulled her as close as her thickening body allowed.

Her tears confused the young men around the table who had been laughing and enjoying one another over the buttery *rømmegrøt.* Each cinnamon-laced bite of sour cream porridge brought back memories of home. Kristine had taken extra care with Norwegian foods to make up for the many Christmases that Fredrik had spent away from family and Norway. Between her pregnancy fatigue and homesickness, she was overwhelmed by his embrace. Seeing her mother's tears, Odny began to cry, too.

Before they could all start thinking of what they were missing at home, Alf changed the mood again.

"Boys, let's wash the dishes for Kristine, and then it's time to dance around the Christmas tree."

Everyone got busy. When she bent to wipe the tears from Odny's face, Kristine felt Fredrik wrap his arm around her pregnant middle. The traditional activities that he had not celebrated in so long had made Fredrik affectionate. Even though she was bent over with a toddler standing between them, Kristine returned his tenderness and wanted to just rest in his arms. Reaching around her, Fredrik picked up Odny and helped her straighten up. They stood, arms around each other, and their child for a quiet moment.

"Are you homesick, Kristine?" Fredrik asked.

"No, Fredrik, I am with you and our daughter. This is home." As she said these words, all thoughts of Førde and her family there were replaced with a deep sense that this is where she was meant to be, with Odny, enveloped in Fredrik's embrace. A clatter from the kitchen broke their tender moment.

Kristine left Odny with Fredrik and bustled into the kitchen to supervise.

"Do not use the homemade soap on the silver *rømmegrøt* spoons. Be sure to use really hot water." Kristine surveyed her kitchen not trusting these young bachelors with her best flatware and dishes.

Fredrik pulled the Christmas tree out from the corner and plugged in the electric lights, cautioning Odny not to touch. Fairly new to shops, the lights replaced the dangerous candles so many used. Kristine would have liked to have had traditional candles, but it seemed disloyal to her electrician husband to even think about that.

"*O, Jul med den glade, vi klapper henden vi.*" Kristine's soprano blended with the young male voices in the folk song that their families in Norway had no doubt sung hours before, holding hands and walking around the tree, just as they were doing. The words spoke of love, joy, and family.

"*Vi svinger og vi le, så glad er vi, så glad er vi.*" Odny clapped her hands in glee as she watched Fredrik link arms with Kristine, twirling her until the pleats in her wool dress belled out. The color rose in her cheeks. Kristine glowed with contentment and love. For this day, at least, she had made a family of four Norwegian young men, her daughter, and Fredrik, her husband, with whom she was celebrating her very first Christmas as a married woman.

Chapter Eleven

No Home Without Children

Fredrik to Mikal, March 1926:

I have stayed at home because I have some good news to tell you about. You see, we have gotten another daughter. I would have preferred a boy this time, but I guess we do not have a choice. It was on March 7, a Sunday. Everything went fine. I'm still here in Waukegan and may remain here for some time. So, I guess we will stay here until we travel to Norway, and that we will do whether it is foolish or not.

* * * *

"Kristine, what shall we name this child?" Fredrik asked as he handed the swaddled infant to her.

Settling the baby girl in her arms, Kristine had to smile to herself. Fredrik handled the baby as if she were one of his fragile light bulbs.

"Edith, I like the name Edith. What do you think?"

"Edith, that's not very *Norsk*. Who is named Edith?"

"American girls. I think she should have an American name," Kristine said, holding Fredrik's eyes with a challenge.

"American? With me for her father, she is a *Norsk* girl. Shall we name her after someone in one of our families. How about Anna? We both have Anna in our family."

"No, not American enough." Kristine's answer was quick and firm. "I don't want anyone to think she might be German." Kristine had seen how the Germans were scorned in her immigration classes and at the YWCA, where she had begun to go for knitting circle.

"But Kristine, one day we will be back in Norway. Do you want her to be left out there? Edith is not *Norsk* enough."

"Well, what then?" Kristine said. "You should decide. I picked Odny and that is certainly *Norsk*. Think of something that is *Norsk* enough for you, but sounds a bit American."

"Why are you so worried about how American it sounds?"

"Because we are living here in Waukegan, not Førde, and we will be for a while. You said so yourself." Kristine was exasperated, more upset than she wanted to be. "You are Fred to everyone you meet. Simple to say and remember. We already have a hard last name for Americans. Why make it harder for her if we don't have to."

"I don't have time to talk about this now. The nurse is here, dressing Odny. I have a sales call to make. See you later!"

The baby stirred, mewing as only hungry newborns do. With a sigh, Kristine turned her attention to feeding the infant, her frustration replaced by fatigue. She was learning that when she stood up to Fredrik, he often would leave. He always seemed to have someplace to go, someone to see.

"She nursed well before she fell asleep." Kristine said when the nurse, Clara, came in to see to her and the baby.

"You must wake her up. She needs to eat more," Clara said, disapproval written on her face. "Take her blanket off, she is too comfortable."

"But, she's sleeping," Kristine protested. " I think you should put her in the bassinet."

Clara sniffed, "Yes, ma'am. She is your baby, but my other mothers find I know best. Maybe it is different where you come from?"

Kristine was too tired to stand up to Clara, who seemed so certain of what to do. Her eyes welled up with tears. Not even two years ago, surrounded by her mother and sister Elise, she had given birth for the first time. She remembered Elise taking the baby so she could rest. And later, when Kristine was up and about, how many hours had her mother held Odny and rocked, the newborn and the grandmother in harmony.

On the one hand, it was quite grand to have a professional nurse, but when she tried to put them on a strict eating and sleeping schedule, Kristine wanted to be done with Clara's services.

"I'd like to get dressed now," she called. She was feeling stronger every day. It had not been a hard delivery. Nevertheless, Clara insisted that she must stay in bed for two weeks.

"I'm on my way. Don't get out of bed until I am with you." Clara said, crossing the hall from Odny's room. "Are you sure you are strong enough to get dressed and be up?"

"I am. I was up over an hour yesterday and felt quite good afterward. Today I would like to stay dressed until Fredrik comes home."

"Oh, no, that is too long.

"Why? You won't be with us forever, I need to be able to take care of this family soon."

"There is no rush. Mr. Hjelmeland told me just this morning to plan on at least another week."

"He did?" Kristine grew quiet as Clara held out her corset and slip to put on. Fredrik told her how expensive it was to live, and then he hired this nurse. He still talked about going home to Norway, but he also talked about building a house. She never knew how many of his plans were just talk and how many would actually come to be.

Language was still a problem, but she was learning. "Baby, diapers, sleep, bleeding, milk," were all words Kristine could use now. When Kristine didn't understand some direction, Clara shouted at her and looked stern, which made Kristine even more uncertain.

"Clara, where are you from?" Kristine asked. She had learned to ask that in English class.

"From? What do you mean? I'm American, I'm from here." Clara jerked Kristine's stockings up and clipped them to garters hanging from the corset.

"From Waukegan?" For some reason she wasn't sure of, Kristine persisted.

"No, no, I grew up on a farm in Wisconsin. There were too many girls in our family. I had to find something else to do."

Clara helped Kristine thread her arms through an everyday dress. "When I finished high school I went to Deaconess Hospital and learned to become a nurse."

"You come to Waukegan how?" Kristine's limited English was running out.

"Oh, when we finished our class, my cousin told me about Victory Hospital. None of the Lutheran hospitals in Milwaukee had any jobs."

"You work at hospital?"

"Sometimes at night, before I come here, but only when they need me." Clara helped Kristine stand and move to a chair.

"Where you sleep?"

"I rent a room from my cousin." Clara was about to say more when Odny, almost two years old, came toddling into the room.

"*Mor*, I have my doll, where is your doll?" Odny had dolls and babies confused.

"Your baby sister is sleeping. What is your doll doing? Has she had breakfast?"

Odny climbed up into Kristine's lap, to better show her the doll. Breathing in Odny's little girl smell, Kristine stroked her wavy hair and felt calmer.

"Your mother must rest." Back to being the nurse, Clara scooped up Odny. "Let's find some blocks to play with."

"No, I want mommy." she cried, but Clara shut the door behind them.

Kristine leaned over her sewing basket, picked up a dress that she was hemming, and wished she had asked for Odny to stay. Alone in the bedroom, she thought about her years of caring for her sick mother and her brother's young children in Norway. How different that was from Clara and how much the same. A woman had to find her way, and sometimes the choices weren't the best. Now she had two girls. What would become of them without cousins or grandmothers, other Norwegian women to teach them what was important? How to be a woman, a wife, a mother?

Fredrik had been very concerned about the baby. Even though she'd had a home birth with Odny in Norway, he'd insisted on the doctor coming. The nurse was his idea. Fredrik told her this was the modern way to have babies in America.

Mostly Fredrik didn't get involved in the details. He talked about work, about the contracts he had that would help him buy more land and build a house. What things cost. He knew what to do next. Clara seemed to know exactly what to do. Why didn't she? A year ago, leaving Førde, she had been certain that coming here was the right thing. Now her breasts ached and she could hardly walk from her bed to the living room. Would she ever get her energy back? She felt older than her thirty-four years. Tears dropped on the little cotton dress.

* * * *

Fredrik to Mikal, March 28, 1926:

Let me not forget to congratulate you on your new little daughter. You have one of each, a boy and a girl. I only get girls. Kristine has recovered and is doing her work as usual.

She has a lot to do. We are going to move May 1, to another
house. This one upstairs in the summer is too hot. Kristine
had a letter from her brother Karl asking me to lend him
6000 kroner; I believe his business is not going too well.
What do you think I should do? I am working hard for my
money. But you know how it is. If he should lose the place
just for 6000 kroner, that would not be very nice either.

When she heard quick steps coming up the stairs to the flat,
Kristine knew Fredrik was home. Neither Alf nor Gudmund
took the stairs so fast at the end of the day.

"Kristine, I'm home." He stopped short, finding both Odny
and her in the front room.

"*God kveld* (Good evening)." Kristine was pleased with
herself. It was the first week she had been without Clara. She'd
convinced Fredrik she didn't need a nurse. Having the baby fed
and asleep and Odny ready for bed showed she could manage.
"How was your day? You are late tonight."

"I was working on a big job, and I rented a new place for us.
You can start to pack. We'll move May 1," Fredrik replied as he
picked up Odny and swung her around until she squealed.

"Shh, you'll wake the baby," Kristine warned but with a smile.

"You and baby will have a very nice room," he told Odny,
ignoring Kristine. "And you, my good wife, will like the porch
out front to sit on when the weather gets warm again."

"Fredrik, where is this new place? Is it a first floor flat?"

"No, we'll have a little house on Elmwood Court, all to
ourselves. A mile or so from here."

"How little is it? Are there rooms for Alf and Gudmund as well as the girls?" Kristine wished she had seen it.

"Of course. Three bedrooms, plenty of room. On Sunday, we will all drive by it."

"Ride, Daddy?" Odny hugged his neck. She loved to go out in the car.

"Not now, it's bedtime."

Later, after Odny was settled into bed, Kristine and Fredrik shared supper. She had missed this time together, as it was the only time of the day that she could speak Norwegian and really talk with someone. After the baby was born, the nurse, Odny, and Kristine ate before Fredrik got home.

"I didn't know you had a place in mind," Kristine said. They had been talking about needing more space now that the baby was here.

"Well, I was talking to a fellow about a building site, and he told me about this place he had for rent. I paid him what he wanted for his lot, and he gave me a deal on the rent. I'll have to install electricity, but that's easy enough."

"Did you actually go inside the house? Is it in good shape?" Kristine didn't know much about Waukegan or deals, but she knew that she wanted sturdy floors and a kitchen she could work in.

"Um, not yet, but I will." Fredrik was very interested in his split pea soup. "There are people living there now. From what the owner tells me, we will need to get some more furniture. You can go back to Blumberg for those things you looked at when we bought the table at Christmas."

"What about helping my brother Karl? Is there money to

do all of this? I don't need new furniture if it means we can't help Karl. He mustn't lose the house I lived in my whole life." Kristine knew that to Fredrik that seemed far away. She didn't know whether it would irritate him if she talked about it when he was excited about his deal.

"Didn't I tell you? I wrote to Mikal and asked him to talk with Karl. If he thinks it's wise, he will help him right away. Then I will send the money. Karl can work with Mikal."

Kristine frowned. She knew that Karl did not think much of the hard-driving Hjelmelands. He had been the one most against her marriage. She hoped his pride would not stop him from negotiating with Fredrik's brother. A new baby, a new place to live, worry about her family in Norway. She lost her desire to talk.

"Thank you, Fredrik, I will wash up in the morning. Would you put the dishes in the sink?" Kristine pushed herself up to standing. "I think I must try to get some sleep before the baby wakes. It's already been a few hours since she last ate."

"You go on now, Kristine. I have some paperwork to do, but I do not have to leave so early in the morning."

"Good. Have you thought more about her name? We can't call her baby forever. We should think about setting a date for her baptism, too." Kristine's voice fell to a whisper.

"*Ja, ja,* lots to think about." Fredrik was already moving toward the front room. "*Sove godt,* sleep well."

"You too, good night."

Kristine lay awake trying to sort out all her conflicting feelings. When she had imagined life in America, she had imagined a home like her friends had. She had not really known that Fredrik would make decisions to move them as easily as he changed shirts. For her, making a place a home was about more than the building and a roof over her head. It was a place to be family, where history was honored. It was a safe and *koselig* (comfortable) place where people could be welcomed. She was frightened to realize that she didn't know Fredrik well enough to know whether a safe, *koselig* home for family was less important to him than making money or whether it was important, but he trusted her to do the homemaking.

She fretted over her baby girl who had yet to be baptized. What if the child died without being baptized? In Kristine's experience, too many babies died. Kristine and Fredrik didn't even have a proper church with a pastor they could go to. She hadn't expected that there would be so few Lutheran churches. Was Fredrik not concerned because the baby was another girl? No, that was silly. He had been nothing but kind and generous.

She pressed her eyes tightly shut. She had said her usual prayers before getting into bed but now she squeezed out an extra one. *Please God, help me to learn how to live with Fredrik, to make such a good home for him that he will not move us all the time. Help me to love him as Jesus loves us. Amen.*

* * * *

Fredrik to Mikal Hjelmeland, June 1926:

We have a nice little house all to ourselves now and have bought furniture for more than $500. Alf and Gudmund are *staying with us. They are both nice boys. Some three weeks ago I went to Canada again. I have gotten the deed for my land. If the harvest [on his homestead in Saskatchewan] is good, I might sell it...Since I returned I have bought some more home sites and some other land here for approximately $6,000. Maybe I will settle here where I am now, at least for some time. You know, we have been thinking about going home to our native country[Norway], if we will live for a time.*

Kristine heard a door slam when she stepped out onto the back porch to hang some diapers she'd just gotten from the washing machine. She was enjoying having a clothesline so handy.

"Alf, is it you?" she called. Fredrik's nephews had both gotten jobs that paid a bit better than Fredrik was able to pay them. Since Alf worked second shift, he was often home during the day before work.

"It's me. Is there anything to eat?" Fredrik answered.

"Fredrik! I did not expect you. Are you sick?" Kristine was flustered. He had just gotten back from a trip to his homestead in Canada. She wasn't really used to him being home, especially not in the middle of the day.

"What? Sick? No, of course not." He seemed indignant at the idea. "I was talking with Delco about a dealership and maybe a store to sell light fixtures and electric pumps. We met downtown."

"Odny and I had bread and cheese and jam before her nap. Is that enough, or shall I heat some *grøt* (porridge)?" Kristine hurried to put the kettle on for tea.

"No, no, cheese and *knæckebrød* (thick rye cracker) are good. I'm only here for a few minutes. Where are the girls?" he asked.

"Napping. Odny still sleeps a bit in the afternoon. Today the baby is sleeping, too. It doesn't happen every day. She's growing so fast. It's different every day. One of them will be up soon. Are you done for the day?"

"No. I need to get back out to Grayslake and finish the installation I was working on. I decided to stop and give you the letter from Karl that you've been looking for." He lay the thick envelope on the table as Kristine brought a steaming cup of tea and plate of cheese, sausage, and rye krisp. "As long as I was in town, I picked up the mail."

Kristine sat opposite him and quickly scanned her letter.

"Oh, thank you. Karl has gotten the loan that he needed for the business. He is so thankful. It helps a lot. He writes that he will send you a letter and first payment as soon as Mikal brings the contract to him to sign." She continued to read down the page, skipping Karl's complaints about Mikal's bargaining on Fredrik's behalf. "He says that Mikal has postponed bringing the papers twice because your father is not well. Did you know that?"

"What? Let me see." He took the letter from her and read to himself. He put down the letter and said, "I had not heard. I suppose Mikal is too busy taking care of *Far* and his business to write to us."

He sounded so bereft, Kristine leaned across the small table and put her hand over his. "I'm so sorry, Fredrik. Maybe it is just a summer cold. He may have recovered now. It's been two weeks since this was written."

"Maybe, but he is seventy-eight. That's old. Between building roads and the farm, he's had a tough life."

"*Ja*, that he has. If he is not better, will you try to get home?"

"I don't know. My money is all tied up, and I just took those weeks to go to the homestead. It is not a good time. Besides, it is too soon to travel with the baby, isn't it?"

"It would be hard, but we could if we had to. What are you thinking?"

Fredrik straightened his shoulders with a quick shake. "I cannot think about this now, I must think about the fellow waiting for his electric lights to work."

"But you've hardly been here fifteen minutes."

"And that's more than I should have taken. I am behind in my work."

"If you must go back there today, try to get home a bit earlier than you have been. Please? Odny is missing you," she said. "For that matter, I miss you. We have not had much time together since you were in Canada."

"If I don't leave now, it will be very late tonight." He gave her a quick kiss and was out the door.

That evening his supper was on the back burner. The June sun had set, and Kristine sat reading her Bible when Fredrik returned.

"You're home." Kristine stood to greet him with a kiss. "Are you very tired? I thought you'd be home before dark, but it's after nine!"

"*Ja*, but the job is done. I don't have to go back tomorrow. The worst is that I'm hungry."

"If you want to wash up, I'll put it on the table."

Moments later they sat together, Kristine with tea and Fredrik digging into his stew.

While he was gone to his homestead in Canada, Kristine had found the energy to begin to make curtains for the new rental. They had moved only two weeks before he and Alf drove to Saskatchewan. The days they were gone passed faster than she had expected, but she'd missed Fredrik. To have him so far away made her realize how alone she was in America. It was a long walk to her neighbor Maggie. She hadn't found a Lutheran church nearby. With the newborn and no car to drive her, she had to depend on Gudmund. He was gone most days to his new job. Even the young men who stayed with them were Fredrik's nephews, not her relatives.

Even so, the lilac bush in the yard had bloomed, and she was able to have the baby in the pram and watch Odny play outside. She felt less confined physically than she had at the flat on County Street. Whether it was spring, the baby getting bigger and sleeping longer, or the new house, she was happier than she had been.

With a crust of homemade bread, Fredrik wiped the last of the stew gravy, from his plate and pushed back his chair. "I had a good day today. How about you?"

"After you stopped by, I began a letter to answer Karl before Odny woke from her nap. I'm so grateful that Mikal agreed you should lend him the money. Then when Odny woke and I was feeding the baby, I began to think about scheduling a baptism. Have you thought anymore about a name?"

"No, but I'm guessing that you have. Do you still like Edith?"

Kristine laughed, glad for the twinkle in his eye. "I do, but not if you don't. What do you think of Ruth instead?"

"Ruth? How did you come up with that? Is someone in your family named Ruth?" Fredrik mused.

"No, but my Bible reading today was from the story of Ruth. She's the woman who left her homeland to be with her mother-in-law. I think Ruth fits with being the first born in America." Kristine even tried to give the "th" a softer sound than the Norwegian pronunciation which was more like "Root."

He didn't say anything, just rubbed his forehead with his calloused workman's hand.

"Fredrik?" Kristine's voice was soft, uncertain.

He raised his head and reached for her hand. "I don't know as much about the Bible as you do, Kristine, but I know how much you miss home." His voice was low.

"Oh, thank you Fredrik, you must have been thinking about home, too. You do want the baby to be baptized don't you? I think God just wants her to have a name and be baptized. To me, that's more important than which name." While her thumb caressed his hand, she noticed the lines beginning to show on that broad forehead. "Do you like Ruth any better than Edith?" Her gentle smile lifted the heavy emotions in the air.

Before Fredrik responded, a cry from the yet-nameless baby took Kristine out of the cozy kitchen. By the time she came back, Fredrik had settled in the living room to read his Norwegian language newspaper, *Decorah Posten*.

"*Ja*, it is probably time to name her. Ruth is a better name than Edith, but let's not decide tonight." Fredrik's gaze was tender as Kristine opened her blouse to nurse. "After we have arranged for the baptism, we will see if we have come up with any other names."

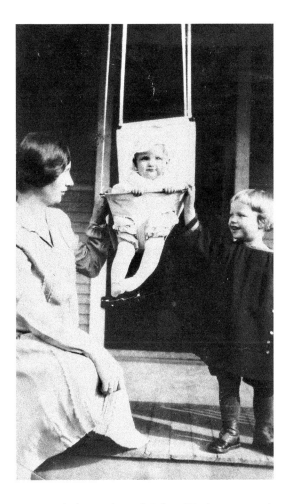

Kristine, baby Ruth, and Odny, Waukegan, 1926.

Chapter Twelve

Førde Calling

Kristine Kristiansen Hjelmeland to Petrina Hjelmeland Eide, January 1928:

> *Ja, Hjemmet* (home) *is not the same for me as it was. Because mother's place is now empty. Now I am glad that I have made myself my own home, a home for myself... Odny and Ruth are both growing little girls, healthy and obedient. For Christmas we bought them a little table and two chairs. The table is white with all the alphabet and numbers painted on it. Odny can already recognize most of the letters...I wish that you were close enough that you could come and visit us. It's a little sad to not have anyone who knows me and my people.*

* * * *

"Mama, is this the O?" Odny asked pointing at the green O on the child-sized white table.

"It is. Where is the R for Ruth?" Kristine said, joining a game that had begun as soon as the girls had started to use their Christmas present.

Odny studied the tabletop. Not yet four years old, she was fascinated that all the designs had names like O and R and were connected to words. Kristine was glad that Fredrik had thought to move the table from the sitting room into their bedroom so she could keep an eye on Odny. Since Christmas, Kristine's legs and feet had been in such pain she'd stayed in bed. It was Fredrik's slow season, so he was able to be home with them more. After almost three years in Waukegan, she had made some friends who were helping with marketing and cooking.

If it weren't for her feet, she would have enjoyed these quiet days at home. Fredrik had even made porridge and *lefse* (potato flatbread) by himself.

"Look who is up from her nap." Fredrik came in carrying rosy-cheeked Ruth on one arm and diapers in the other.

"She needs a change," he said, handing the cuddly toddler to Kristine.

Smiling, she made a space for diaper changing on the bed. He had impressed her with how much housework he was able to do, but diapers were not something he was willing to handle. Fortunately, whatever was causing her foot pain did not prevent her from moving around on the bed or in a chair. Soon the offending diaper was taken care of, and the girls were playing on the floor.

"You are good with the girls, Fredrik. I was just writing to Petrina that she would be surprised at all you do."

"Surprised? I was always her favorite brother, I'm sure she wouldn't be surprised." He grinned.

"Favorite? What she really said is that you were not the worst," Kristine said laughing with him. "Will you post this letter tomorrow, please?"

"Ah, tomorrow. Are you well enough to take care of the girls? I cannot miss another day of work. Gudmund is on a job that needs my help, and I must go to Delco in Chicago. Their delivery didn't come today."

"I'm better, but I'd hoped to spend most of tomorrow off my feet so I can go to night school. We're studying government and grammar. It's really hard to catch up if you miss." She reached out and took hold of his hand. "Do you think we could hire someone to come to watch the girls?"

Fredrik scowled and didn't respond.

Kristine dropped his hand and let the silence grow. She hated this part of being in a new country and new town—there were no relatives or old friends she felt she could ask for this kind of help. Still, many women had it much worse than she did. Not many men would have chased toddlers for a day-and-half. Pain or no pain, she would have had to cope.

Fredrik lit a cigarette before he spoke, a sign that he was not happy. "How about this? I will go over to Wally and Lena's and ask if Lena can come tomorrow. Unless I can telephone, but I don't suppose that cheapskate Wally has put in a phone."

"Fredrik, they are our friends. You mustn't speak badly of someone you are going to ask a favor of." Kristine scolded without any anger, "No, our friend does not have a telephone yet. I would like her company and help, but Wally will want his supper."

"*Ja*, maybe he will come here after work for supper if I offer to drive him home."

"Okay, but Lena must not feel we are asking her to work. Only help with the children and supper." Kristine began to worry about the cleaning and laundry she'd not done for several days.

Fredrik turned to Odny. "Want to go for a ride?"

* * * *

The next morning Kristine was up long enough to get breakfast for everyone and have Fredrik move the girls' table and toys before Lena came. Fredrik left later than usual but still in the morning, determined to drive to Chicago and help Gudmund on their job before his day was over. He dropped Lena off on his way out of town. She let herself in, humming a Norwegian hymn, "Children of the Heavenly Father."

"*Velkommen,* Lena, I'll be right out," Kristine called from the girls' room.

Odny raced past her mother and sister and hugged Lena around the knees. Even though Lena had only been in Waukegan a year, she'd spent a lot of time with Kristine ever since they first met in English classes at night school. Lena was from the east of Norway and married to a Swede, Wally Johnson. Her Norwegian was a different dialect, but even so, Kristine could speak Norwegian with her.

"Kristine, what is wrong with you?" Lena asked as she hung

up her coat. "Fredrik couldn't tell me. All he said was that you were in bed and hurting."

"I've had such pains in my feet. Maybe it is rheumatism. It has been so cold and damp since Christmas," she said, walking with short, slow steps as Ruth wiggled in her arms. "They have been hurting ever since the New Year but got worse on Sunday. This is my third day of resting, and there seems to be less pain when I'm up."

"Oh, I could have come sooner. You should have asked. I love to come over. It's lonely in our little apartment all by myself."

"*Tusen takk*, Lena. Do you want some tea?" Kristine was embarrassed when Lena talked about being alone. She knew that Lena would love to have children, but so far she had not. Ruth and Odny crawling all over her seemed to emphasize that.

"I'll have some tea, but you must sit down so that we can both go to class tonight. I came to help. I think I will start some soup for supper, too. Do you have any split peas? I brought a hambone."

Lena settled Kristine in a chair with a footstool and began to bustle around. A petite redhead, she seemed an odd companion for older, proper Kristine. In Norway, even if they had met, they probably would not have become friends. Here, a common language, distance from home, and night school brought them together at first. Lena's cheerful energy encouraged quiet Kristine to seek her out often. Sometimes they simply had tea and did handwork together.

"*Tante* Lena, is this the letter O?" Odny asked in English, pulling Lena toward the little table.

Kristine chuckled. "You're a new recruit for Odny. If you let her, she will make you stay there until she has recited the whole alphabet."

"Maybe she can be my tutor, I'm still struggling with some words."

"You do well, but that history of the Civil War assignment was hard. I still don't understand Con-fed-er-acy. Is that how you say it?"

Lena put fresh tea in front of Kristine and began to hum, "When Johnny Comes Marching Home Again." Every week they learned a new song.

Kristine joined in, "…and the ladies, they will all come out, hurrah, hurrah…"

Odny and Ruth start to imitate mama and *Tante* Lena. "Hurry, hurry."

They giggled and sang while the girls played and Lena started the soup.

When Ruth toddled past Kristine, she got a whiff of her diaper.

"Lena, I'm sorry but this is what gives me pain, carrying Ruth to change her diaper. I will change her if you carry her. Do you mind?"

"You sit. I worked as a nanny at home before I married Wally. This will take just a minute," Lena said.

When Lena brought Ruth back to Kristine, she was also carrying a bucket of dirty diapers.

"Lena, no, I did not expect you to come wash diapers for me. It is too much," Kristine said.

"Nonsense, there's a washtub in the basement, right?"

"Yes, but I could show you how to use the electric washing machine. It's so much easier. After the wash, just feed the diapers through the ringer and hang them on the line."

"No, no, you stay up here with the girls. It's enough that we have running water. Isn't it nice that we don't have to pump it and heat it on the stove? When you are better, I will come back for a lesson on the machine. This won't take long. Call if you need me."

Not even a half hour later Lena came up with the basket filled with wet, clean diapers.

"Where do you hang these, Kristine?"

"They'll dry best in the kitchen. This time of year, I string the line from this corner to that one, in front of the back door."

"I'd like to hang them outside, but it's started to snow."

With Kristine's help, the diapers were hung and Lena went back to making soup for supper.

Kristine sat down again in the chair where she could keep an eye on the girls but close enough to the kitchen to chat. She picked up her knitting.

Lena glanced at her, "You really have it nice here with hot water, an ice box, and a machine to do the wash."

"*Ja*, indoor plumbing and electricity help a lot, but Fredrik is already talking about building a house instead of renting. I hate to think of packing things up again."

"I thought Fredrik was going to build a house when you go back to Norway."

"He says that he can build here and make enough money to buy land in Norway."

"Really? So much? You are lucky, Kristine."

Baker Kvål's house buit 1939   Alfred Kristiansen   Baker Gundersen (Astrtids parents)   Førde Hotel

rl Kristiansen →

Førde, Norway, 1920s.

"Mmm, what do you miss about home, Lena?"

"I miss walking in the mountains and good fish. What about you?"

"I miss my friends and some of my family. It's hard for me that no one here has heard me play the organ in church or remembers the trips with friends to *Jølstervatn* (Lake Jølster) on Midsummer night. I would like to help my sister with so many children on that rocky farm of her husband's family," Kristine said with a wistful smile.

Lena raised an eyebrow. "Did you say some of your family?"

"Oh, of course I meant all of them, but before mother died, my brother Karl expected so much—cleaning, cooking, and childcare. Without Mother at home, it would be hard to go back there. I do miss *Far*, and Anna and Alf, though."

Ruth toddled up and pulled on Lena's skirt.

"Ruth, what do you want? *Er du sulten* (Are you hungry)?" Lena bent over and handed her a rusk. Ruth had eight teeth and was working on another. She took the sweetened toast eagerly. "I don't know if I want to move back. Wally has a good job, and I don't have to milk cows for someone else."

"We do have it *hyggelig* (cozy and comfortable) here. I still dream about a proper Norwegian home."

"Kristine, you already have a proper Norwegian home. It is so much nicer than my home or Wally's in Norway. And you have made it *Norsk*. I love to come here.

"I am so glad, *mange, mange takk* (many, many thanks). Sometimes I think Fredrik wants to go back to Norway even more than I do. He works all the time and tells me it's for that home in the Norwegian mountains."

"Really, I'm surprised. After all his years here?"

"It's a dream of his, to go back as a rich landowner."

"I hope he doesn't get too rich, too soon. I would miss you a lot if you left Kristine," Lena choked up a bit.

To hide her embarrassment, she went over to Odny at the little table, "Will you teach me English please? Where is the L? For Lena?"

Kristine watched them play and wondered about *hjemmet*. Was it a place or people? She probably could not learn that in night school.

Chapter Thirteen

We Are Getting Along

Fredrik to his brother, Mikal, December 8, 1929:

Well, brother, I am doing the same kind of work as before and that is to go by car out to the countryside to try to sell. It isn't always that easy, but I am getting along. This year hasn't been so good for me. We are having bad times so people aren't buying...Brother, I often miss you. I have no one to consult. I am just the same person I used to be—rush ahead and start thinking afterwards, and many times I have had to pay for that.

Kristine sat in Fredrik's chair in the dark living room gripping a letter. In the two weeks since the telegram had come with the shocking news that her father Andreas had died in his sleep at home in Førde, she had both dreaded and yearned for this letter from her brother Alfred. This afternoon when the post came, she'd put it in her apron pocket and made the girls an early supper. Ignoring their complaints that it was too early to go to bed, she'd closed their door and sat reading and re-reading the description of the funeral until it became too dark to see the painful words anymore. Even in the dark she could see, without photos, the newly dug grave to the side of the white frame church. She saw her somber family assemble in front of the shop and walk the short distance to the church. What she couldn't see were the children, who in the years since she'd been gone, had changed more than she could imagine.

So she sat, turning the images in her heart, gripping her tear-soaked handkerchief.

The door opened, letting in a blast of cold, November air.

"The girls are in bed. You are late tonight." Kristine's voice was barely above a whisper.

"*Uff a meg*, you scared me. What are you doing sitting in the dark?" Fredrik yelped.

He switched on a lamp.

"Even my brother, Hjalmar, got shore leave. He was there and I was not. Oh Papa—" Kristine dissolved into tears. She held out the letter.

He scanned the flimsy blue sheets quickly. Andreas Kristiansen had not been ill and had been to church the night before he died. The funeral had been well attended, with people from all over the region coming to pay their respects to a longtime merchant and community leader.

"*Stakkers* (poor), Kristine, I'm so sorry. It was not possible for you to go." Fredrik tried to put an arm around her hunched up shoulders, but she curled further into herself. He could see from her blotched face she had been crying for some time.

"Have you eaten? Come into the kitchen and we will talk while I eat."

"Please, Fredrik, leave me alone. I don't want to talk and I don't want to eat."

* * * *

In the days that followed, a dark cloud settled over Kristine and, by extension, the whole family. The fact that their routine did not change—Fredrik working, the girls growing, the meals to cook and clothes to wash—seemed wrong to her. Her life had changed. Her parents were both dead and she was thousands of miles away from the people who knew her best. She stopped smiling, snapped at Ruth and Odny, cried while ironing.

"I'm home," Fredrik called.

"Daddy, it's still light out. You don't usually come home when it is light." Odny pulled him toward the picture she had been drawing. "Can you play?"

Thin-lipped and quiet, Kristine nodded toward him, not asking why he had come home early. She turned back to peeling carrots for the stew she had on the stove.

"I will play with you after Mama leaves for school. Now we must hurry and help her so she can get ready," he said to Odny but looked at Kristine, raising his eyebrows.

"*Ja, takk*, Fredrik. But there is no rush. I'm not going tonight. I have missed too much," she said.

"You will never finish if you don't go to school," he said.

She gazed at him, opened her mouth to say something but then clamped it shut.

Fredrik raised his voice. "You love night school. Until a month ago you never missed."

She shrugged. "Not much point. Classes won't bring me any closer to Norway. Class might push me farther away."

"We have been over this and over this. Now is exactly the wrong time to move back to Norway. I could lose everything we have worked so hard for."

"What is all this hard work for if we will never see a fjord again or walk in the mountains with our brothers and sisters? We have no parents, either one of us. And now you have moved us again to this run-down house on the edge of Waukegan."

"What kind of man am I if I take you back there now? There are no jobs for electricians. There's no building going on. I will fix up this house when I build my store next year. Things have only gotten worse in Norway since my father died. Mikal told me not to come then, two years ago."

"Exactly, two whole years ago, now both our fathers and mothers have died without us, and we are no closer to going home than we were when I came here almost five years ago." Once again tears streamed down her cheeks. She put down her paring knife and moved to leave the kitchen.

With a hand on her arm, Fredrik stopped her. His voice raised, he said, "No, tonight we will have supper together. Then the girls and I will drive you to school. I don't want to talk about this anymore."

Eye to eye, Kristine studied his angry face. The only times

she'd heard Fredrik use that harsh tone was with people who had cheated him. Why couldn't she shout back? It was she who felt cheated by empty promises. But it would take so much energy to defy him, and there stood the girls, not really understanding, but listening to their every word.

She shrugged. "Then I must finish the carrots, please."

That night and every week afterward, Kristine went to night school but did not hum while she did her chores or join Fredrik for supper. She stopped making curtains for the rundown house he had moved them to at 1826 Grand Avenue just before she got the news of her father's death.

"Kristine, why did you not tell me the steps to the house were broken?" Fredrik usually did not use the front door.

"Does it matter?" Kristine's voice was neutral.

"Of course it does. Someone could be hurt."

"No fixtures for the lights, dingy paint, rattling windows don't seem to matter." Her voice remained cold.

"I told you, Kristine, it is just for a short time. We will fix it up, I promise."

She stared at him, not smiling, not frowning.

She could not explain to Fredrik why she had lost interest in anything but basic, everyday needs. Even with the girls, she was remote. She went through the motions of day-to-day living.

On a night in early fall, Fredrik came in late. She was waiting with a smile and had changed into a Sunday blouse.

Over the *labskaus* (cabbage, potatoes, and ground lamb) a favorite of Fredrik's, she said, "Lena, was here for tea today. They are going to Norway in May, on the *Bergensfjord*."

"Really? I didn't think that tightwad Johnson had saved up so much money. Are they moving back?" Fredrik chuckled and kept eating. "This is really good, Kristine. You make *labskaus* just the way I like it."

"*Neida*, no, they are going back for a visit. A visit, Fredrik. Do you think we could go, take the girls?"

"What? Go to Norway? In May? Just when the building season has begun?"

Odny and Ruth, 1928, Waukegan, IL.

"But Lena said the round-trip tickets were less than the cost of the one-way tickets when they came four years ago. Please, Fredrik?" she pleaded.

"No, not possible. I have the land and drawings for my store and to remodel this house. They will start laying the foundation for the store as soon as the ground thaws enough to dig a basement. I thought you wanted some improvements here."

"I did but…" her voice trailed off. "Couldn't we go once the construction started? Maybe you wouldn't stay so long. The girls and I could travel back later with Lena and Wally. They're staying most of the summer." Begging, she felt her cheeks redden, but she did not cry.

"*Kjærligst* (My love), I will think about it, but do not count on it. I must consider what I would lose from not working for weeks even as the money goes out the door," he said. "I've promised a lot of people installations and have the construction workers all lined up."

"*Takk,* Fredrik." Kristine saw from the set lines of his face that she could not push him anymore.

Still not cheerful, she did begin to join him again for supper. Over the meal, she reported the latest bad news from Norway. The widow of Fredrik's middle brother Marthin was struggling with two small children. Her brother Karl wrote that the business was doing poorly and he needed her niece Anna, the one whom Kristine had raised until she emigrated, to quit school and work. Elise wrote that the crops had failed and they were selling their cows. Her sister-in-law Petrina wrote of her depression after the influenza death of her teenaged son.

"Kristine, do you think I don't understand what you are doing?" Fredrik said in heavy dialect. "Every night about Førde and Norway. Can we talk about night school or the girls or my work?"

"*Ja*, Fredrik, I am still interested in home even if you want to forget it," she said without looking up.

After weeks of relentless news from Norway, Fredrik proposed a compromise. Even though it was not exactly as Kristine had hoped, it was more than she had expected. She and the girls would go to Norway for the summer while Fredrik stayed in Waukegan and worked. They would travel with their friends Lena and Wally, who could help with the girls and transfers.

She had dreamt of returning with Fredrik, but he had given up some of his plans to allow them to go. He had installed so many generators in Northern Illinois and Southern Wisconsin that he had built up a demand for electrical light fixtures and appliances. A retail store to meet that demand was Fredrik's dream. Their trip meant that he had to sell more of his investment property than he wanted and trim some of his plans.

Once the tickets were bought, Kristine returned to her more cheerful self, especially when Fredrik actively helped with arrangements. He decided that the girls should see more of Norway than Bergen and Førde, so he bought the railroad pass for her to take the girls to her brother in Oslo and his sister in Brekstad, near Trondheim. Now Kristine sang as she collected gifts to pack. Sometimes she caught Fredrik frowning, a crease between his brows. She tried not to be so happy about going without him, but in so many ways, he had never really been a part of her life in Norway. She had only lived with him a few weeks after their wedding and never in their own home. Their life in Waukegan had little in common with the life she had led in Førde. While she could hold both lives side by side in her imagination, she could not actually picture him in Førde with her friends. She found herself wondering if she would miss him.

Because she was generous and knew that a guest should help, but also to show what a good life she had in America, she chose personal gifts for each member of her family and many of Fredrik's. One whole suitcase was filled with blouses and dresses, lengths of fabric, shaving brushes, leather belts, dolls, and toy trucks. She sewed new coats for herself, Ruth, and Odny. The long winter nights were filled with hemming dresses and imagining summer in Førde with the girls. By May, everything was ready to go.

"I wish you were going with us, Fredrik," Kristine said the night before they left.

"I do, too, but you would miss me if you were here. I will be very busy, gone a lot."

"You must remember to eat. Promise me you'll go to Mrs. Peterson's. She said you are welcome."

"*Ja, ja*, I will manage."

"Just think how much has changed in five years. I can speak enough English to find trains by myself. We have two daughters instead of one. You are known throughout the county for your work."

"Now, Kristine, will you be bragging about me?" His eyes crinkled as he teased her.

"Of course I will, to everyone I meet! You know, you are something of a mystery to most people in Førde. Not to your family, of course," she said pertly.

"You must talk with Mikal. Tell him to be on the lookout for a place for us in Førde," he said. "What did you do with the cash I gave you for him?"

"It is in the lining of my coat. In a pocket I have sewn in for carrying such envelopes. A place for us in Førde? Are you ready for me to talk about that?"

"Well, only to Mikal. He understands how it is." He raised an eyebrow and turned serious. "You will come back to me, won't you?"

Kristine caught her breath. Could he read her mind? Had he suspected her half-formed thoughts? She stepped into his embrace to avoid his knowing gaze.

"Of course, Fredrik. We are a family," she said into his shoulder. "The girls would not stay without you."

"Kristine, I promise you one day we will all be in Norway together, maybe to stay," Fredrik said with a catch in his voice.

"One day. God willing."

Chapter Fourteen

The Bergensfjord Again

Kristine Kristiansen Hjelmeland, St. Olaf College report, as told to her daughter, Odny, 1943:

Mother, Ruth, and I left Waukegan on the 14th of May 1930. Ruth was four and I was six. I wasn't very happy because we had left Dad at home; I cried for half a day... We had a wonderful time on the boat because there were so many people that knew our friends and relatives. It was on this boat that Ruth and I saw our first movie. I can remember they had all kinds of games on the deck. None of us got seasick; therefore, we had a wonderful time.

"Odny, take Ruth's hand and stand right there." Kristine turned from the girls to the bus driver putting their bags on a cart.

"Here you are at *SS Bergensfjord*. That right?" the brusque driver spoke in an accent unfamiliar to Kristine.

"Thank you for your help." She gave him a tip. The bus ride itself was included in their passage ticket.

Looking toward the gangplank, Kristine saw a young sailor approach. He greeted them in Norwegian.

"Welcome to the *Bergensfjord*. Your names please?"

Switching from English to Norwegian, Kristine gave their names. How much easier it was to go home, she thought, feeling the weight of the journey lift.

"Here you are, *Fru* Fredrik Hjelmeland with Odny and Ruth, traveling tourist class, second deck, cabin E17," he said, consulting a clip board. "And *Fru* Johnson?"

"She is on another bus. We were separated at the train station," Kristine replied, finding it a relief to speak Norwegian after two days on the train and negotiating the transfer to the docks all in English. "I'm sure she will be here soon, but all the English at the train station was confusing. I don't know exactly when. Can we wait for her? There's time, isn't there?"

"Yes, but you should wait on the ship. Follow me please." He led the way up the gangplank pushing a cart with their travel bags.

Kristine took a girl in each hand. Odny had finally stopped crying for her daddy and was looking around at all the people coming and going. Ruth skipped up the ramp with excitement.

"Here's a good place to wait. You can see everyone boarding." The porter unloaded their bags in a small pile next to the railing on a middle deck. "When your friend comes, someone else will show you to your cabin."

Looking down on the dock, Kristine scanned the people who were being spit out of buses and taxis. She straightened her traveling coat and wiped the girls' faces with her handkerchief. It seemed everyone was dressed in their finest on sailing day. Burly men shouted as they loaded trunks and directed traffic. She could see the open jaw of the ship's hold being filled. She did not see Lena and Wally. What if they had taken the wrong bus? What if something had happened to them?

"Mama, what is that? Odny pointed at big barrels being loaded onto a lower level.

"I don't really know. I think it's something to eat. By the time we leave, there will be five hundred people on this ship. It takes a lot of food to feed all of us."

"Won't you cook, Mama?"

"No. For eight days on this ship, we will just eat and play."

"Play? Play what?" Ruth joined in.

"Well, I think we will find a lot to do but right now, we must watch for Lena and Wally."

"I think I see them. Is that them?" Odny waved at one of the many couples standing at the gangplank waiting their turn to board.

Just as Kristine began to say no, she didn't think so, she turned to see Wally scoop Ruth up onto his shoulders. Lena bustled up behind him.

"Ooo, Wally, will you play with me?" Ruth giggled.

"I am so glad to see you. I thought you were lost." Kristine reached out to hug Lena, but she had turned to consider the luggage.

"Lost? We're right here." Lena replied. "You haven't been to our cabin yet?'

"No, I was waiting for you." Kristine saw that Lena traveled the way she lived, straight to the point and as simply as possible.

On the Bergensfjord, Lena Johnson,
Kristine, and Odny and Ruth, 1930.

They both turned toward the porter, talking over each other
with their directions.

To save money, Kristine, Lena, and the girls were sharing a
cabin while Wally bunked with single men in a dormitory-style
room. Kristine smiled to watch Lena cluck around like a hen
until she had them all moving toward the tiny cabins with the
luggage.

In the narrow hallway, they moved aside for a couple
maneuvering the other direction until the woman recognized
Lena. Dropping their bags, they hugged one another and began

to ask where they were going, where they lived in America, and how much they had missed their homeland. When they could no longer hold back the surge of people trying to get past them to their cabins, they parted, agreeing to meet again at dinner.

"Kristine, that woman's sister and I were in confirmation together. Can you imagine? They're headed home because her husband has inherited the family farm. We will go all the way to Oslo with them. I must find out where her sister is now." Lena chattered away.

"Do you write to her?" Kristine asked as they found their cabin. Two narrow benches with a cushion along the back ran the two-thirds the length of the narrow room. Under these benches were drawers as deep as the beds were high that could hold a small suitcase or belongings if they were unpacked. Above each bench were fold-down, hanging canvas cots. Kristine looked doubtfully from four-year-old Ruth to the suspended cot.

"No, I only write my mother and Wally's if he is writing to his dad. I'm not much of a letter writer."

"Mama, what is this for?" Ruth stood on tiptoe and pushed on the handle over the tin bowl that would be their hand-washing basin.

"Don't touch. Only Mama can touch that." Odny was feeling her role as the big sister.

Everyone talking at once began to give Kristine a headache. If they had to spend much time in the cabin, it would not be a pleasant crossing.

"Girls, put your bags over here and sit on this bed so Lena can come in the room."

"*Ja*, maybe I should wait. We cannot all be standing up at the same time in this cabin," Lena said. "Girls, come with me. Shall we look for the lounge?"

"*Takk*, Lena, I'll find you in a minute. Hand me your bag, I'll set it on your bed."

Alone for a moment, Kristine thought back five years. She hadn't appreciated how unusual it was to travel first class. Her stateroom then was twice as big as this one. But she hadn't known anyone on that journey. She'd been alone with her baby. Now she had her girls and her friends. And she was going home, not to an unknown place. She hung her coat on a hook on the wall, washed the grime from her hands, and headed out to join Lena, Wally, and the girls.

Soon the adults were immersed in stories of home in Norway and what was taking them back now. Meanwhile, the children found each other and began discovering the games available to them. The adults fell into an easy rhythm of gathering in the lounge before and after meals to knit, read, socialize, and play with the children. When the weather was good, the deck provided even more space.

On the third day out, Kristine sat on the deck in the weak May sun of the Northern Atlantic, watching Ruth and Odny try to play shuffleboard with two boys. Their mother was telling Kristine that they were on the way to her family farm.

"Are you visiting your parents? You are lucky to be able to," Kristine asked with a sigh. She would only be able to visit her parents' graves.

"Actually, no, we are moving back," the woman said. "My

husband died in a farm accident last fall. I had to sell our farm in North Dakota."

"Oh, I am so sorry," Kristine said, ashamed that she had been envious. "It must be very hard for you."

"*Ja*, life is hard," the woman said, not elaborating.

"How long has it been since you were home?" Kristine asked kindly. "You must be happy to see you parents again."

"Maybe my mother—she needs my help—but not my father. He sent me as a twelve-year-old with his uncle to make my own way in America. He was struggling then and is still struggling. He wrote to ask how I expect an eight-year-old and eleven-year-old to help, boys, who don't even speak Norwegian." The last words came out in a whisper. "He says he cannot feed us all."

Kristine could not tell if it was grief or bitterness that choked the woman up, but the exchange made her uncomfortable. She had been so sure that this trip was what she needed to come to peace with America and her lot in life there, but now doubts were creeping around the edge of her awareness. Had she minimized her meager life in Førde before she left? How boring and limited it could be? Had her sadness over *Far's* death overcome the excitement of all the people Fredrik had brought into their life? What about Fredrik? He didn't always explain things, but he was good to her and tried to please her.

As Kristine talked with more people, she became aware that as many people were on this trip because of some kind of setback as there were people who were just visiting. Her house in Waukegan and Fredrik working so hard for even more came to mind often. She wrote a letter telling Fredrik how grateful she was to be able to come for this visit. She would post it in Bergen as soon as they got off the ship.

Near the end of the crossing, Wally told the girls he had a surprise for them.

"Can you guess what it is?" he asked, eyes dancing.

"A movie that talks!" Odny exclaimed.

"You are such a smart scamp. How did you know my surprise?"

Odny blushed, embarrassed. "The other kids were talking about it. It's tonight. Can we go? Please?"

"Please, please," Ruth echoed, not really understanding what they were talking about.

"What is the name of this movie?" Kristine wondered if it was proper.

"It's called *No, No, Nanette*. A musical," said Wally.

When Kristine didn't respond, Wally took advantage of the girls and Lena sitting there.

"It's a movie that talks, the latest thing. We should all go. If it isn't right for the children, you can leave," Wally said, voicing Kristine's concerns. "We'll be there together."

Kristine looked at the eager faces, then at Lena, who shrugged as if to say, "Why not."

No, No Nanette made pietistic Kristine squirm, but she did not leave when wives tricked their husbands and Nanette danced in dresses that looked more like a slip than a dress. The girls didn't seem to understand the plot but loved the singing and the glamorous women. The rest of the summer when they were being called on to do something "American," they would break into singing "Tea for Two" imagining high heels and handsome dancing partners. The movie wrapped up their week of so many first-time experiences.

Right on schedule, the ship docked in Norway's busiest harbor, Bergen. After Kristine bid farewell to Lena and Wally, who were going on to Oslo, she took a deep breath and a girl in each hand. As they walked through the cold drizzle onto the dock, she didn't look back. She was home.

"*Velkommen, er deg Fru Hjelmeland og jenter?* (Welcome, are you Mrs. Hjelmeland and girls)?" A man in a dark green sailor's oilskin raincoat stood waiting at the foot of the gangplank. Fredrik had arranged for his cousin Jens to meet Kristine and the girls, but she had never met the man or his family.

"You must be Jens Iverson." Kristine moved to the side to shake his hand in greeting and acknowledgement.

"This is Odny," Kristine nudged her to put out her hand as they had practiced.

"*God morgen* (Good morning)," Odny said as she shook hands obediently.

"And this is Ruth."

"*God morgen,*" Ruth copied her sister.

After additional formalities and retrieving luggage, they were settled into a taxi with their small trunk, four suitcases, and the travel bag. As Kristine looked out the window, she thought about how much smaller Bergen looked to her than it had five years before when she was departing. Compared to Chicago, there were fewer private cars. Iverson's family was typical in that they took the trams and buses that dominated the city streets.

When the driver stopped in front of Iverson's apartment up the side of Fløyen, one of the five mountains that surrounded Bergen's city center, Kristine took out an envelope Fredrik had given her. She handed it to Iverson.

"Can you arrange for him to pick us up for the boat to Vadheim in the morning, please?"

Iverson quickly counted the cash in the envelope and looked relieved that hosting Fredrik's relative did not include paying taxi fares.

Another flurry of *velkommens* and introductions to Mari Iverson and their daughter brought them into day-to-day Norwegian life. In the middle of the living room was a table set for *kaffe*. Painted roses edged the luncheon plates, and lit candles warmed the dampness. Inhaling the familiar smell of fried herring that permeated the air, Kristine was distracted from thinking of how much she had missed these tastes by Odny.

"I will not eat whatever it is that smells so bad," she declared in English folding her arms across her narrow, six-year-old chest.

"Odny, *snakke Norsk nå* (speak Norwegian now). We are in Norway," Kristine said and followed it with a stern order. "You will eat whatever you are given."

"Yes, Mama, but I don't know the right Norwegian words. What is Norwegian for stinky fish?" Odny pouted, still speaking English.

"Mind your manners and take your sister to wash your hands."

During *kaffe*, Kristine kept close watch on Odny and Ruth. She did not want word to get back to Fredrik's family that American children could not behave. She regretted all the freedom the girls had had on board ship. In Waukegan, they were obedient and never talked back. This behavior was frustrating to her. Didn't they understand she expected better in the land of their birth, their family?

Coming home might be more complicated than she had thought.

Chapter Fifteen

Førde at Last

Odny Hjelmeland, St. Olaf College Report, 1943, regarding summer in Norway 1930:

The next morning we took the boat to Vadheim I Sogn and a taxi from there to Førde...

When the taxi crossed the bridge onto the road where she had grown up, Kristine was flooded with memories, her breath coming in little short gasps.

"Mama, are you all right?" Odny asked, wondering what was wrong.

"Oh, so all right," Kristine said as she took in the small group gathered outside the house to greet them as if they were visiting dignitaries. "We're home now. This is where you were born!"

Karl and the children, her brother Alfred, her sister Elise, and a few of their children stood waiting, dressed in their Sunday best. Miraculously, Kristine, the baby of her family, had come back from America. Few who left returned. Her sister Elise hugged her as if she would never let her go. Kristine rested in her embrace but also took in how much older Elise looked.

Her best friend and sister-in-law, Alfred's Anna, cried and laughed and spun her around until Kristine's elegant hat fell off. The niece Kristine had mothered from birth until she left, also named Anna, shook her hand. A blush rising from blotches on little Anna's neck to her broad cheeks belied her excitement and shyness. Little Anna's older brother Alf had not lost the slowness that had marked his early childhood. Fourteen years old now, he stood off to the side staring with his mouth hanging open, not quite sure how to greet these strangers. When Kristine approached him with her arms open, he took a step backward. She put her arms down but continued to stand in front of the man-sized child.

"Alf, how tall you have grown since you used to help me with the potatoes. Is it you?" she said.

"Oh *Tante*, I didn't know you?" He stuck out his hand for her to shake, not comfortable with a hug, but his grin gave away his relief that this stylish looking woman was his *tante*.

"Who else could I be?" They shared a laugh before Kristine said, "your father tells me that you are helping in the shop. Tomorrow will you give me a tour?"

Alf dipped his head. "Of course, *Tante*."

Then there was an awkward pause. No one knew what to do. Kristine looked from one familiar face to another, but they could only stare back as if she was not one of them.

The genuine excitement and joy at seeing Kristine again was tinged with a touch of caution that stemmed partly from her well-cut coat and assured way, but also from the thought that she might be a different sister, aunt, friend than they remembered.

The whole group made its way down the lane and across the river to Alfred's home, for an authentic boiled meal of beef, carrots, and dry, flaky potatoes. Before they could all eat, Alfred proudly showed Kristine the workroom in the front of their house. Bolts of material for dresses and shirts, pants and jackets, the drawers of pins and needles, the racks filled with yarn for knitting and for weaving crowded into one end of the large room. In another corner, there was a stitching area that included a variety of embroidery floss and tapestry yarns as well as the wool and linen to stitch flowers, *Hardangersom* (elaborate cut work embroidery), and cross-stitch. Kristine lingered over the array of patterns and colored threads.

"Alfred, how many workers do you have here?" Kristine asked as she considered all the tables and benches.

"Some days we have at least twelve workers in here." Her brother said, pacing back and forth, "That is why I hope to build a store very soon. Have you located such workrooms in America?"

"Not like this where the knitters, stitchers, and tailors work together. I have been approached about doing some sewing piece work but not in a work-place like this. They really weren't interested in my kind of sewing. There is no shop near me that sells the Aida cloth for *Hardangersom* or the fine flosses that you have here. I have longed for a shop like this." Kristine turned to his face so like her own, sudden tears clogging her throat. Not only did Alfred look like her, but of her four brothers, he was the one who most shared her love of fine things and had a vision for an easier, refined life.

Odny and Ruth with Alfred Kristiansen family, 1930, Førde, Norway.

"Mama, Mama." Ruth was tugging at her skirt. But Kristine had been so absorbed with her brother's workshop that she was startled to see her.

"What is it?" she said. "Where is your sister?"

"Odny says *Tante* says, it's time to eat."

"Oh, my goodness, I suppose they are all waiting for us. Alfred, have you gotten me in trouble already?" Kristine teased her brother.

Alfred knelt down next to Ruth and began to speak in soothing Norwegian. Overwhelmed by this man she didn't understand, Ruth hid her face in her mother's skirt.

"Kristine, you must ask her in English if I can take her into *middag* and if she will be my girl while she is here, since I only have sons." he said with a smile, still kneeling.

In a whispered exchange between Kristine and Ruth, it was

arranged. Alfred held a now smiling Ruth's hand as they joined the others gathered around the table.

The midday meal passed in a blur of conversation of whose children were whose, who had gotten married or died, or other news that Kristine might have missed. When Ruth began nodding over her plate and Odny had asked twice to please be excused, Kristine's brother Karl pronounced that it was time to go.

After making plans to go out to Elise's early the next day, Karl, Anna, Alf, Kristine, and the girls walked back to the Kristiansen house. Kristine had thought perhaps this would be the time that she could talk with Karl about life since her father had died, maybe even tell him how sorry she was that she had not been able to come sooner. Karl sent Alf ahead to warn Maria the housekeeper that they would have *kaffe* as soon as they finished the short walk from Alfred's. Then he shut himself off by taking big strides and not looking left or right.

Kristine trailed behind as in the old days, except that she now had her own girls to watch as well as Karl's children. She was relieved that Anna seemed to enjoy taking care of Odny and trying to talk to her in simple Norwegian phrases as they walked along hand in hand. With one ear listening to their progress, she encouraged Ruth, who was so tired from the traveling she could hardly put one foot in front of the other.

When she walked through the front door and stood in the hallway that separated the front room from the shop, Kristine was struck by how narrow and dingy everything looked. Worn, in fact. Inside the living area was no cheerier. All the furniture stood in exactly the same places as five years ago but somehow seemed to sag and droop. The kerosene lamps had not been cleaned, and there were half-burnt candles instead of the fresh ones she would have had out for visitors from so far away. Kristine was about to start talking about installing electricity when Odny said she needed to go to the outhouse and would only go with Kristine.

"I'll take her," said Anna, so wanting to be noticed by her *tante,* whom she had thought was lost to America.

Odny stood shaking her head no. A flush crept up her neck.

"Odny, you can go by yourself then. Anna will only show you the way."

"No, I won't go without you. I want you."

''What? Be a big girl. You don't need me."

"I do need you. Pleeease…" Odny whined.

Ruth was screwing up her face to start crying, too, when Kristine said, "Okay, let's go together all of us this time, then you will be able to go by yourselves after that." And she led them out the back door to the outhouse.

Even before they were outdoors, Odny was whispering her complaints.

"This smells worse than the other place. What is the terrible smell. Is it fish? Mama, why do we have to come out here? There are spiders in here. I want…"

Kristine held up her hand. "Stop, do not say anymore. You are a little girl who is lucky to be here. I grew up in this house and you were born here. This is where we lived until we went to Waukegan to join your daddy. You must be *skikkelig* (respectful)." She reached out and pulled the outhouse door open. "Now, you first, then Ruth. No more whining."

Odny looked at her, her upper lip quivering. She had not heard such sternness from her mama very often. "It stinks in here," she whispered but went in and came out scowling. Ruth then refused to use it at all until Kristine went in with her.

Much of the happy energy that began the day waned. *Kaffe* was a dreary time, with Karl, Kristine, and the children served by Maria the housekeeper. Every time Maria poured coffee or *saft* for the children, a nervous giggle escaped from her. Karl fixed her with a sour look before she scurried away.

After asking about the business and complimenting the children, Kristine searched for something to talk about. Answering with only one-word responses, Karl did not follow up with questions about Fredrik or seem interested in the girls.

"It is so strange without *Far* asking for his herring," Kristine said, looking at the meager table with just rolls and jam and a few small shortbread cookies.

Karl grunted but did not speak.

"We only have herring for breakfast now since *bestefar* (grandfather) died. Father says that it is extravagant to have fish twice a day," Anna said, as if her father weren't sitting right there. Indeed, Karl's expression did not change. "But I go every day to get fresh rolls from Fru Kvål."

Kristine wondered that the cheapest of fish was so extravagant as to be limited to once a day. Were times so bad for Karl? Instead of pursuing memories of her father, Kristine asked Anna to play something for them on the organ.

Anna squirmed. "*Tante*, I am so sorry. I have forgotten how to play."

Turning in her seat, Kristine asked Karl, "Has Mr. Stram stopped giving lessons?"

"No, but she did not seem to do so well with him, so there didn't seem to be any point to keeping on. I stopped her lessons when *Far* died."

Pulling one of her dark braids across her mouth as if it would keep her from saying something she shouldn't to her father, Anna stared at her lap.

Compassion for her overcame Kristine's irritation with her brother. "No one is good when they first learn to play. I will be here for a few months. Tomorrow I will play with you. Maybe you would like that?"

When Anna nodded, Karl stood up. "Anna, clear the table. I will be in the parlor." Kristine waited for a good night or nod to her presence, but Karl had left the room. Her heart sank that this was the way they passed their evenings in the household. When Odny and Ruth followed him, she thought about stopping them but decided to just let them go.

She and Anna quickly cleared the table and were ready to wash the dishes, but Maria said it was her job.

"*Takk,* Maria, tomorrow you and I will figure out how we can work together while I am here, but for tonight, I think I must say good night and wish you a good night's sleep." She could hear Ruth's little-girl voice from the other room.

Maria gave another nervous giggle before saying she would like that and handing her a pitcher of warm water for the bedroom washbasin.

"There you are, finally," Karl said when Kristine went into

the living room and found Ruth standing next to him, going through his pipe collection on a stand. "I don't understand a word this child is saying. Is she speaking Norwegian?"

Kristine laughed at his befuddlement. "Oh, Karl, I'm afraid she mixes Norwegian and English. She hears both at home. Maybe you can teach her."

"Humph. How old is she?" Karl asked and peered over his newspaper at Ruth as if some not-quite-tame animal had invaded his parlor. Frightened, Ruth hid behind Kristine.

Odny sat on a stack of old newspapers and ignored her sister and gruff uncle, studying a paper for words she could recognize.

"She's four." Agitated, Kristine moved around the small room, straightening up pillows, lifting doilies to look at the dust, and picking up small tools, a few coins, and bits of pieces of paper. Dismayed at his whole manner, she tried to find a way to reset the tone.

"Mama, why won't *Onkel* Karl answer me?"

"He doesn't quite understand your Norwegian, and he is not used to little girls."

"And I don't like children who touch my pipes," he barked and hid behind the newspaper again.

Kristine opened her mouth to protest, but after a look at the girls' wide eyes, she said nothing until she waved Odny to come to her side, too.

"Ruth, say you are sorry for touching *Onkel* Karl's pipes, and both of you say *God Natt, sove godt* (Good night, sleep well)," she said instead of the reprimand she wanted to give her brother.

Transfixed by the strained note in their mama's voice, Odny

led Ruth in saying good night. Karl responded with a nod and a thoughtful pull on his unlit pipe.

"*God Natt,* Karl." Kristine's voice held a question. "Tomorrow?" Was he happy to have her? Pride kept her from asking.

For his part, Karl kept up the appearance of indifference. He looked up from his paper as if he'd already forgotten she was there.

With his curt, "*God Natt,*" Kristine felt dismissed. She turned and led the girls out into the dark-paneled hallway that not only separated the house from the shop but also held the stairs to the second floor.

"Mama, you didn't bring a lamp. Shall I go back for one?"

"No, maybe Anna will bring us one," Kristine answered. "Besides, it is still light outside, it's just dark down here with no windows."

Kristine and the girls climbed the steep stairs to her old room under the eaves. Pallets had been made up on the floor for the girls, and Kristine's bed was pulled taut with a freshly ironed sheet topped with a down-filled comforter that smelled of sunshine and sea salt. Kristine set the pitcher on the washstand and tried to supervise the evening washing up.

"Mama, I will hit my head if I stand up in bed." Odny demonstrated by walking her hands across the slanted boards that made up the ceiling of the room.

"Why would you stand up in bed?" Kristine asked as she rescued her stockings from Ruth, who was busily filling the bottom dresser drawer while also trying to sit in it. "Don't sit there, it is not strong enough for a big girl like you."

Grabbing their nightgowns, she pushed the suitcase up against the single bureau in the room, finished the washing up, and tried to settle both girls next to her on the big bed.

"Tomorrow we will finish unpacking and..." Kristine was stopped by a tap on the door.

Before she could say, "Come in." Ruth had flung the door open.

Anna stood there holding two steaming cups. "Maria thought you might like some warm milk before bed. I told her that you used to bring me milk at bedtime."

"Come in, Anna. How kind of you. Did you put honey in the milk, too?"

"Of course, just like always. May I?" When Kristine nodded, Anna gave a cup to each of the girls.

"None for you, Anna?" Kristine asked.

"Not yet. I am not quite ready to go to sleep," she said with a shy smile.

"Then come join us on the bed for evening prayers."

"Okay. It will really be like before," Anna said, smiling, as she sat next to Ruth, who climbed into her lap.

Kristine told Odny to pray first. "You must thank God for bringing us back here. This is the very room that you were born in."

Odny looked anything but thankful, but prayed as she had been told.

When she had finished and it was Ruth's turn, Ruth said, "Thank you, God, that I was born in America with Daddy."

The bickering began.

Whether it was fatigue or her own mixed emotions, Kristine

surprised herself by laughing. "Ruth, you are so right. We must thank God for both our homes but most of all for your daddy, who made all this possible. We will write him early tomorrow. Now *sove godt* (sleep well)."

Anna, who had been looking uncertain throughout the prayers, was so relieved when Kristine laughed that she leaned over and hugged each girl, a happy surprise for them all.

"We'll be just outside the door. I don't want to hear a peep from you. Go to sleep now."

Kristine and Anna closed the door and sat side by side on the top step, whispering about plans for what they would do while Kristine was home, the people they would visit, the hikes they would take. From the room under the eaves, there wasn't a sound.

Chapter Sixteen

Storehesten, Big Horse Mountain

Odny Hjelmeland, St. Olaf College Report, 1943:

It took Ruth and me only two weeks to pick up the Norwegian language. We traveled all over Norway visiting relatives for four and a half months. We went to Førde, Hjelmeland at Bygstad, Trondheim and Oslo. We had many picnics in the mountains especially Storehesten behind Hjelmeland.

In the morning, Kristine was in the kitchen before Maria, putting the water on the coal stove for morning coffee and eggs.

She inspected the cupboards, pondered the cold storage instead of a refrigerator, pumped water at the kitchen sink, and searched for a fresh cloth for the breakfast table. The meager food supplies distressed her, but she greeted Maria with what she hoped was an encouraging *God morgen*.

"*Fru Hjelmeland, God morgen.* You are already cooking?" Maria turned one way and then the other, her hands fluttering and eyes not quite meeting Kristine's. Petite and plain, Maria made Kristine think of a brown sparrow.

Only twenty-one years old, unmarried, and unschooled in the household arts, Maria scurried to make the meals, do the laundry, and clean for the Kristiansens. After Kristine had left for America five years earlier, Maria had been hired to help out. She did the best she could but had never been to *husmorskole* or even had any woman to mentor her in what to do. She irritated Kristine running around like a mouse but never seeming to accomplish anything. Even as Kristine noticed that the order and cleanliness were not up to her standards, she felt sorry for the young woman.

"Maria, thank you for taking care of Karl and the children and for Father when he was alive," she said. "I have worried about how you all get along here with no woman in the family to help take care of things. Do you do the shopping from the market?"

"Usually. Sometimes Karl asks me for a list and he goes," Maria answered in her thin, squeaky voice.

"Maybe, I could help with that while we are here," Kristine said. "I'm sure the butcher and baker are still the same. And we are so many now."

"Ja, maybe we could go together some days so you could show me what is best?" Maria's voice trembled, and she turned away from Kristine to drop eggs into a pan of boiling water. "Will you be here for *middag* today?"

"*Nei,* but tomorrow we will be, and we can go to the market in the morning. This morning I need to wash clothes. The girls and I have been away from home for two weeks, so we are running out of clean stockings and dresses."

"But Fru Hjelmeland, we don't wash clothes on Wednesday." Maria sounded shocked.

* * * *

To Kristine, her home had become a place where strangers lived together rather than the lively family center it had once been. Using the long summer afternoons and evenings for visiting family and friends helped her overcome her sadness.

She quickly relaxed into giving her daughters over to family so that she could resume some of her old roles. She was dismayed to see how dreary the once bright, cheery parlor, where the family had entertained and gathered in the evenings, had become. Mostly during the recent years it had been used by her father and Karl, the only adults left in the house. A thick film of smoke from their pipes seemed to dim all the color in the room. The red geraniums she had nurtured through her mother's illness were gone, replaced by a growing stack of newspapers. The English ivy curling around the windows looked dry and brittle. The oily pungency of smoked fish mixed with the smell of stale pipe tobacco, kerosene lamps, and burnt coal even though there had not been a need for the heating stove since she arrived. The woven tapestry on the table under the big window was so dusty the orange and blues looked brown and gray.

One morning, Karl left the shop to visit the outhouse and

found all his parlor furniture outside. Kristine was beating rugs as if they were her worst enemies.

"Kristine, Maria should be doing that," Karl said, trying to assert himself in this domestic activity.

"Mmm, how long has it been since she did this, Karl?" she asked, hoping that he would hear her certainty that the housekeeper had not done this monthly task for years. "Besides, she is working on another task I have given her."

When he made his way back inside, Maria was scrubbing the floorboards with homemade, lye-based soap. "Maria, that smells terrible. What are you doing?"

"*Fru* Kristine told me to clean the floors and baseboard with this. Do you not want me to?" Her eyes flickered nervously from the floor to him.

"Humph, go ahead. She will guide you while she is here, but finish quickly and dump your water near the outhouse." Karl retreated to his shop.

At *middag* that day, they had *risyngrøt,* rice porridge, *spekekjøtt,* and *flatbrød.*

"I like this, simple, like you used to make for us on Saturdays," Karl said.

"*Ja, takk,* it was cleaning day today." Kristine was cautious about saying any more.

"Was it necessary to move everything around? I thought it was fine the way it was."

Kristine held back from telling him that it was awful that he should live like that, unhealthy. Instead she brought up a tender subject. "*Far's* pump organ, do you ever play it? I tried it today.

The leather in the pedals seems very stiff."

Karl stared stonily at her before saying, "You know I do not play. It is wrong to use what was *Far's.*"

Kristine chose her words carefully, trying to be respectful of the old man her brother had become. "*Far* had both Alfred and me take lessons. What if we gave the organ to Alfred?"

"Kristine, what is wrong with leaving it here? Must you change everything?"

Before she had left for America, this would have been the last word, but Kristine found herself arguing. "It is not change to take care of the nice things you have. Karl, it has become a sad place. For the children's sake, you must bring some light and music back into this house."

"Kristine, this is my house and they are my children. I will do what I see fit to do."

* * * *

Her first visit after settling in was to Bergum, the farm that Elise lived on with her husband, Olav, and their four children, two girls and two boys. She and her girls, including little Anna, walked there carrying the gifts Kristine had chosen specifically for them. Odny and Ruth ran ahead.

A few yards behind them, Kristine smiled to hear Odny pelt little Anna with questions.

"Why does the spray from the fjord taste so salty?"

"How can a road go through the mountain?"

"Those boys are fishing. Can we go fishing in a rowboat?"

Little Anna tried to understand, but mostly her answer was a smile.

All three girls yodeled and shrieked to hear their voices echo off the damp rock walls of a short tunnel.

At Bergum, Elise had taken time from her daily chores in the dairy barn and the house to lay out an embroidered tablecloth and make *fiskekaker* (fish cakes) with potatoes and carrots, for their *middag*. Even though the food was humble, the table was meticulous, with lilacs and silver spoons for their vanilla custard dessert. This was the kind of welcome Kristine had expected from Karl.

"Elise, how did you find time to do all this?" Kristine asked, her arm still around her sister's shoulders.

"It is *ingenting* (nothing)." Elise replied, her smile belying her pleasure at being complimented.

When Olav came to the table, Kristine took in his shiny red cheeks, thick-fingered hands, squinty blue eyes, and gentle smile. She saw not only a farmer but also his utter satisfaction with his lot in life, no matter the difficulties. She realized that he probably did not spend time thinking about how life could be—all his energy went to providing for his family the same way his father had on this meager plot of land near the sea. Did she want more than she was supposed to? She pushed the thought from her mind as they ate and laughed. When they were finished, the older girls washed the dishes and took the young ones out to look for berries. The afternoon flew by. Kristine was surprised when Elise put down her mending to prepare *kveldsmat* (a light evening meal).

"Elise, is it that time already?"

"*Ja*. Olav and Paul are milking. I wonder where those girls have gotten off to."

"We must start walking back. Karl will think he has been abandoned." Kristine wound up her knitting and stuffed it into her bag.

"You don't need to leave, stay for *kveldsmat*. You must. Karl knows where you are, and Maria will take care of Alf and him."

"Shall we call him and tell him?" Kristine walked to the back door to look for the girls.

Elise stared at her sister's back. "Kristine, have you been gone so long? Things have not changed that much here. We have been saving for a phone line, but with Leif being born and the poor barley crop last year…"

At the note of defensiveness in her sister's voice, Kristine turned to see a flush on Elise's placid face.

"Of course we can't call. I forgot that the old road is too narrow for the phone lines. Alfred's Anna told me yesterday." She said too much, trying to cover her embarrassment.

"Mama, look what we have, a whole bucket of *tyttebaer*, a Nordic cranberry." Odny ran through the door, already speaking a bit of Norwegian. "We're hungry. Can we eat the berries now? Please?"

"We're hungry," Ruth piped up.

"Judging from your pink mouths, I'd say that you have already had some berries." Kristine laughed, and Elise smiled at the picture the three little girls plus the older ones, Anna and Margit, made. Maybe a roll and some cheese to go with those berries?

On the walk back around the fjord to town much later, Kristine thought about Elise working every day within the limits of the farm, the way things had always been done. Tending the chickens, cleaning fish, preserving berries. Life in America must seem easy to Elise. Kristine promised herself not to talk about phones or private cars and the radio Fredrik had bought just before they left. She hoped she could slip back into her role of youngest sister, but somehow the years apart had changed that dynamic.

"Mama, I am so tired, carry me?" Ruth interrupted her musings.

"Too much berry picking in the mountain fields for your little legs?" Kristine picked her up and carried her a short way, but Ruth was tall for four, and her long legs made their progress too slow.

"Anna, will you take one of Ruth's hands and I'll take the other?" Kristine put the sleepy girl down. Odny came over to Kristine's other side, and they made their way the last mile or so back to Kristiansens', four abreast on the narrow road.

* * * *

The next afternoon while Anna was with the girls, Kristine walked across the river on the one bridge in Førde to visit her girlhood friend, Fru Astrid Kvall. Astrid welcomed her with coffee and almond cake. The rich smells of baking breads and buttery cookies permeated Astrid's apartment above the bakery that she and her husband owned. Astrid had married later, like

Kristine. Despite the letters Kristine had sent her, Astrid asked many questions about what it was to live in a town where no one knew you. As they talked, Kristine realized she was not the newest person in Waukegan anymore.

The coffee cups were refilled several times as Kristine told Astrid about her life. In Waukegan, factories opened and new people from Poland, Ireland, Italy, and Armenia came to work. Kristine's newest friend, Helena, was one of those whose husband worked in the factory. Kristine told Astrid how comforting it was to help someone else who struggled with language and how to manage in a foreign place. Astrid was amazed that apartments and duplexes were built on streetcar lines so that hundreds of men could work in one place. She thought she understood the shipping on the Great Lakes, but the trains that transported everything from cattle to steel or fabric through Chicago were more than she could imagine.

Another day, after a morning of tackling more cleaning in the upper rooms of the family home, Kristine took the girls and little Anna for a visit to Alfred's Anna at their home behind the store.

Kristine and Alfred were the two youngest siblings and looked very much alike, favoring their finer boned and compact father, Andreas, with light brown hair and straight, small noses set in oval faces. Closest in age to her, Alfred had married Kristine's best friend from confirmation class, Anna

"*Velkommen, takk for sist,* welcome, it has been too long since we were last together." Alfred's Anna drew them into her cozy *stue* (parlor). Her fair round face, soft blue eyes, and halo of brown hair spoke of serenity and calm despite the youngest of her four sons clamoring for attention. "I have put the *kaffe in* the garden. It will be easier to talk if these noisy children have some space."

In minutes, they were settled around a small table holding teacups and *boller and mandelkake* (cardamom rolls and almond cake). The garden bordered the Førde River, making it an interesting place for the children to explore while their mothers knit and talked.

"I have missed this, Anna. The river flowing into the fjord is not something I have found in America." Here Kristine did not feel the need to explain so much. Alfred's Anna understood on some level that life was different in America, but that Kristine was still her friend and sister-in-law with whom she could both laugh and cry.

After getting Alfred's Anna's perspective on their friends and childbirth and the most interesting changes in the neighborhood, Kristine jumped into a family matter weighing heavy on heart.

"Anna, I am worried about Elise. She looks so much older to me. Do you think they are doing well on the farm?"

"*Ja,* I think so. I haven't seen much of her since Leif was born." Anna was counting stitches and didn't look up from the sock she was working on. "Then your father dying like he did, so unexpectedly. She never says much."

"She seems happy to see me, but also angry."

"At you, Kristine? No, but you certainly remind her of *Far.* You and Alfred are so like him. I think she has too much to do much with the baby, the family, and the farm. "

"Does Margit help now that she's thirteen?"

"I think she has been helping a long time. When your father

died last year, Elise stayed at the house for several days with baby Leif and sent little Anna and Alf out to do her regular chores on the farm. I think that little Anna and Margit were responsible for the children, the cooking, collecting the eggs, everything. A lot for two girls only ten and eleven then." Anna broke off her yarn with a snap. "Speaking of children, where are ours?"

In a flurry of arms and legs, two boys and two girls came around the corner of the house, chattering away about fish.

"That was a huge fish, mama, the biggest ever!" Ruth was panting.

Not to be outdone, Odny held out her hands about two feet wide.

Johan laughed. "It wasn't so big. We catch bigger ones all the time."

"*Nei*, trout do not grow that big!" little Anna corrected the younger ones.

"Did you catch it for our supper?" Alfred's Anna asked with a smile.

"We didn't. Torleif said he was in charge of that," Odny said.

Kristine got caught up in the back and forth because, to her astonishment, after only two weeks in Førde, the entire conversation was in Norwegian. She marveled at how easily her young girls adopted another language when she was still struggling with English after five years.

On their next visit to Bergum and Elise, the children were sent to wander up the mountainside in search of more berries to preserve for the long, dark winters when fruit was not available. Berries—*tyttebær, moltebær* (cloudberries), raspberries, blueberries, currants—were plentiful in the temperate mountain bogs of Western Norway. The summer of 1930 was a good year for *blåbær* (blueberries).

"Are you coming with us, Mother?" Ruth asked.

Odny's eyes lit up when Kristine said, "No, you are fine with Margit and little Anna. They know where the best berries are. You must listen to them." She could see that Odny and Ruth were thrilled with the freedom to wander without her.

Kristine was less thrilled with picking peas in Elise's garden, but it gave her a chance to talk to her sister about her concerns. "Are you fine, Elise? You seem a bit sad."

Elise looked up from the peas she was gathering, startled that Kristine would be so bold as to comment on her mood. "I am fine, of course." When Kristine didn't say anything more, Elise added. "I have been quite tired since Leif was born. Maybe I was too old to have another baby. At forty-four, I should have been done with that."

"Oh, my, I suppose so. I forget sometimes the difference in our ages," Kristine said.

Elise shrugged and kept picking.

"Was it terribly sad for you when *Far* died?' Kristine had not been able to get anyone to tell her about those days.

"It was a shock. I miss him almost more than I missed you when you left," Elise admitted in a voice that shook with unshed, choked tears.

"Poor Elise, you have been so alone." Laying her basket of peas to the side, she hugged her sister close. She was ashamed she had not seen how the losses of both sisters, one to early death, the other to emigration, and both parents left Elise so lonely, caught in the unremitting work that is the farm and family.

Elise indulged in some brief crying but soon was embarrassed by the show of emotion in her vegetable garden. She straightened and wiped away her tears. "*Ja*, you are here now. We must make the most of our time together."

Kristine was saddened but grateful that Elise had let down her guard. They passed the afternoon doing simple chores and reminiscing about happier times. Hours later the girls came bounding into the house with buckets of blueberries and waving a fistful of coins.

"Mama, we have sold berries on the road. Look at all the *kroner*, Norwegian money, that we have."

"You sold berries? Are you saleswomen like your father?" Kristine asked with a smile.

"Well, Margit helped," Odny admitted.

"Should she have the money, then?"

"She has most of it, but she says this is our part for picking so many berries." Four-year-old Ruth seemed to understand this concept of sharing.

Kristine thanked Margit for her kindness and vowed to repay her double for sharing this experience with her cousins.

* * * *

Just ten miles away by bus, over a mountain and past Langeland, a mountain meadow and lake, was Fredrik's family farm, på Bygstad, the township. Fredrik's oldest brother, Mikal, now owned the dairy farm in the section known as Hjelmeland. He was working hard with his much-younger wife to use the efficiencies he had learned in his twenty years in America to make this small plot support his growing family. Since his return from America in 1919, he had taken over the farm, married, and followed in his father's footsteps in the road-building business. By 1930, he had four children and a wife on the twelve-acre farm. The red, hip-roofed barn that he built in the American style with concrete foundation—two levels plus the haymow—became a landmark on the road to Bygstad. With the landmark mountain Storehesten rising behind it, Hjelmeland with its American style barn stood out as a progressive place.

With the girls, Kristine felt more at home visiting Fredrik's family than she had years before when Fredrik's father lived there. Because Mikal had mentored Fredrik in their shared years in America, he was very interested in their lives. Most of her family could not imagine her life in Waukegan. Fredrik wrote often to Mikal and sought his advice, especially on financial matters related to property. Mikal's wife, Maria, was fun to be with, and Odny and Ruth found many playmates among these cousins.

"Are you writing to Fredrik soon, Kristine?" Mikal asked at breakfast during their first visit to the farm.

"I hope to finish a letter this afternoon. Can you carry it to the post for me tomorrow?" Kristine didn't know where the nearest post office was.

"I can, but not tomorrow. Perhaps Gunnar will ride his horse into Bygstad for you. I am off to Sogn for some business today," he said. "Will you add a note from me to your letter?"

"Of course. Do you want to write it?"

"No, I must leave soon, but tell him that I have my eye on some property in Førde and that he must let me know what price he is able to pay." Mikal spoke just like Fredrik. "And tell him I will send him details as soon as he lets me know if it is possible."

"I think he will want details before he tells you about money. Isn't that how you brothers do a deal with people?" Kristine had begun to understand a bit about the brothers' approach to real estate.

"With other people, yes, but between him and me, he knows what I am asking," Mikal said.

"Yes, well, have a good trip." Kristine felt she had just been put in her place. "Who will take care of the farm while you are gone?"

Mikal looked at her, surprised, "Maria of course."

"By herself?" Kristine thought of the five children ranging in age from nine to infant and the twelve cows Maria milked every day.

"She has help. Now, I am off." Mikal seemed annoyed with Kristine's questions.

Kristine was not offended by this dismissal, but rather it so reminded her of Fredrik's quicksilver ways that she found herself missing him. Shaking those feelings off, she pitched in churning butter and making yogurt, cooking for the men working in the fields, keeping an eye on the baby, but not milking or riding the horse-drawn hay wagons. She drew a firm line at barn work.

"I don't think you girls should get in the way in the barn," Kristine told Odny and Ruth when they began to follow Maria the next day.

Maria cocked her head to one side, wondering about this woman who had come from America with such views about barns and children. "They are welcome. Goodness knows, my brood is in there."

"But your children know about barns, my girls do not. They could easily get in the way."

"Not that much to learn about the barn," Maria said with a laugh. "If they play in there too long, I will give them a chore to do. I expect they will be outside more than in the barn."

Hjelmeland was not on the *sol-side* (sun side) of Storehesten, the mountain that shadowed the farm. After months during which the sun never made it high enough on the horizon to shine in the farm's side of the valley, when Kristine was visiting, the sun shone twenty hours a day.

The third day that Mikal was gone, Maria came in after her morning chores and said, "Today Kristine, I think we will walk to the *sæter* (summer pasture for the cows). Will you start some coffee, please? There is a thermos in the cupboard to put it in. I will get some crackers and oranges. That will be enough. They have food for us when we get to the *stoylen* (small huts for the milkmaids)."

"No *middag*, then?" Kristine had already begun to peel potatoes for the meal.

"No, it is a long walk up and back, so we will leave as soon as we can."

"I'll be ready. I must just pack up a few things while the water boils. Will we be over night?" Kristine loved walking in the mountains. She was hoping to go for days.

Storehesten, Big Horse Mountain, and Hjelmeland Farm, Bygstad.

"No, I can't be gone so long, but with the light, it will be late before we have to be back." Maria smiled at Kristine's eagerness.

Within a half hour, the oranges and crackers had been packed and the children called in from the barn and the nearest field. Kristine and Maria each carried a big basket. Maria also carried her infant, Oddborg, in a sling on her hip.

Gunnar, the eldest, led the way, with Odny close on his heels. Finn, Jofrid, and Ruth tried to keep up and the moms walked and talked, not allowing anyone to stray too far from the cow path worn over decades of use.

"Mama, carry me?" Ruth held up her arms as they climbed hundreds of yards above the farm.

Kristine stroked the blond head leaning into her. "I think maybe you need a rest, little one." She called to the group who had gotten ahead, "Maria, we will follow you in a few minutes. This one is not used to your mountains."

"I'm not tired, may I just go on?" Not waiting for permission, Odny scrambled after her cousins as if she were a lamb. She hopped from rock to rock when they came across blueberry bogs. She did stop long enough to refuel with a few berries.

Maria stopped, too. "Come up here Kristine, the *lyng* (heather) is soft here. I could use a stop, too. No need to rush. We have all day."

"Oh, then I will stop, too," Jofrid said. Mikal and Maria's middle daughter was exactly Ruth's age. They were becoming fast friends.

After a brief interlude, drinking from a nearby mountain stream and munching on *flatbrød,* they climbed the rest of the way to the *sæter* (summer pasture), and found the rest of the children talking with the milkmaids, who were laying out their summer picnic. Cheese, *rømmekolle,* (a yogurt-like porridge), and the crackers that Kristine and Maria carried filled out their mountain picnic amongst the cows.

"Girls, what do you think of our summer pastures?" Maria asked Ruth and Odny.

"It is very far to walk up here. When do the milkmaids come home?"

"They stay up here about six weeks with the cows. The grass is better here."

"Six weeks without their mothers?" Ruth looked around for hers. From behind her, Kristine patted her shoulder.

"I thought the *rømmekolle* was very sour," Odny said before she caught Kristine's glance that warned her about her behavior. "But the berries and *flatbrød* were very good."

Kristine relaxed into the day, the place, and the company.

While Maria consulted with the milkmaids about which cows were doing well, the calves, and the limited milking. Kristine, Ruth, and Odny leaned against the side of the hut, absorbing the warmth of the sun against the wood and rocks. She felt Odny grow heavy against her side as all the exercise, fresh air, and excitement caught up with her. Soon both girls were napping, cushioned against their mother.

Much later, after they had their coffee and some sweet cookies, they gathered the children and walked down the mountain to tumble into bed. Days like these assured that Odny and Ruth would return to Fredrik knowing his home and a piece of their heritage.

* * * *

"Karl, which bus should we take to get to the ferry to Bergen?" Kristine asked over breakfast one day late in July.

"Are you going to Brekstad?" he asked. After their tense beginning, Karl had gotten used to having Kristine around and could see that his children and even the housekeeper, Marie, liked having her around. "How long will you be gone?"

"A few weeks for sure. It takes three days to get there. The train connections from Bergen to Trondheim are only every other day. Petrina wrote that her Andreas will fetch us in Trondheim, but she felt if we are coming so far, we must stay for some time. We will stop to see Hjalmar in Oslo on the trip home."

"So much travel—you are adventurous." Karl peered at her. "What has Fredrik done to you? You were afraid to go to Bergen alone, and now you travel all over the country with children?"

"I don't know when I will get to come home again. When we move back, I will be just like everyone else, too busy and too poor to travel around," Kristine said with a laugh. He seemed to be complimenting her, but something about this exchange made her feel defensive.

After several bus rides, ferry rides, and two different trains, they finally arrived in the town of Brekstad in Ørlandet, just west of the bigger city of Trondheim.

"Kristine, you have really come." Petrina shook her hand, patted her shoulder, and finally hugged her close. Among the many sisters, wives, and cousins in Fredrik's family, Kristine felt closest to Petrina.

"We have. These are my girls, Odny and Ruth. Do they favor Fredrik, do you think?" Kristine asked, fishing for Petrina's approval.

"This one looks just like my sister Anna did as a girl," she said, shaking Odny's hand solemnly.

"*God dag, Tante* Petrina." Odny responded to the formality of this petite woman.

"But this one is all you," she said turning to Ruth. As usual when meeting new people, Ruth tried to hide behind her mother.

"Are your boys here?" Kristine asked.

"Soon they will be home from the egg center. Perhaps Andreas told you he is working on establishing a center to provide the city of Trondheim with eggs. The boys help him with that in addition to the dairy and agricultural school when it is in session."

"My goodness, you may be too busy to have us as guests," Kristine said with a laugh.

"Never too busy for you, Kristine!" Petrina laughed. "You are the one who saved brother Fredrik from a wild and lonely life in Canada."

"Such foolishness. He was doing fine without me." Kristine flushed at the unusual compliment. "But he does wish he could be with us."

"I remember when you wrote to ask about him." Petrina and Kristine had been friends since before either of their marriages. Petrina had encouraged Kristine when the long years passed after her engagement to Fredrik. Since both lived so far from home, they shared a bond of a certain kind of loneliness and spirit of adventure.

"Mama, are we still in Norway?" Odny asked.

Before Kristine could answer, Petrina said, "You are very clever to wonder. This is so different from Bergen or even Førde. No tall mountains, only one big fjord, fields of crops. I wondered if I had wandered into a strange land when I first came here, too. But yes, you are still in Norway."

The days in Brekstad were filled with following their boy cousins, Gunnar, Gudmund, and Leidulf, around, picking strawberries and walking late at night to the sea to watch the sunset. Unlike in Førde, this house was filled with music, books, and art. When the chores were done and they had written to their father, the girls got to draw or try out the piano.

One evening, enjoying the late summer warmth in the garden, Andreas was trying to teach Gudmund the guitar.

"I want to play." Ruth sat down on the ground in front of the boy and his father. "Please? Will you teach me?"

"You do? Stay right there." Andreas hurried off into the house, leaving a baffled Ruth, until he emerged with a smaller, child-size guitar.

"Is that for me?" Ruth asked, delighted.

"It is while you are here." Andreas was so kind to children.

Kristine and Girls with Petrina Ede and sons, Gunnar, Leidulv, and Gudmund. Brekstad, Norway, 1930.

Here, too, they helped with the day-to-day work but interspersed the chores with walks and concerts at the church and time to learn of one another's lives.

When it was time to leave, everyone was tearful.

"I am so glad you will get to see Nidaros cathedral where all the kings are crowned before you get the train in Trondheim," Petrina said sniffling.

"Will the king be there?" asked Odny, who had become very interested in kings and queens.

"No, but his palace is in Oslo, where you will go next." Petrina reached out and hugged Kristine close.

"*God tur, kjære søster,* (Travel well, dear sister)," Petrina whispered.

Kristine could only say thank-you a thousand times, not trusting herself to think about goodbyes to Petrina, who had indeed become like a sister to her. She knew that it could be a very long time before they would see one another again.

From Trondheim, the travelers took a train to visit Kristine's brother, Hjalmar, and his small family in Oslo. Hjalmar was a waiter on cruise ships that went primarily across the North Sea to Germany, Denmark, and England. He, too, had ventured out of the confines of Førde and Bygstad to see a bigger world. It was Kristine's first visit to Oslo, the growing capital city of Norway.

"Is your ship in the harbor, Hjalmar?" Kristine asked. He had taken them around the city, and they were finishing with *smørbrød*, open-faced sandwiches, near the train station next to the expansive harbor at the top of the Oslofjord.

"Why are there guns on those boats?" Odny asked.

Hjalmar seemed pleased at so much interest. "No, my ship will be in the harbor tomorrow morning. I rejoin the crew the next day."

"Odny, why do you think there are guns on that boat?" Hjalmar turned to the six-year old, taking her seriously.

"To keep the bad guys away?"

"Not exactly. Because this is where the government and the King are. Oslo is an important city. The guns are here for the same reason Akershus fortress is here. To protect the city. Anyone who wants to take over the city will probably come by ship through the water."

Odny had heard enough and skipped off to play with Ruth in the small park near the docks.

"Really, Hjalmar? Was there fighting here during the war? I hadn't thought about this harbor." Kristine realized her brother had not been home at all during World War I. She hadn't thought about it before.

"*Ja*, we never had any fighting here, but those cargo ships I was working on then were shot at plenty in the North Sea. It could happen."

Kristine looked around at the sun glinting on the blue fjord and the festive leisure boats next to Navy vessels and commercial ships and shuddered. "Hjalmar, don't say that. I can't bear to think of another war."

"Who would want to attack Norway? We are a small, poor country. Even if the big countries start again, they won't waste lives in Norway." Hjalmar sounded reasonable. "But now we need to go back to the apartment, or we will be late for *kaffe*."

"It's been so kind of you to have us here with you, Hjalmar. I know Marta is not used to so many people." Kristine did not really understand Hjalmar's wife, but she felt it was important to acknowledge that she appreciated their visit.

"You are right that she is not comfortable with visitors, but we have been very happy to have you," Hjalmar said. "She will talk about the American visit for a long time."

The next morning, Kristine and the girls boarded the train for Førde. As with most trips in Norway, the trip involved a train over the mountains and a series of ferries and buses. By the time Kristine had managed to get the girls and their baggage as well as herself to Førde, she was missing the convenience of a personal car.

In their last two weeks in Norway, Kristine and the girls re-visited friends and family in Førde and Bygstad. On a sunny afternoon, she sat with Alfred's Anna in their garden, knitting.

"Kristine, are you really leaving us? This summer has been wonderful for me to have you back. Your girls are truly Norwegian."

Kristine glanced at Odny, who was dangling her feet over the canal from the river that flowed behind the garden. Odny was chattering away in Norwegian to her cousin Johan while he fished. "*Ja*, Fredrik will be surprised. They both will have a better idea of what we mean when we talk about going home to Førde."

Anna chuckled, "They have had a grand tour. You have been places I have never been and met so many people."

Kristine concentrated on her stitches. "I must give Fredrik thanks for that. I love to go around and see things, but if I had not first gone to him in America, I would not have ever gone farther than Bergen. What would have drawn me to Trondheim or Oslo?" She omitted her awareness that she would not have had the money to travel to those places.

"I keep forgetting Fredrik. Is that terrible of me?" Anna laid down her stitching. "I suppose he is missing you."

Kristine looked past Anna at the water and mountains surrounding Førde. "He writes he misses us. I'm sure he misses the girls. He is a good father and wants everything for them."

"And you, Kristine? Are you happy there?" Anna saw something in her childhood friend that she couldn't identify— longing, homesickness?

"It is confusing. When I am here, I feel I'm home, but I do miss Fredrik. More than I expected. I think I have caught his restlessness." She smiled, "He is a good husband, but I don't think he can keep his promise to come back to Norway."

"Why ever not?" Anna said.

"Anna, it is as if I am two people, the Norwegian Kristine and the Kristine who is learning to be American. But Fredrik, he has been there so long now, twenty years. He has become mostly American."

"Is life so different there?" Anna asked without showing any real interest.

Kristine was disappointed in her friend, but how could she imagine Kristine's life in Waukegan? Not everyone knew everyone. New buildings went up all around them. Their markets and shops had a variety of things, so much more than Førde. People came from the country and other places in Europe. There was even talk of a World's Fair in Chicago. Even though the images of Fredrik, her friends there, and the town itself rolled through her mind's eye, Kristine merely said, "Some things are different, but I try to make our home as much like here as I can."

Later that day, after *kaffe* with Karl, Alf, Anna, and the girls, she took out her trunk and put most of the gifts that they were taking back to Fredrik, her father's hymnbook, and the fabric and patterns that she had bought from her brother's store into the trunk. In a suitcase that she would carry, she put her mother's favorite teacups, wrapped in a tapestry that Karl said she should have. As she worked, she thought of her conversation with Anna. She admitted to herself that she missed Fredrik most of all. She missed his energy, his spirit, his willingness to try new things and be modern, his love for the girls. She missed that he treated her like a woman and not someone's daughter, friend, or sister.

Their last morning in Førde was filled with tears but also with laughter. At breakfast, Karl even teased Ruth that he would miss her help with his pipes. Over and over, Alf thanked them for coming. He presented both Ruth and Odny with pink rubber balls as if they were precious jewels. The girls responded by giving him a cap, which he put on immediately and refused to take off. Anna and Kristine had stayed up late the night before talking, but avoided one another's eyes lest they start to cry again. Maria fussed and fluttered around them. She had come to depend on Kristine to help and guide her.

A smaller and happier band of people than when Kristine had left with Odny gathered to say good-bye: two of her brothers, Elise, and their families. The young cousins all clamored to go with Ruth and Odny to America. There was even a taxi to take them to ferry. Happy thank-you's, come again soon, and waves rang out as they waved and waved until they were out of sight.

After four months with the people she had so longed to see and be with, Kristine said good-bye to what she had imagined she had left behind and to what was.

Chapter Seventeen

Another New Place

Kristine to Fredrik's sister, Petrina, 1930:

Our entrance paperwork went quickly and then we were back on American soil again. Next we had to find our suitcases and have them inspected, but that did not go so smoothly. I had to look for over an hour to find one of my suitcases. While getting the three suitcases inspected, I also had to look after Odny and Ruth. By the time that was done, I was so tired I could have fallen over…A taxi took us from the docks to the bus to the train station, where we boarded the Chicago train that went through Washington D.C. After some hours in Washington we got back on the train to continue to Chicago, and there was Papa. Ja det var fest. (It was so wonderful.) He was so happy we were back.

Fredrik paced the platform, up and down, wondering if today was to be another wasted day at Union Station in Chicago. Yesterday, when Kristine and the girls had not been on the train from New York, he had not known what to think. Maybe they weren't coming back after all. When he got home and found the telegram saying that they had been delayed by a problem with the train, he'd calmed down some. However, the telegram went on to say they'd be on the next day's train from Washington, D.C. They were supposed to come directly from the *Stavangerfjord* ship to the train to Chicago. After four months in Norway, they detoured to Washington? The thought of Kristine managing Odny, Ruth, and their luggage on a trip to a strange city made him reach for his cigarettes. Just as he lit up, he heard them announce a train from Washington on Track 5. He strode across the cavernous terminal. As he scanned another platform for his family, four cars down the track he saw Odny take the conductor's hand to step onto the platform. Kristine, holding Ruth's hand, was next to step down. By that time, he was there to scoop them all up in a hug, hand luggage and all.

"*Far, far, hør på oss* (listen to us)!" Odny and Ruth chattered away in Nynorsk, his Norwegian dialect.

"*Neida*, who are these tall girls who are speaking Norwegian? Kristine, what have you done with Odny and Ruth?" He was so happy to see them again that he couldn't stop touching them, patting a head, grabbing a hand to hold. Over the long summer, he had wondered what he would do if Kristine decided not to come back. She had been so sad before she left.

He held out his arms to her. She stepped into his embrace, laughing. Four months had been longer than he'd imagined when they booked the trip.

"*Ja*, Fredrik, these milkmaids must have sneaked in and

replaced our girls. Let's find the trunk and see if we can find our English-speaking daughters."

Giggling, they collected a small mountain of luggage and soon were in the car driving to Waukegan. Odny talked steadily, telling him stories of names and places he had never dreamt she would know. She was telling him a complicated story about being chased up the mountain by a goat when he caught Kristine's eye. She smiled back. When he saw the light in her eyes, he could smile himself. The sadness had left her eyes. Had she left it in Norway?

"Now, we are home!" he announced as he pulled into the dusty driveway off Grand Avenue on the far western edge of Waukegan. He stopped in front of a square brick building with big glass windows. The sign on the building read, SERVICE ELECTRIC, F. Hjelmeland, proprietor. He watched Kristine's face. Did she like the new store? What did she think?

"Daddy, is this your store? Whose car is that? Is someone meeting us? I'm hungry." Ruth began to cry from exhaustion. It had been a long journey.

"Fredrik, you have been very busy while we were gone. Look at all you have done. A building where there was only a foundation." Kristine responded more slowly. "What kind of help did you have with this? How did you decide to call it Service Electric?"

"I wanted to have an American name, one that tells what we do. What do you think?" he said, smiling but wary. "As to the construction, I was lucky. Some of the big companies have begun to lay off. I was able to get day workers fairly cheap."

Family in front of new house at 1826 Grand, 1930.

After depositing their trunk and suitcases in the house, they walked over to the new store. Fredrik talked the whole way.

Kristine thought he was talking like a nervous schoolboy as he pointed out what the building still needed and of his plans to expand the inventory in the store from electrical fixtures to appliances.

"Do you think you would use a new electric washing machine, Kristine?" he asked.

"*Ja*, I surely would. I did so much wash at Karl's house. I missed the one I have here. That housekeeper of Karl's does not know how to wash and iron linens very well. Everything needed to be done. A newer washer would be wonderful. Does it automatically feed the ringer? I heard they are coming out with an electric iron, too. Could you stock those?"

"I will check. Thanks, I hadn't thought about an iron, but I suppose if you get the clothes clean, you need to iron them." He draped his arm across her shoulders and let her know he was finished with business talk. "Fru Hjelmeland, would you be so kind as to make us a cup of coffee?"

Kristine grinned at him. "It would be my pleasure."

As they walked back to the house, his nephews Alf and Gudmund arrived and were waiting to greet Kristine on the new front steps to the remodeled house. They asked immediately about their mothers and siblings.

"I have letters from both your mothers and fathers and some packages, but they are buried deep within the trunk. You will have to come back tomorrow to get those. For now, you must stay and have coffee," Kristine said.

Fredrik realized he should have gotten some more food in. He'd had the neighbor woman buy some bread and rolls, and he had fresh milk, but not much else. He hoped Kristine would manage as well as she usually seemed to.

"*Vær så god* (help yourselves), will you have coffee or tea?" Kristine was gracious as she served the simple meal of bread, cheese, and coffee. A crisp white cloth embroidered with red and yellow flowers covered the table, and somewhere she had found strawberry preserves. The men munched the bread and cheese and slurped their coffee as if it were an elaborate banquet. They'd had no one to cook for them or pour their coffee and steam the milk since Kristine had left. They listened as the girls told story after story about their families, the places they had played as children themselves.

"*Onkel* Alf, we hiked all the way to the *sæter,* the summer pasture on *Storehesten,* the mountain named Big Horse," Ruth said proudly.

"Wow, that's a long way up the mountain. You must have been hungry," said Alf.

"We were, and do you know, they gave us *rømmekolle* for lunch," Odny interjected.

"Did you like it? Do you want to live on the mountain and tend to the cows all summer?"

"Oh, no, I didn't like that porridge. They didn't even have sugar to put on it. And Daddy wasn't there." Odny looked as if she might cry.

"Alf, don't tease the girls. They've been traveling for over a week. They don't want to go much of anywhere except to bed," Kristine said with a smile.

Everyone laughed and said good night even though it was barely evening.

When Kristine returned from getting them settled, she poured more coffee for everyone and sat down with the men.

"So, how did you find things at home, Kristine? Everyone healthy? Was it as wonderful as the girls say? Has much changed in Førde?" Alf asked.

"The children made it fun. My niece, Anna, is quite grown up now that she's twelve. She was with us every day we were in Førde. Elise's two girls, too. They kind of adopted Ruth and Odny, taking them everywhere, even when they picked berries and hiked in the woods." Kristine looked over their shoulders as if she saw something they didn't. "The mountains and the fjords are so beautiful. Førde hasn't changed much, but oh how I missed father. The music has left the house. Karl is so gloomy. Because business is bad, he wants Anna to quit school and do the things that the housekeeper does. I gave Karl some money so Anna could stay in school. I'm glad I was able to get her out of the house and shop.

Fredrik frowned. "Kristine, let's talk about this later. Maybe I can have Mikal look into how we could help, man to man."

"Oh, we must write to Mikal very soon. He had so many questions about you, your business, the homestead in Canada, and people I don't really know. Most of the time he spoke English when he talked about America. He misses you and his life here. Since you were there, they have had a girl, Jofrid, Ruth's age, a younger son, Andreas, and a baby girl. Four children in seven years. It is a good thing his wife Maria is young. She needs to be to take care of the farm and all those children."

"*Ja,* do you think he would come back to earn some quick money? There's a lot of building going on with the World's Fair opening in Chicago in a few years."

"*Nei,* I doubt that he will leave Maria with the babies. Without your father there, Mikal must supervise the farm work while he continues the road building. Except for the day we arrived, I hardly saw him. Only for the midday meal. But he is clever. He has used some of the techniques he learned here to improve farming there. You should see his beautiful American-style barn. I have pictures in my trunk."

"Did you see my mother, *Tante* Kristine?" Young Gudmund had not been in Waukegan as long as his cousin Alf and was still homesick.

"I did, but not much. She was very busy at their farm. You must send her what you can of your earnings. The hay harvest failed this year. Your father is doing some fishing to earn what he can, so she must do more of the farm work."

"Oh, that reminds me, Uncle Fredrik, the job you sent me on today. I had the wrong conduit for the main lines to the barn. So, I have to go back tomorrow. Do we have more line in the shop?"

"I think we do, but I can't understand that you went out there without it. Let's go check the store and the truck and make sure you're ready for tomorrow."

"*Takk for kaffe, Tante* Kristine, I need to leave now, too. May I come back tomorrow for my letters?" Alf asked.

"Of course, see you tomorrow."

"You'll see me again tonight," said Fredrik with a grin as he followed the younger men out the door.

When he returned an hour or so later, he found that Kristine had unpacked from their trunk a leg of *spekekjøtt,* and left it out for him with some bread and boiled potatoes. He breathed in the salty smoky essence of the *spekekjøtt.* No one could cure mutton like Mikal. As he shaved a curl of the rich meat from the hank and laid it on a slice of boiled potato, Kristine strode into the small kitchen with a bucket of sudsy water. Her hair was pulled up tight away from her face and her everyday housedress was covered with a flour sack apron.

"Kristine, now, tonight? After traveling all the way from

Washington, D.C.? Aren't the girls sleeping? Sit with me while
I eat."

"*Nei*, Fredrik, you did not touch this floor the entire time
we were gone. I can't sleep until I can walk through here without
sticking."

Fredrik put his knife down. Kristine always joined him for
supper, even if she had already eaten with the girls.

"Come, this will wait until tomorrow, won't it? Besides, your
soap stinks, I want to enjoy the *spekekjøtt* since Mikal was so
good to send it."

"Humph, too much will wait in your mind, cleaning the
house, finishing remodeling this house, moving back to Norway.
When are we going to talk about that? When does that go with
spekekjøtt?" she muttered from her hands and knees. She waved
her scrub brush toward the bedrooms without doors, the rough
shelves that held the pots and pans, before digging deep into the
wooden floor.

Fredrik watched her scrub on her hands and knees, not
knowing what to say. Where was the happy woman who had
stepped from the train this morning?

"Now, now, Kristine, I thought you liked this place? *Ja*, it
needs some more work, but building the store took most of my
time while you were gone. I have to catch up with orders, and
more selling, to make it a go. If we are going back to Norway, this
store will need to be a success."

Kristine sat back on her heels and looked at him as if
considering whether that was worth responding to. Without
a word, she moved her bucket and started scrubbing another

section of the floor. Her shoulders began to shake and tears dropped into the wash water.

"Kristine, is it so bad as all that? Why are you angry? You said you had a good trip?"

"*Ja*, we did. So good, it's hard to be back here where the only thing that's changed is this new store. It looks like it will be only more work for you, more hours away from us. Does it make any difference to you whether the girls and I are here or there?" She began to cry in earnest.

His patience wearing thin, Fredrik bent over and pulled her up abruptly. Hands on her shoulders, face to face, he said quietly, "Now you must stop talking nonsense. Of course, I missed you and the girls. Every day I thought of you and wanted to be there with you. When you weren't on the train yesterday, I imagined all sorts of terrible things. Without you, it was easy to work all day, every day, because there was nothing to do here at home. I missed you too much. Did you miss me?"

"Too much?" Sniffling, Kristine raised an eyebrow.

"*Ja*, so much that all I did was work. I didn't cook. I didn't take care of the house, but I built a store and made money for us." His voice rose, as did the color in his cheeks, "That's important, too."

Kristine bit her lip and looked away from him. She knew this was as close to an apology as she would get. She had missed him and had really missed her life and friends in Waukegan. But she had enjoyed being a special visitor in Norway, enjoyed being the center of attention.

"Say something, please." His voice was softer. "This house

and moving home to Norway, we will talk, just not tonight, when we are both so tired."

"Fredrik, you must promise to work on this house if the girls and I are to live here."

"I said that I would, but you must show me what it is you need. What have I done that is so wrong?"

She rolled her eyes up at the bare bulbs hanging from the ceiling, but the beginning of an impish smile on her tear-streaked face changed the mood. "Well, one good thing about your running out with Gudmund, I had time to change the sheets on our bed." She had given up the argument for the time being.

Fredrick pulled her close, murmuring, "*Kos deg, jeg er så glad i deg* (It's okay, I love you so)."

She leaned into his solid shoulder, with a sigh. His cold supper and her floor scrubbing were finished for that night.

Chapter Eighteen

Ordinary People, Extraordinary Times

Letter from Fredrik Hjelmeland in Waukegan, Illinois, to his brother, F. Mikal Hjelmeland, in Bygstad, Norway, September 3, 1933:

For more than three years now, we have been having bad times here in America and it isn't any better now as far as we can see. Activities within the building trades have completely stopped...Brother it is hard to understand that this can be America. I have never seen a mess like this.

I haven't done any electrical wiring for years. I'm trying to be a salesman. Mikal, you never thought I could be a salesman. If there is a job that's hard, it's being a salesman when no one will spend any money. But, I have made it up to now. I go out to the country every day. I drive about 30,000 miles a year.

I'd like to compare the situation with an abyss or bottomless pit. If you had bought a house, you lost it. If you had put your money into a bank, you lost it. On properties

I had bought, I lost about $10,000. The properties are of no value today. I had $650 in a bank, and it is all gone and just the same with about $1500 in work I have done and don't expect to get paid for. About $12,000 is gone forever. But still, I'm much better off than many in my class.

Roosevelt is a good President; he is trying to do his best. During the past years the entire country had been badly governed...Worst of all are the people in their middle age, now when there is nothing, they have lost everything they have built up in the banks on the stock market, and in what they thought were good investments. Most of them found they are completely broke. This is hard for an ordinary man to understand.

Kristine watched Fredrik trudge across the yard from the shop to the house. It was early for him to be coming home. She wondered if there was to be more bad news. With a wave, she turned back to taking the wash down from the line. A soft breeze from Lake Michigan had given the towels a clean, sun-baked smell. She folded a dress, considering whether it was too faded for Odny or Ruth to use for school. It was one of Odny's two school dresses from last year. Ruth was nearly as tall as her sister now. Kristine had hoped to have sewn at least one new dress for each of them before school started, but she'd been sewing for the Wilsons. They had heard she was a seamstress and asked her to sew for their three girls. At least the money they paid her was enough to buy nice fabric for her own girls.

Lost in thoughts of keeping the family in shirts and dresses,

Kristine laughed as she felt a kiss on the back of her neck. "Fredrik, what if someone sees you? Acting like a teenager."

"What if they do? A man can still kiss his wife, can't he?" Fredrik said as he turned her around, arm around her waist. "What were you staring at? Did you expect the dress to speak to you?"

"*Ja*, I was hoping it could tell me how to keep our growing daughters in decent dresses," she said.

"What's the matter with these?"

"The dress is too short for Odny. A nine-year-old should not have her knees showing, but Ruth is almost as tall as Odny so I'm not sure it's any better for her. It's not a big problem. I'll just let the hem down."

"I don't want them looking down and out. It will be bad for business. People won't come to me for work if they think I'm on my last legs."

Kristine looked at him more closely. Did he have more gray hair? The lines between his brows seemed deeper. What was making him so touchy about the girls' dresses?

She reached out and stroked his cheek. "Fredrik, no one will pay attention to what your girls wear to school, but of course they will be clean and neat. Did something happen at the store today?"

"Only more of the same. I went to collect from Henderson, and he told me his bank went under. He can't make any of his payments. He'll pay us with potatoes if he can, but I'm not the only guy he owes."

"Potatoes! We are barely half through last year's potato payments. I guess we won't starve. How much longer do you think people will be paying you with their crops?"

"I don't know. You're right, we won't starve, but potatoes won't put gas in the truck. I need to go out to Mueller's farm tomorrow. Not only do I…*Uff da,* who is this strong person?" Fredrik's voice lifted as Odny hugged him around the waist.

"Daddy, you're home! Is it time for supper already?" she asked.

"Not quite. Your mother needs some help with this laundry, and isn't setting the table your job?"

"You know it is, Daddy," Odny grinned. "Does Ruth have to help, too?"

"Where is she? You're supposed to be watching her," Kristine asked.

"She's right there." Odny pointed toward the house.

Around the corner came Ruth, her straight blond hair flying behind her. Two other girls were running right behind her.

"Ruth, come over here and help Odny carry this basket of sheets," Fredrik said.

"Yes, Daddy. Can Rosemary and Lucy stay?" she asked.

"Not today. It's a school day," Kristine said. "And I think I hear your mother calling." Kristine wished Fredrik was kinder to Ruth. He expected a lot of a seven-year-old.

Younger than Odny, Rosemary and Lucy were also sisters. Their family lived on the street just to the north. Walking home together was a favorite after-school activity. Nine-year-old Odny could supervise the two-block walk. Both moms knew to look at the other house if they didn't see the girls as expected.

"Yes, Mrs. H. See you tomorrow, Ruth. Coming, Mom." Running and shouting, they turned toward home.

"Rosemary, I made potato bread today. Take some home to your mother."

"Odny, pick out a loaf and wrap it in some brown paper from the cupboard, you know where it is. Then practice your piano. I don't think your dad has heard your newest songs. After supper, you can play for him." It was very important to Kristine that her girls play piano, both because she thought that was a skill all girls should have, but also because she hadn't had a piano growing up in Norway. She'd learned to play on the church organ. She was happy that she'd insisted Fred buy a piano from neighbors who were forced to sell for some cash.

"Kristine, you know we can't keep paying the piano teacher if I don't get some more jobs that pay me," Fredrik said.

"Don't worry about it. We haven't paid him for two months. I've been making baby clothes for his first child in exchange for the lessons. He's grateful for that. I don't think his wife is a very good seamstress. I'm not sure what will happen once the baby comes. Maybe I can pay him in potatoes," she said with a smile.

She handed Fredrik another clothesbasket, but before they could follow the girls into the house, she put a hand on his arm to hold him back.

"I saw Louise Wange at knitting club today. Hans still can't find work. I worry about their children. They look hungry to me. Maybe I'll cut down one of your shirts for Eric and Signe can use Ruth's dress from school last year. She's such a tiny thing," she said.

"I wish I had something for Hans, but I'm barely keeping Gudmund in work." Fredrik shook his head. "Besides, Hans is a machinist, not an electrician."

"Is there nothing we can do?" Kristine was persistent. Besides Lena, Louise was one of her few friends from Norway. They had met at the YWCA group for newcomers to Waukegan shortly after Hans took a job at the Cyclone fence company. Most immigrants either worked in Chicago or had relatives on farms in Wisconsin or Minnesota.

"Not much that can be done. Invite them to Sunday dinner. I'll give him some money. At least we can do a little for other Norwegians.

Kristine started toward the house. "I know you've given him something already. Louise is very grateful."

"Five dollars a week and a meal doesn't seem like enough, but I can't let the family starve. Hans is a hard worker. There just isn't any work to be had right now." Fredrik shook his head in frustration.

"I think what they need right now is hope. I'll walk to their house in the morning. If I get another seamstress job, she can help me, and I'll share the money with her. My sign in the shop has brought in some work," she said.

"Has it now? Should I be getting a share of that?" Fredrik teased.

"You have gotten a share. When was the last time I asked you for market money?" she said and patted his belly. "Let's see, if we have the five of them for dinner plus Ben, Gudmund, and Sverre, we'll be twelve on Sunday. Can you get some chickens? It's too early for farmers to give you any squash or cabbages. I hate to invite them if we don't have enough food."

"For heaven sake, any food is more than they can muster up. They'll be grateful for whatever you can give them," he said.

Kristine did not say anything but fixed him with her steady gaze. Blue eyes met blue eyes. She knew he could do better than that.

"*Ja, ja,* I'll see if that German guy, Mueller, out near Brown's Lake, will want lights put in and throw in a couple of his birds as part of the deal. Is that enough?" Fredrik looked down at the basket.

"*Takk,* that will help a lot. I'll make extra *lefse.* Thank goodness we have plenty of green beans and beets," she said to his back as he headed into the house.

* * * *

It was after dark when she heard the car pull into the driveway. "Aauugah" the horn of the 1932 Packard blasted through the quiet evening. Even after the engine was turned off, Kristine could hear clucking, angry chickens combined with Fredrik shouting. She rushed outside.

"Kristine, these damned birds have made a fine mess of the back seat of the car." Fredrik held two fat brown and russet hens by their bound feet behind his back as he bent to examine his precious car.

"Fredrik, your language," but her smile softened the rebuke. "Now that the whole neighborhood knows you're home with chickens, you can give them to me," she said, taking the hens from him while trying to avoid beaks and flapping wings. "Didn't they have a sack or something to put over their heads? Poor birds are frantic."

"*Ja*, you would be, too, if you were on your way to becoming Sunday dinner." Fredrik backed out of the car and straightened up. "I'll put them on a peg until morning if you go get something to clean up the car."

Kristine considered her husband for a moment and shook her head ever so gently before handing over the hens, still cackling and flapping. Even after eight years of living in America, he could surprise her.

"You're right, we should try to clean up the droppings right away, but you don't need to shout." Kristine peered into the back seat. "Did they peck the leather seats? *Uff da*, it stinks."

"Turn on the yard light when you go in, and don't forget the whisk broom for all these feathers."

As she fetched a bucket of soapy water and some rags, she fought between amusement and annoyance. This evening delivery was not what she'd had in mind when she asked for chicken for dinner. Where had he been until so late? But he had delivered on her request. In his own way.

"Fredrik, have you been drinking?" Coming back outside with the cleaning supplies, she sniffed, suspicious about this noisy, smelly delivery. Even before the hard times had come, Kristine was a teetotaler. One of the first groups she joined in America after the church was the Women's Christian Temperance Union. They had their headquarters close by in Evanston, Illinois. Despite Prohibition, too many men were leaving their families with even less as they drank away their meager belongings. Kristine was afraid of that kind of suffering.

"*Ja*, well, not really drinking, just some home-brewed beer.

That's what it takes, Kristine, to make a sale." He swayed a little and didn't quite look her in the eye.

"What does drinking beer have to do with electrifying the barn?"

"Mueller's wife, she fixed us a fine *middag* of pork and cabbage and potatoes. It would have been rude to refuse their beer. They're German, so, of course, they had beer."

"You had this beer at *middag?*" Disapproval hung from her question.

"*Ja,* well, Mueller is a stubborn old guy. He sent me away and told me to come back after milking." Fredrik stuck his head inside the car and began scrubbing.

Kristine found herself talking to his backside. "You made the sale?"

"*Ja, ja,* and got a deposit, cash besides these damn birds. But it took a lot of talking." Fredrik stuck his hand holding the rag out. "Hand me the whisk broom."

"Here." She slapped the broom into his hand. "A lot of talking and drinking?"

"*Ja,* more talking than drinking, but his wife helped." His voice muffled as a feather came floating out around his knees. "She really wants electricity in the house. Mueller only wants it in the barn."

"She helped?" Kristine probed.

"She wouldn't let me leave until Mueller agreed to doing both the barn and the house. It took a while. Every time she had a new argument or asked me another question, she poured more beer. It seemed to help."

"Uh, huh…" Kristine let her voice hang there.

Fredrik emerged from the back seat, faced Kristine, and chose not to notice that her bemused help had turned to disapproval.

"When we finally worked out the price and details, we sealed the deal with the chickens and a little brandy." Fredrik had warmed to his story. His eyes were glassy and his cheeks flushed.

Kristine was sure that it was more than a little brandy, but she had her chickens, so she gave up the interrogation. Picking up the bucket, she dumped the soapy water and took Fredrik's hand.

"It was a good day, then. Let's go inside and let the chickens enjoy their last night of pecking," she said with a sigh, wondering what he had really agreed to with the Muellers.

The next morning, while she and Louise stood over a steaming pot in the back yard, ready to pull the first gutted and cleaned hen out to be plucked, Kristine told of the poor birds' noisy delivery, omitting the beer and brandy that had lubricated the transaction.

As a farmer's daughter, Louise laughed until she could barely pull out the chicken. "Kristine, you're a great friend and I'm so grateful for all your kindnesses, but you know nothing about chickens. How did you get this old without knowing how to handle a chicken?"

"*Ja,* you know, in Norway there was always someone else to do it. Those last years, Elise would bring the occasional chicken, plucked and dressed, from her farm. Otherwise we almost always ate fish, or eggs." Kristine pushed some hair out of her flushed face with the back of her hand. "What now?"

"I'll get you started plucking this one before I scald the

second one." Louise carried the chicken over to a newspaper-covered table under the oak tree in the tidy backyard. "You want to pluck as quickly as possible. The feathers let loose as long as the skin is hot."

Louise's fingers were quick, and soon feathers were scattered all over the table and ground. She handed the half-plucked bird to Kristine.

"Here you go. I got the pin feathers. Those are the hardest. Your turn."

Kristine held it delicately between her thumb and index finger. Pulling with tentative jerks, she got a few feathers to release, but many did not.

"Lay it down like I did, hold the feet with your whole hand, and yank at the feathers with your other hand." Louise was trying not to laugh. "It's not alive anymore. You won't hurt it."

Kristine bit her lower lip and tried again. It went better. By the time Louise joined her with the second scalded chicken, she was almost done with the first one.

"Well, Louise, you're really working for your *middag* today," Kristine said blowing at a feather that had stuck to her upper lip.

"It is my pleasure, Kristine. I wish we would be able to have you for dinner one day."

"You will, I'm sure. They say with the new President, times will improve." Kristine hoped this was true.

"It might not be soon enough for us. My cousin in North Dakota has written. He needs help on his wheat farm. He can't pay but he has a small house for us." Louise flipped the chicken over and attacked the other side.

"North Dakota? Have you ever met this cousin?" Kristine held her bird up by its legs. It looked like a pale pink pincushion with feathers sticking out like straight pins.

Louise laughed, "Here, I'll trade you. The last feathers are the hardest," reaching for the mostly plucked chicken. "No, this guy came to America when I was still a little girl. He's married to a Swede he met here. They don't have any children to help with the farm."

"And Hans wants you to go?" Kristine tried not to judge. "What if you get there and it's awful?"

"It will take the last of our money to move there. We will be stuck." Louise concentrated on her plucking. "Besides, Hans is not a farmer. We left Norway because he couldn't put his heart into it."

Not wanting to give false hope, Kristine bent her head over the chicken. As hard as her choices had been, she had never had to worry about feeding her children. She took refuge in talking about the children.

"Do your children like *lefse*?" she asked.

"Of course, why do you ask?" Louise was cautious, too proud to say she hadn't been able to make it lately.

"Well, I have so many potatoes. I thought maybe I could give some to you with enough flour. If you would make *lefse* for dinner on Sunday, it would help me a lot."

Louise knew that her friend was being kind but decided to let it go, since she felt useful.

"Of course. I love to make *lefse*." Louise set aside the now clean and fully plucked chicken before looking at Kristine, still pulling one tiny feather at a time from the chicken. "Here, let me finish that one."

By the time Kristine had emptied the scalding pot and was ready to gather up the feathers and soggy, smelly newspaper, Louise had finished the second chicken. She handed Kristine the two chickens, fully cleaned of feathers to put into her electric refrigerator.

In the house, Kristine started the teakettle and began to gather potatoes and a packet of flour to send home with Louise. What would she do in her shoes? She prayed she would not have to face that.

Hjelmeland family with Lena Johnson and Norwegian friends,
Waukegan, 1933.

Chapter Nineteen

Where Do We Belong?

Fredrik writing to Mikal, 1935:

We took a trip to Whitehall, Wisconsin, to see Judge Anderson and his family. We stayed with the Fred Fredrikson family even though Fred died last spring. Mrs. Fredrikson, Selma, their son, George, and their daughter, Hazel, are managing the farm. They are very nice people and were very glad that we came and visited. Kristine and the children were there for ten days. I was there only one day. They want to go back next summer. It's nice to have a summer place to go, especially a farm. They are very hospitable people and the food is real Norwegian.

Kristine wrapped bread in a damp towel before putting it in the basket that held a bottle of juice and thermos of coffee. Butter, sliced ham, and cheese, rested in a separate package. A knife to assemble the sandwiches and spoons for the jar of canned peaches completed the picnic supplies. She stood back to try to think whether she had anything she could take to share with the Fredricksons. Even though they hadn't been on a trip to Wisconsin since Fred Fredrikson had died, Fredrik hadn't said anything about going until she came home from knitting club yesterday afternoon. Ten years after coming to America, Kristine still wasn't used to Fredrik's sudden plans to pick up and go somewhere.

It would be good to see how Selma and her grown children, Hazel and George, were getting along, but the Judge was another matter. He seemed to disapprove of most everything, especially their living in Waukegan. And his wife, Berthe, who came from the same family as Fredrik, acted as if she were royalty.

"Mama, I put in pajamas, clean underwear, two blouses, one skirt, and coveralls for each of us. Should I bring anything else?" Odny interrupted Kristine's consideration of the provisions.

"So far so good, but also put in your Sunday dresses, your white anklets, and summer good shoes. Put in more underwear. We might be up there a week. Add some washcloths and a towel so we can clean up along the way. Where is Ruth?"

"Mama, are we going to see the judge?" Odny asked.

"We are. I must remember our hats."

Odny groaned.

Kristine gave her a stern look. "You will be respectful. Judge Anderson is a very important person in Whitehall." It always surprised her how Odny could pick up on her feelings. She didn't look forward to the obligatory visit either. "We'll visit them tomorrow, and then the rest of the time will be on the farm. It will be fun.

"Yes, Mama, but their furniture is slippery, and Mrs. Anderson smells funny," Odny whined.

Kristine didn't respond immediately. Odny could argue all day. After a bit, she said, "When you finish putting everything into the valise, find Ruth." She set the food basket next to the kitchen door.

"Even if we leave soon, it will take us all day, and I don't want to get there after dark. I don't like to be on those country roads at night," Kristine said as much to herself to encourage Odny to hurry. Finished in the kitchen, she went to pack some clothes for Fredrik and herself. The broad fields of Wisconsin made Kristine uncomfortable. There were no fjords or mountains to orient her.

* * * *

"We're off. Next stop, Fredriksons' farm." Fredrik started the engine of his brand-new Chrysler sedan and backed carefully onto Grand Avenue.

"Daddy, all the way, no stopping?" Ruth sounded worried.

"Well, maybe if you are good and don't ask about how much farther we have to go, I'll think about stopping," Fredrik teased.

Kristine smiled but didn't get involved. After the flurry of packing and arranging to be gone, she was happy to sit back and watch the scenery go by. In moments, they were out of Waukegan and into the farmland of Northern Illinois.

"Fredrik, do you like your new car?" Kristine asked when they weren't passing houses anymore. She knew it was easier to have any conversation before the paved road turned to bumpy dirt and gravel. Wisconsin had better roads than Illinois, but she didn't like to talk when Fredrik drove fast on gravel. She still felt that horses were safer.

"I do. It's got a lot more pickup than the old one," he said.

"Was the 'old' car even two years old?"

"No, but it had a lot of miles on it, over 60,000 by the time I traded it in last week."

"Well, the leather seats are very nice," Kristine said betraying not only what mattered to her but how little she knew about cars. "It's very fancy for riding to the farm. I wish you could stay with us, too."

His smile faded, "You know that I can't afford to be away from the business. As it is, on the day to take you and the day to pick you up, nothing much will get done."

"What about Gudmund and those other two fellows? I thought you were keeping them busy?"

"I am, but it is only because I am out there every day looking for work, selling generators and parts. I'm the only one who does that."

"*Ja*, you do work very hard. I'm glad you're getting away even if it is a lot of driving back and forth." Not wanting to upset him, she closed her eyes and let the warm July air blow across her face.

After a half hour of riding past tidy farms and stopping for tractors crossing the roadway, Fredrik glanced in the back and said, "Windows up, dust ahead." They were headed off the paved road and onto gravel.

Her nap interrupted, Kristine asked Fredrik, "Will we see Judge Anderson tomorrow?"

"Yes, he's expecting us."

"Do you want to take us or just go by yourself on your way home?"

"I wrote that we would all be there for tea in the morning."

"So, all of us." Kristine could not hide her disappointment. "Why is it important for us to come? I don't know what to talk about with Berthe, and the girls have nothing to do."

"Ah, they need to learn to behave with grown-ups. Besides, I want the Judge to see what a fine family I have."

"And I am to…?"

From the back seat Ruth whined, "Daddy, can we open a window? Puh-leeze, I am so hot."

"And it smells like onions in here. Ruth, stop breathing so hard," Odny said.

"Girls, you may roll the window down one inch, not more. But, if we get close to a car or truck, roll it back up right away." Fredrik was firm.

"But I can hardly breathe," Odny persisted.

"You are fine. Think about something else," Fredrik said.

"So, you were saying, we need to learn something from Judge Anderson and his wife?" Kristine said, trying to keep the sarcasm from her voice.

"Kristine, are you teaching these girls to complain? If you don't come with me tomorrow, they will make up some story about our 'troubles' and how I don't know how to run a family."

He sounded so weary that Kristine relented. He was proud of them; she didn't want to make life harder for him. "Okay, thank you for making it tea and not a whole meal."

"Every time we visit, he gives me a talk about how much better life is in Whitehall than Chicago. I don't think he has been there since he emigrated forty years ago," Fredrik half laughed.

"Why doesn't he like Chicago?"

"He talks about gangsters and tenements and speakeasies."

"He must come to visit us. We don't have that in Waukegan."

Fredrik's laugh sounded more like a bark. "That old goat leave Whitehall? Not likely! He has too much sway over everyone to risk being an ordinary fellow somewhere else."

"Daddy, did you see a goat?" Ruth piped up.

Kristine smothered a giggle as she heard him sputter something about hoping that the Fredriksons had gotten one. She wondered, though, what hold did the Judge have on Fredrik? Why did he feel obligated to visit if he had so little regard for the Judge?

Hours later, when Fredrik pulled into a schoolyard with a pump and outhouse, the girls tumbled out of the stuffy car like kittens from a basket. Kristine took out her picnic supplies and handed Ruth a small, clean bucket with a handle.

"I get to pump!" Odny ran to the metal pump between the side of the schoolhouse and the set of swings blowing back and forth in the breeze.

"I want a turn," Ruth called, running after her.

"You're too short," Odny said leaning down on the curved iron pump handle.

"I am not. I'm almost as tall as you are."

"My gosh, she is." Fredrik sounded amazed.

Kristine looked up at him from the patch of grass where she

was spreading a cloth out for their picnic. For once, he didn't have his hat on, and he seemed almost relaxed.

"They are both changing and growing. Another good thing about today, you get to really spend time with them." Kristine turned toward the pump when she heard the girls' shrieks, just in time to see an arc of water from the bucket land on Odny's head. Odny must have started the water fight, since Ruth's blouse was already sticking to her lanky body.

Fredrik marched toward them in mock sternness until he got within reach and pumped the handle so furiously that water began to fly everywhere. The girls giggled and splashed with this unexpected play from their daddy. After making sure that everything got splashed except their lunch, they mopped their faces and had their picnic. Fredrik stretched out on the ground and closed his eyes for five minutes. After a quick trip to the outhouse, they were back on the road.

Hazel Fredrickson had *kveldsmat* of homemade bread and jam, sausage and *spekekjøt*, sardines, cheese, *knækkebrod,* and *lefse*, scrambled eggs, and stewed apricots set out for them when they arrived at the farm, after milking, but well before dark. George's hair was slick from cleaning up after chores, and a chorus of Norwegian rang out.

"*Takk for sist, velkommen.*"

"*Tusen takk? Og deg? Hvordan har du det* (And you, how are you)?"

Ruth tugged at her mother's skirt and whispered, "Mama, I don't know what they are saying except *takk*."

"It's okay, you will learn. Remember when we were in Norway?

Norwegian will come back after a few days. You can speak English, too, but they might forget and answer in Norwegian."

The next morning the obligatory visit to the Judge went off as planned. The Judge once again extolled the virtues of living in the Norwegian American enclave of dairy farms nestled in the coulees of western Wisconsin. Berthe quizzed Kristine about people in Chicago that Kristine had never met, her house in Waukegan, and her childrearing skills. Odny and Ruth said "please" and "thank you" and did not speak unless spoken to. When requested, they sang the folk tune "*Per Spellman*" in Norwegian. Odny played a section of Grieg's *Peer Gynt* on the out-of-tune piano.

"That was a long two hours, Fredrik," Kristine said as he drove back to the Fredrickson farm from the Judge's big white house in town.

"Thank you, Kristine. I was proud of the girls. You are doing a wonderful job with them." He stole a glance at her and continued in almost a whisper. "Anderson once told me I wouldn't amount to anything."

Kristine turned her head to see if he was serious. "Why would he say such a thing?" surprised she had not heard this before.

"When I first came from Norway, Mikal and I were working here, and Judge Anderson wanted to sell us some land. We told him no, and then a few months later I needed a loan."

"Did he give it to you?"

"Only after Mikal guaranteed it. As he gave me the money, he told me I couldn't expect to ever succeed if I wouldn't follow his advice." Fredrik glared at the road. "And in some ways, it feels as if I have been paying for that one loan ever since."

"My goodness, was it such a big loan?" Kristine asked.

"What? *Neida,* only a hundred dollars. I paid it all back right after the lumbering season was over, but he never lets me forget that fall."

"Fredrik, you're almost fifty years old. Surely he knows you're no longer a twenty-two-year-old boy." She stared at her husband as if he were a stranger.

"Daddy, may we get out?" Ruth's voice sounded small to the preoccupied adults.

Fredrik stirred in his seat as if he was unaware that they had arrived in the farmyard and the girls were listening.

Kristine responded automatically, "Go straight to our room. Lay your dresses and hats on the bed. Put on coveralls and ask *Tante* Selma if you can help her. Odny, unbutton Ruth's dress for her. I'll be up in a minute."

Even after the girls got out, Fredrik sat behind the wheel. Kristine tried again, "What do you mean about paying him back?"

"*Ja,* it is foolish, but I somehow feel I still have something to prove to him."

"Well, that is foolish, because you are here with your family and new car. That's not proof that you are a success?"

"He acts as if I have betrayed my family by living near the city and going into business, not dairy farming. I know he wrote my father that I was reckless."

"And that troubles you?" Kristine was puzzled. Fredrik was normally so decisive. She didn't understand why he wasn't proud to have nice things, talented daughters. Traveling out of the city to the country was a luxury most people couldn't afford. So many of her friends in Waukegan were still struggling. President Roosevelt had helped, but many were still in need of food and a place to live. "What more could you do?"

"More. I need to do more so we can go back to Norway."

Kristine raised her eyebrows. "Fredrik, must you drive to Waukegan today? I think you are too nervous. This has not been a pleasure trip for you." She needed to think about this part of Fredrik that she knew so little about. It worried her that he would be alone and working without them to care for him during the next week.

"I must, Kristine. I promised a fellow near Madison that I would stop to talk about electrifying his barn. If I leave soon, I can be there before his dinner."

"Madison? That's hours from here and from home."

"Closer to home. I think he has a very big farm. It could mean a lot of work for me. Don't worry, look how happy the girls are." He jumped out of the car to meet Odny running down the steps from the house. "Where are you off to?"

"The barn! Will you go with me, Daddy? *Tante* Selma wants to talk to George. I'm supposed to look for him."

"Okay, but after that, I must start if I'm going to get back home tonight."

Kristine watched their dark haired heads bent toward each other as they walked the lane to the barn. Quick, moody, and impulsive, Odny was certainly his daughter.

Within the hour, Fredrik gave the girls a hug and embraced Kristine a moment longer than usual.

"Girls, I want you to take care of your mother. She's not a

farm girl. You must help her and listen to her until I get back."
The familiar teasing in his voice and the crinkles around his eyes
lit up his face. He hopped in the car and was off. The little family
standing on the lane waved after him.

"*Uff da*, is Fredrik not staying for *middag*?" Hazel came up
behind Kristine.

"No, he hopes to get all the way home tonight, so he needed
to leave now. He wasn't hungry after tea with Mrs. Anderson and
the Judge this morning."

"*Ja*, but such a long journey without food," Hazel said as if
she made the trip often.

"You are kind to worry, but Fredrik has made this trip many
times he tells me."

"I remember before he married you, Fredrik would show up
and tell us where he had been working and where he hoped to go
next. It always made Mama happy to hear about his adventures
and to feed him. Father bragged about his clever cousins, but I
think he talked more about Mikal." Hazel sounded wistful.

"You couldn't have been very old when Mikal went back to
Norway." Kristine smiled to hear the young woman reminisce.

"I was only five the last time I talked with him. Shortly after
that, he went back to Bygstad," she said. "I remember he pulled
on my braids and seemed very handsome to me."

"I think both the Hjelmeland brothers are handsome,"
Kristine said with a chuckle. "Does your mother need help with
the *middag*?"

"Oh, I completely forgot. I was on my way to the milk house.
She wanted some cream."

"You go on. I'll go back and see how I can help. If you see the girls, remind them that they must listen to George and come when he does for *middag*."

From then on, the rhythm of Norwegian American farm life enveloped them. In the mornings, the girls helped with chores, collected eggs, rode the hay wagon, and played with the barn kittens. All things they didn't do in Waukegan. The people who came to the farm to visit, the man who collected the milk each morning, the young boys who came to help with the haying, all spoke a mixture of English and Norwegian. Unlike at home in Waukegan, the girls did not have to explain what *lefse* was, or describe a *fjord*, no one made fun of their mother's accent.

One morning, after the children left with George to work in the hay fields, Kristine stood smelling the earthy barnyard blending with the wild roses growing around the farmhouse. She sat down on a painted stool under an apple tree to prepare the green beans she and the girls had just picked. Hazel and Selma were in the kitchen sterilizing the canning jars on the wood stove. Sighing, she shooed a chicken that tried to roost next to her. No breeze stirred the midsummer air. It was so much cooler out here than in the steamy kitchen. Snapping the ends of beans steadily, she found herself wishing for her modern, efficient kitchen in Waukegan, where they could catch some lake breezes from time to time.

"It's nice out here," said Selma, red faced and walking toward her. "Can I help?"

"*Ja*, is there another stool?" Kristine stood up quickly out of respect for the older woman.

Selma sank down onto it and pointed toward the clothesline poles where there was another one.

When they were both settled, snapping the beans, Selma said, "So, Kristine, is Fredrik still talking about moving back to Norway?"

Startled by the direct question, Kristine laughed before saying, "*Ja*, talk, Fredrik talks about lots of things, but I'm not packing our things yet. Did he say something to you?"

"Not exactly. He asked what I had heard from my family. If times were any better for them. It made me wonder what he might be thinking."

Kristine hesitated. She had not expected to talk about such private things with Selma, who was Fredrik's relative by marriage.

Kristine, Fredrik, and girls with Selma Fredrickson, Pigeon Falls, WI.

"You might know more than I do about his thinking. He doesn't tell me," she said more sharply than she had meant to. "When I took the girls to Førde five years ago, it had changed a lot. It seemed so sad and small."

"You mustn't worry about this." Selma put a gentle hand on her arm. "I think coming here reminds both you and Fredrik of home."

To her embarrassment, Kristine felt her eyes well up with tears. Selma was wise and too kind.

"I try to do what Fredrik wants, but I don't always know what that is. If I talk about going back to Førde, he tells me why that isn't possible. Times are bad, housing prices are expensive, no work over there, better schools for the girls here. But if I talk about the girls' American friends or improving our house, he reminds me that we need to save for a store in Førde. Our goal is still to move back. It's confusing."

"I can see that." Selma swatted away the flies that began to swarm in the still hot air.

"Do you ever think about moving back?" Kristine asked.

"Me, move to Norway? Gracious sakes, no. I was born just up the road. I have never been to Norway."

"But, your *Norsk* is just like at home."

Selma grinned. "Thank you. No one spoke English at home. Even church is still in Norwegian out here in the country. What would I find in Norway that I don't have here in this valley?"

Kristine didn't know if that needed an answer. She took refuge in their task. "Is Hazel ready for us? We're finished snapping these."

"So we are. I'll go see if the blanching water is boiling. You take the beans over to the old well and give them a rinse."

Later, after putting up quarts and quarts of green beans, accompanied by the soft pop of the jars sealing, preparing two more meals, the haying and the evening milking, the adults sat on the porch trying to catch an evening breeze while the girls chased fireflies. The inky blue sky and the heat seemed to cast a hush over the evening. Quiet talk turned to the upcoming church picnic and whether they would finish the haying before it rained.

A wave of homesickness pushed Kristine back in the wicker chair. Wiping tears from her eyes, she wondered if it was not Norway that she was missing but Fredrick and her home in Waukegan. As welcoming as Selma and her children were, she was a guest, not part of the fabric of this place. She thought about Selma's question. Why would she go to Norway? What would she find? Somehow she and Fredrik were both looking for more. With him, she had become aware of new people, new ways of doing things. Being together, seeking more with Fredrik had become a kind of home for her. She knew her role was not here doing what had always been done. What part of being at home is knowing how you fit in?

Hazel interrupted her reverie. "You're awfully quiet, Kristine."

"I was thinking about how nice it is to be here with all of you, but I am missing Fredrik tonight."

She stood up and stepped off the porch. "Look at all the beautiful stars. Girls, do you see the Milky Way?"

"Can Daddy see it too?" Odny asked.

"The Milky Way is over Waukegan, too, but he probably isn't sitting outside all by himself."

"Poor Daddy, when is he coming to get us?" Ruth asked.

"The note I got from him said tomorrow. Can you remember to bring him out then to look at the stars?"

Ruth nodded but didn't say anything, just bit her lower lip.

"If Daddy is coming tomorrow, when are we going home?" Odny voiced Ruth's worry.

"We will leave the next morning, Sunday, before church."

"No, I want to go to the church picnic." Ruth began to wail.

"We aren't finished with the hay. Are we, George?" Odny asked George, who had been dozing in a chair.

He sat up with a start. "What? The haying? No, not quite finished. Maybe tomorrow."

"George, maybe if you ask, Daddy will help you with the haying, too. Please."

"Well, I don't know if Fredrik has time for my haying."

"Girls, you mustn't ask that. Your father has decided, and he wrote that he needs to be home by Monday for a new job he is doing."

"But Mama, doesn't Daddy want to throw horseshoes at the picnic? Mr. Monson from the dairy said that all the men like that." Ruth had not given up on going to the picnic.

Kristine had a smile in her voice as she said, "We'll talk about this in the morning, but right now, I think it is bedtime for the Waukegan people." She put an arm around each girl, "What do you say? Odny, Ruth?"

"*God natt, takk for idag* (Good night, thank you for today)," they said with unhappy looks at their mother.

"Yes, *takk for idag og sove godt*," Kristine called over her shoulder as she trundled them up the stairs to their room.

The next day Fredrik arrived by 1:00 p.m. in time for the midday dinner.

"Goodness, Fredrik, we didn't expect you so soon." Kristine greeted him with a chaste kiss on the cheek and light in her eyes.

"Daddy, Daddy, you're here!" Odny and Ruth came running. "Did you miss us?"

"I did. I missed you so much I started on my way before it was light this morning."

"Just like George getting up to milk the cows?" Ruth asked.

"Well, not exactly." Fredrik chuckled, looking from one rosy-cheeked girl to the other. "I think you have grown in ten days."

"Daddy, George is not finished with the haying. Can we stay longer to help him?" Odny asked, not wasting any time.

"I don't think so. It's too quiet in Waukegan without you, and I need to go back. People are counting on me to start a project next week."

Odny looked crestfallen and pulled away from her father.

"Maybe you can go back out with George after *middag* and show Daddy how you have been helping all week," Kristine added.

Selma came out of the kitchen, wiping her hands on her apron. "*Velkommen*, Fredrik. Dinner is ready. *Vær så god*, I put another place on for you."

The afternoon passed quickly, and soon Ruth had her daddy out looking at Orion in the night sky.

Knowing that the early morning would be busy with chores

and leave-taking, Kristine began her thanks and good-byes to Hazel and George, but especially Selma. "Thank you so much. It is wonderful for us to come to your farm and be away from the city. The girls learn about so many things they never see or get to do in town. Speaking Norwegian and catching up with the news you have of home makes me feel like family."

"Ah, Kristine, you are family," Selma said handing her a small square of *Hardanger* stitching, Norwegian cutwork embroidery.

"Selma, I have been the guest and you are giving me gifts?" Kristine examined the fine, even stitches and intricate cuts, knowing how much precise work went into even that small piece.

"I want you to always remember to come back here. Maybe when you use that, you will think of us."

"*Mange tusen takk*. I feel that even without this beautiful doily, but knowing you made it is important to me." Kristine gave the reserved, modest farm wife a lingering hug.

When Sunday morning came, before George finished the milking, the Hjelmelands were off with many hugs, a basket of farm treats tucked into the back seat, promises for another visit soon, and Ruth and Odny waving madly until the farm was out of sight.

"Was it a good visit, Kristine?" Fredrik asked.

"*Ja*, it was, but I missed you, and I am anxious to get home," she said.

"To what home, Kristine?" he asked sharply.

"To our home, yours and mine in Waukegan."

Chapter Twenty

How Much is Enough?

1937

Fredrik to Mikal, 1937:

*Time flies, one year after the other. We plan many things,
but we do not always succeed in accomplishing our plans. I,
for my part, am not as good to work (with my hands), any
more. But I keep the balance as long as I can work with my
head. I have made many mistakes that have cost me a lot,
but I have always come out of it nevertheless...I do not have
any son that can help me in the business.*

Kristine coughed and held her handkerchief over her nose.
Fredrik had turned from the paved road to a rutty dirt road. As
the dust and gravel flew through the open car, Kristine rolled up
her passenger side glass window.

"Fredrik, you did not tell me this house is in the country. Is it
a farm house?" she asked, a small furrow creasing her broad brow.

"No, no, we are not in the country, we are on the edge of town. Look at all the houses. We've passed at least four on this road."

"Humph, really?" Kristine's friend, Lena, said from the back seat.

Kristine twisted in her seat and raised her eyebrows with a quick shake of her head as if to say, "We'll talk about this later."

Turning back, Kristine looked out at bare spring fields, some worn-looking houses, and a few mailboxes. They met no other cars or horses, but Kristine noticed a workhorse tied up behind a shed. She'd rarely been to this part of Lake County where Fredrik worked most days.

She thought back to the night last week when Fredrik came home late, after dark. She and the girls had already eaten, but it was their pattern for her to join him with a cup of tea while he ate supper and catch up on their days.

Fredrik was telling her that he thought the economy was improving. "I have two orders for new generator systems and another for redoing the system I put in five years ago to make it more modern. Business is looking up."

"Is it?" Kristine said, not really paying much attention.

"I am working with two other fellows in Libertyville for possible jobs. While I was there, I bought that house."

"What house?" Kristine asked, alert to the way he slipped this in at the end of a general chat.

"The one I told you about last week," he said, becoming very interested the potatoes on his plate.

"Fredrik, you have talked about a store or office in Libertyville but not a house." Her voice wobbled. "Do you have plans for this house?"

"I thought I had told you this. I was looking for property to build, and the banker said they had just taken over this property. When he quoted such a low price, I decided to take a look. I'm sure that once these terrible times are past, Libertyville will grow to be bigger than Waukegan." Fredrik stood up and began to pace, as if moving helped him to think. "When he took me to see it, we made a deal."

"So, you'll build another store?" She remembered thinking there was more to his story.

"I was thinking that maybe it makes sense for us to move out there and get a feel for how much traffic there would be before building another store," he'd said, avoiding Kristine's increasingly suspicious gaze.

"Move, move who? Our family?"

"Well, we'd need to do some work. The house needs paint and fixing up."

"So, you are telling me that you expect to take the girls out of school, find a new church, and leave this house, just when we've finally got it all furnished and improved?"

"I'll take you out there one day next week, and you can tell me what you think needs to be done." He'd spit this out all at once without addressing anything she was saying. "You are good at this, some cleaning and fixing up. I'm sure that you can make it as nice as here. We won't move until summer, plenty of time to install electricity and have a well dug."

"But what will you do with our house here? It has been

my favorite of all our places, so close to St. Paul's and Whittier School. Such nice neighbors."

"I'm sure I can rent it for a good price. You've made it look so *koselig,* comfortable." Then he'd asked, "When is a good day next week?"

Looking grim, she'd replied, "I think I will ask Lena to come along. She is good at cleaning and seeing possibilities."

After five years, she had finally gotten the house on Grand Avenue behind his store up to her standards. She was proud of how she mixed the best of their Norwegian traditions of fine china and silverware for serving fish and buttery baked goods with the most modern of American life. For her, the electric lights and stove, a radio in a beautiful wooden case, a telephone, central heat, and a modern bathroom were all marks of success. This house, more than the others, affirmed that she had been right to leave her family and marry Fredrik.

Now Kristine wasn't so sure. Reluctant but resigned, she'd agreed to look at this house that was to be their next home. The edges of dread crept into her thoughts. She sighed and tried to focus on new curtains to make and floors to finish.

"Well, here we are," Fredrik broke her reverie. They had pulled up to a walkway leading to the front door of a two-story house.

"Here Fredrik? This is the house?" Skepticism dripped from her voice. She stopped before she said any more about the square, unpainted frame house with a plain, wooden porch.

"I guess it doesn't look like much from here, but it's nice sized and has four bedrooms. What do you want me to carry in for you?"

Kristine and Fredrik, Service Electric,
1826 Grand Ave., Waukegan, IL.

The plan was that Kristine and Lena were going to clean the house while Fredrik was on a sales call. He would pick them up before the girls got home from school.

"Are you sure this is not an old farmhouse?" Kristine asked, near panic. "Where is the school? Stores? Library? I don't see anything but a few houses."

She turned in her seat to find that Fredrik had already gotten out and was walking around the car to get the supplies from the trunk.

Lena followed Fredrik up the walk muttering, "Gray, the fence is gray, the house is gray, even the sky's gray."

Kristine shot her a sharp look from where she had stopped at the drooping fence. It wasn't Lena's place to comment, but she was right. Not only was this house a farmhouse, it looked as if it had not been lived in for a long time.

"Imagine it white with green trim. Would you like green? I'll get one of my guys to paint it." Fredrik was busy trying to get the key to work. "It's a little rusty. There we go." The door creaked open.

Not waiting for Kristine or Lena, he moved the cleaning equipment inside and hurried out to the sloping front porch.

"Fredrik, wait, is that what you want to know? What color paint? Inside, too?" Kristine asked. "What about this yard? Is the roof good?"

"*Ja, ja,* some cleaning and paint, this will be a fine place. The roof is fine. It's a really sound house for the price," Fredrik answered in Norwegian.

This told Kristine that he was nervous. They always spoke English except when they didn't want Odny or Ruth to understand.

"Here's the keys. I'll pick you up in a few hours. Magnuson is waiting for me," he said. "His farm is just up the road about twenty miles. See you later." Without waiting for a response, he was off.

The two friends stood, dazed, and watched the dust cloud behind the big Oldsmobile. Practical and private, they turned and stepped gingerly into the front hall, but did not mention any more misgivings about their task.

"Where shall we start?" Kristine looked down the narrow hallway and up the steep stairway. Cracked linoleum, faded to a dingy yellow with what appeared to be black swirls, peeled in lifted edges from the stairs to the second-floor bedrooms. "Maybe the kitchen. I'd like to see what I'll have to work with."

"Are there any lights in here?"

"No. Fredrik said that he got the house cheap because it doesn't have electricity or plumbing."

"And he expects you to live here? Oh, careful, that floorboard cracked when I stepped on it." Lena followed her to the back of the house.

Kristine went through a door on the right.

"Oh, Lena, this is *fryktlig* (horrible)."

Kristine stood, holding her broom close to her like a shield. She looked from a rusty sink on a wooden platform with a broken leg to the cabinet with a door hanging by one hinge. The single, grimy window had a cracked pane. She heard scratchy sounds coming from the walls or floor. She couldn't tell which. On the small wood stove that dominated the room, there seemed to be the remains of porridge, solidified into rock. Soot from the stove covered most of the wall.

"What is that smell?" Lena covered her nose with a handkerchief. "Something has died in here."

"Maybe whatever is running through the walls. Squirrels?"

"Eek, not a squirrel Kristine! Look at that!" Lena pointed to a gray rat as the long tail disappeared under the sink and behind the stove.

"Lena, we must go outside and think." Kristine sounded as if tears were near.

"Let's see what's out in the back…" Lena strode over to the back door and began to tug on it. Nothing happened. Kristine took a rag from her bucket, wrapped it around the knob, and they pulled together. No movement.

"Let's get out of here."

They scurried out the front door and around to the back yard to find piles of trash, a broken-down outhouse, and a bare pipe trickling water. Two boards were nailed crisscross on the back door.

"How could Fredrik expect you to live here?"

"I doubt that he ever looked inside. According to him, the house is sound." Kristine walked back around to the front porch.

"It's sound, if that means it's still standing after years of neglect," Lena said.

Kristine turned her bucket over, wiped it off with a rag, and sat down. She waved at Lena to do the same. "Lena, I have learned this about Fredrik. If there is something he feels is a good deal, he doesn't think about us or any day-to-day details. He just thinks we will manage. But this, this I am not going to manage."

"Aren't we going to clean?" Lena started to smile. "Fredrik just left."

"I am not going back in that house. Not now, not ever." Kristine shook her head and kicked her heel against the porch floorboards. Her panic had turned into determination.

"What will Fredrik say?"

"He won't be happy. I have always gone along with his plans."

"*Ja*, but usually his plans are about being modern," Lena said, doubtful that her calm friend was actually saying no to her strong-willed husband.

"Lena, what about our neighbors, the girls' school, our church? I must figure out how to tell Fredrik I won't leave that to live out here in the country." Her voice rose with desperation. "It could be years before Libertyville grows as Fredrik thinks it will."

"*Ja*, Kristine, I'm so glad. I would miss you a lot if you lived out here. Besides, this is an awful place. But what will we do now? Fredrik won't be back for hours."

Kristine stared at her feet stretched out in front of her. Only that time when she took the girls back to Norway had she felt so confused. Until this, she'd been willing to believe Fredrik that moving and improving, making money on the moves would bring them closer to moving back to Norway. Somehow this felt permanent. If she went along with move after move, it would never end. Not only could she not imagine living here, she was losing the vision of living as a family in Norway. Maybe Waukegan had become home in a way she hadn't considered. Lena was right. What would they do with at least three hours in this dismal place? Her brooding was interrupted by Lena's laugh.

"Lena, what's so funny?"

"We are all worked up about rats and filth. Stuck here for the day. It reminds me of "*Per Spellman*." Lena began to hum a Norwegian children's song.

Per Spellman han hadde ei einaste kuh,
Per Spellman han hadde ei einaste kuh,
Han bytte bort kuhe, fikk fela igjen,
Han bytte bort kua fikk fela igjen.

Kristine joined her and they sang many verses about the old song about a foolish fiddle player who lost his fiddle gambling.

They laughed even more as the story unwound that he had to trade his cows to get his fiddle back.

Soon they were substituting Fredrik for Per Spellman in the song and singing that he would need to trade his electric generator to get rid of a house to get his family back. As they made up more silly verses, their giggles took over until the two friends collapsed against each other, weak from laughing.

"*Ja*, Lena, you must sing that for Fredrik when he comes," Kristine said when she had caught her breath.

"*Neida,* Kristine, you are his wife, you will sing."

"That's exactly why I cannot. I must go home with him," she said, setting herself off giggling again. "*Ja,* I feel so much better. It must be time for coffee."

After coffee, they did do a little tidying up. They collected the rusted and accumulated trash into one pile in a corner behind the house. They ventured back into the kitchen and hauled out what they could.

When they were done, Lena looked at Kristine and asked, "What next?"

"Nothing. Let's draw some clean water from the well and wash ourselves up. Fredrik should be here in an hour or so. I don't want him to get the impression that I am the least bit interested in moving here."

When Fredrik drove up later, he found them seated primly on their overturned buckets, knitting in hand.

Still oblivious, he greeted them. "I see you didn't find it so much to do. Look at you, relaxing on the porch."

Kristine looked at him with a half-smile. "Oh, quite the

opposite Fredrik. We did what we could, but this place is not in good enough shape to even work on."

"What?" Fredrik could not contain his disbelief. "What did you find? Have you not even tried to clean up?"

"*Neida,* we have not." Krisitne was tempted to burst out all her feelings but knew that was not how to handle Fredrik. He would not want Lena to know any more than she already did.

She glanced a warning look at Lena, who was smirking but not saying anything.

"Fredrik, we must go. The girls will be coming home soon." It was her turn to not address any of the issues.

"They will be fine. In some families Odny would be working at her age. She can keep an eye on Ruth. I am going to see what you found."

So, he led them through the downstairs. Lena pointed out the smell, the soot, the cracked and broken floors, the sounds in the walls. The women waited while he went upstairs. He looked even angrier when he learned that they had not ventured up there.

When he came down, he inclined his head toward the porch and said he would lock up, while they carried their basket and buckets to the car. Kristine nodded and did not comment. Somehow, without overtly battling, a temporary truce was in effect. In the way of couples, they'd silently agreed to sort this out in private.

Kristine and Lena chatted with each other on the quiet ride home. Fredrik smoked one cigarette after another. After they dropped Lena off at her house, Fredrik spoke for the first time since leaving the farmhouse.

"Kristine, it is worse than I thought, but a few workmen and some paint will make a difference."

"No, Fredrik. Paint will not make me want to move to that house."

"Well, of course we would electrify, and there's plenty of room for the plumbing. I checked." He thought he was being encouraging but understood that something was different about Kristine.

Kristine thought he wasn't hearing her refusal, but knew she wanted to be able to explain it. She did not have practice in refusing Fredrik. "We will talk about it later. Now I must check on the girls and start supper."

"*Ja*, and I have work to finish up at the store."

They got out of the car and headed different directions, Fredrik toward the store and Kristine to their house, just as they always did.

Later, when the girls were in their room and Kristine and Fredrick were in the living room together, she said, "We must talk about that farmhouse."

Fredrik peered at her over his newspaper, *"Ja?"*

"We cannot move there, Fredrik."

"What do you mean? I didn't think we would move tomorrow?" He chose to misinterpret her.

"No, not ever. Not that house."

"But Kristine, the deal is already done. It is our house."

She shrugged. "If you could buy it, you can sell it, can't you?" She felt unusually calm. When she saw his brows knit together and his frown, she braced herself.

"Can't you see that moving to Libertyville will help us sell more out there? People like to do business with their neighbors. It is the right thing to do next." His voice rose as he added arguments.

"That is the point, Fredrik. Moving is good for business, but it is not good for this family." Her voice was quiet but deeper than usual. She thought back to the days when she fought to go to Norway with the girls. It was the last time they'd had a serious disagreement. This felt more momentous to her, as if her entire future depended on staying in Waukegan.

"What do you mean? When have I done anything that wasn't good for this family? Why do you think I work so hard?" His scowl had deepened. Voice raised, he sounded as if she had hurt his pride.

"Why do you? Work so hard?" She paused and a flush rose on her cheeks, betraying how hard it was for her to challenge him. "We have enough. You have always taken care of the girls and me, but you are away more and more. Such long days you work without our seeing you. We miss you."

He picked up his paper as if they were done talking.

"Fredrik, look at me." Anger, hurt, and fear prompted Kristine's demand. Blue eyes locked into blue eyes. Kristine saw apprehension. She softened her voice. "We are never going back to live in Norway, are we? You love this life, here in Waukegan."

This seemed to confuse Fredrik. "Just because you don't like the house in Libertyville, you have decided we will never live in Norway again? I asked you to move out there temporarily so we could get established. What is the connection to going back to Norway?"

"It is the connection to how much is enough to make the move back to Norway. I have been in America twelve years and have lived in four places already. The longest has been in this house. Every time you tell me this move will help us get back to Norway. If we are going to start over in a new place, it should be Førde." Ready to say more, she clamped her mouth shut and waited for his reply.

"You don't understand business," Fredrik said. "My money is all tied up. Now is not a good time to sell." This point usually turned the discussion to his advantage. Kristine didn't pretend to know about business.

"I understand that you make that decision of tying up your money. You told me this morning how good business was, but we don't have money to move back to Norway? Is it because you bought more property? Don't you have other property in Waukegan? Didn't you buy some land across the street? How much is enough?" Kristine got up and paced the small room.

Fredrik seemed stunned. "Well, yes, but things are not good in Norway. They are not recovering from the Depression like the United States. I would not be able to make money there like I do here."

"Odny starts high school in January. Neither Ruth nor she can speak Norwegian any more. They have friends in the neighborhood. I am busy with the Ladies Aid at church and the YWCA, my knitting club. I have friends. If we don't leave in the next few months, we must stay here until they are grown." Breathless from her speech and how her thinking was unfolding, she stopped pacing and picked up her knitting. "This isn't just another good deal. You have a family to think about. There's a difference between a plan and a dream." She wiped away a tear that had escaped.

Fredrik waited a long time before saying in a near whisper, "I will not make you move to that house."

Kristine looked at him closely, hoping he would say more, but she understood that giving up the move to Libertyville represented more than a different house to live in.

"You have given me so much to think about, Kristine," he said without anger but no affection. "I am going over to the store."

"Do you want me to walk with you?" she offered.

"*Nei, takk.*"

Kristine never heard what became of the Libertyville property, and she did not ask. Even though nothing in their day-to-day life changed, she was changed. She knew that moving back to Førde might only happen in their dreams.

Chapter Twenty-One

Home: An Unfinished Story

Kristine to Mikal Hjelmeland in Norway, December 3, 1939:

Odny and Ruth are good girls. Today Ruth sang a solo in church and Odny played the piano for her. In January Ruth will finish grade school and will then begin high school. Odny has been in high school two years. We now live in our new house close to our shop. We rent out part of the other house but use two rooms for the business.

April 1940, five months later

Kristine heard the bell jangle as the door opened behind her. "Christy, is it a customer? "

Before the new bookkeeper could answer, Odny was calling to her. "Hi, you're here. I knew you couldn't be far. I'm home."

"Hello to you, too, home so soon?" Kristine said, turning to smile at her oldest daughter. "It's such a beautiful day, warm for early April. Did you get out of school early?"

Odny and Ruth, 1940, Waukegan, IL.

"No, but I caught a bus right away." Odny took a bite of an apple. "May I meet some kids at church to rehearse for the talent show? May I go?"

"Not if you're going to talk with your mouth full." Kristine was a stickler for doing things the right way. "First, help us move this display and the appliances."

"Yes, you're just in time. Your mom and I were able to move most of the hanging stitchery, but I think it will take all three of us to move the linens display case." Christy said.

"Okay, but why are we moving everything?" Odny looked around the store.

"Your father asked me to move my merchandise to make room for a shipment of kitchen cabinets and refrigerators," Kristine said.

"Are we getting new ones at home?"

"Of course not. The cabinets are Youngstown. Just like the ones he put in the new house." Kristine turned to the shelves that held aprons and tablecloths and doilies, embroidered and hand-hemmed. "Do you think we can move this as one without disturbing the display?"

"Sure. With you to guide it, Odny and I can just slide it," Christy said. "Odny, I'll push, you pull. We're going toward that spot next to the sales counter."

Kristine was grateful for Christy. She was practical and strong, no nonsense about her. With a few grunts and stops and starts, they maneuvered the shelves to its new spot, display intact.

"Phew, that thing is heavier than it looks." Christy pulled a shirtsleeve across the sweat on her broad forehead.

Kristine dabbed her face with her handkerchief and then handed it to Odny to wipe off her hands. Fredrik had not consulted her when he hired this independent woman to be his bookkeeper. Christy wasn't as ladylike as Kristine would have hoped, but she seemed honest and hardworking. If only she wouldn't insist on wearing trousers to work.

"Are we finished? Can I leave?" Odny asked.

"May I leave," Kristine corrected her. "No, you may not. Now you need to help Christy move the generators and washing machines. How much homework do you have?"

Odny shrugged, wandering over to the counter. Her interest in electrical fixtures and appliances was mainly in what was the newest model of anything.

"The refrigerators look nice. A separate drawer for 'crisping up your vegetables,'" She read, mocking the newspaper ad she found near the cash register.

But Christy took her seriously, "Your dad has been waiting for these for a long time. We've even got a list of people who are interested. Since President Roosevelt started sending planes and weapons to England, steel refrigerators and anything with wiring is harder to get."

"How much more do we have to do here?"

"We'll move those boilers and generators. The whole area in front of that wall needs to be clear," Christy said waving her arm at the east half of the store. "The shipment comes tomorrow, but the first I heard of it was a few days ago. Odny, pick up that end."

"Where is Dad? Why are we doing all the moving?" Odny asked as they carried the generator across the room.

"You know your father. Today is Wednesday, so he's off to Chicago to pick up parts," Kristine answered Odny, but she studied the big woman Fredrik had hired a few months ago when business was growing. "I'm so glad you are here, Christy, keeping track of things. Fredrik said you are taking flying lessons. Isn't that terribly dangerous?"

Christy stood up from adjusting the fitting of the portable boiler under the generator.

"I love it. Up there with the wind in my face, I feel like Amelia

Earhart." Christy tipped her head back as if she could taste the freedom of flying.

"Oh, my goodness, you are brave."

"If there is war, I want to be ready to help."

"Would they take a woman to fly airplanes for the army? I thought that was a man's job."

"Mom, don't be so old-fashioned. We will all be flying around one day. They say it is very safe." Odny craved being part of everything new.

"Maybe it won't come to that," Christy said quickly, not wanting to cause a scene with her boss's wife and daughter. "If we move these two washing machines, I think we'll be finished with this project."

Kristine swept up behind them. A memory of her old life in Norway helping her dad and brother flashed through her. How different this was and yet…She swept harder, sweeping the image from her mind.

"Now, Odny, do you have homework?" Kristine changed the subject. She didn't want to talk about war if it never came to that. "Have you seen your sister?"

"She'll be here soon," Odny said. "When we're done here, may I go over to church?"

"Who else will be there?" Even though the church was only a few blocks away on Lewis Avenue, Kristine was not comfortable with Odny going off with friends whose parents she didn't know.

"Oh, Mom, everyone. Arlene said she would be there and so did Ecky. The new pastor was moving in today."

"I know. I took soup and applesauce over this morning."

Kristine dusted her hands off. "Will the Reckling boys be there?"

"I hope so," Odny replied with a dreamy look in her eyes.

"Is their mother out of the TB sanatorium?"

"I don't know. May I go?" Odny was persistent.

"You still haven't told me how much homework you have."

"None. The only thing I have is to practice those piano pieces to accompany Ruth at the Booth wedding."

"I forgot about that. I have to finish your dresses before then." Now Kristine was anxious to get back to the house, her domain. She moved quickly to dust off her hands and put away the rags they had been using to clean.

"Do you need anything more, Christy?"

"No, thanks for helping out. Mr. H. will be happy when he gets back to see how much we got done."

"Okay, bye now." Kristine and Odny were out the door and walking across the lot behind the store to the house.

Kristine to Mikal Hjelmeland, 1939 (continued):

It is a long time since we heard from Hjelmeland. We hope everything is well with you. The "world is in an uproar now. I am hoping and praying that Norway can stay on the outside and not get involved…

"Hi, Mom, where have you been?" Ruth met them in the backyard. She had just started high school in January and tried not to follow Odny around.

"We've been working."

"What have you been doing?" Odny snapped at her sister.

"Odny, what is wrong with you?" Kristine held Odny back by her arm to shush her.

Turning to Ruth, she said, "Did you have a snack? Do you have homework?"

"I had some milk and banana bread. And I was working on my homework when I heard you outside."

"Okay, good. Time for us all to get busy." Kristine moved them along as if they were small again instead of in high school. "Ruth, you finish your homework, and Odny, do you want to help me with the hand stitching on your dresses for Saturday, practice piano, or peel some potatoes and carrots?"

"Potatoes and carrots, please," said Odny somewhat less argumentative now that she wasn't showing off. "After that can I, I mean, may I, go over to church?"

A smile tugged at the corners of Kristine's mouth. This was more like Odny. She'd rather do anything than sew. She'd made such a mess out of everything Kristine tried to have her do. "Will you go too, Ruth?"

"Sure, I need to practice, too," Ruth said with an impish smile. "But I think Odny just wants to moon around after Fred Reckling." And she began to run the half a block to the house. Odny chased her with a whoop.

They were each doing their chores when, just a little while later, Fredrik burst into the kitchen. "Kristine, have you heard? Odny where is your mother? Terrible, terrible news."

"Daddy what's wrong? Are you okay?" Odny was startled. "Mom's in her sewing room."

"Why, hello, Fredrik. I could hear you upstairs." Kristine walked in. "I didn't expect you so…"

Flushed and wild-eyed, he interrupted her pleasantries and thrust a crumpled *Skandinaven*, the Norwegian language newspaper, toward her. "*Nyheten er forferdlig*, the news is terrible."

"What?" Kristine scanned the headline while reaching behind herself to feel for something to hold on to.

Ruth had heard the commotion and stood next to Odny, watching the drama unfold. They had forgotten much of the Norwegian from their visit to Førde ten years ago, but they knew that something had gone very wrong. Both their parents had changed from cheerful and ordinary to grim in a moment. What could bring their father home in such a state?

"Daddy, what has happened?" Ruth echoed Odny.

Dazed, he looked from the girls' concerned faces to Kristine, who had dropped down into a chair and was devouring the newspaper account. Running his hands through his hair, he replied as much to himself as to the girls standing before him.

"Everything has changed. The Germans have invaded Norway."

"Invaded Norway? Are they in Førde?" Odny's voice quivered.

"I doubt it," Fredrik said. "It's so small, they wouldn't think it's important."

"But the newspaper says they attacked Narvik, way up north," Kristine said. "That's really small and hard to get to."

"Are Gunnar or Alf, or Karl or Paul fighting?" Ruth began to list all the boy cousins she could think of in Norway.

"We don't know. I wish we could telephone. Fredrik, is

that possible?" Kristine didn't think private people could make international calls.

"I don't think so, not from these party-line phones. We could send a telegram."

"Yes, could we? Just to ask if they are okay and what is happening?"

"The office is closed for today, both here and there, but if we send one first thing in the morning, maybe we will hear."

"I need to do something," Kristine said. "Everyone, before we have supper, you must write one letter. The post might still function through the war. If it is just in the North and Oslo, as the paper says, maybe our letters will get through."

Within the hour, they had several letters written that Fredrik posted the next morning before going to the telegraph office with his message, "Send news. Who is working the farm? Can we help? Fredrik."

No answer came to this telegram or the letters. Like a faucet being turned off, the flow of small packages, birthday greetings, and newsy updates stopped completely. Nevertheless, Kristine continued to send letters and small gifts. Fredrik would not let her send anything the Germans could use for themselves. So anxious for some kind of word, Kristine refused to leave the house until after the daily mail delivery. Just in case something would come. She devoured the *Skandinaven,* which mostly reported news of King Haakon VII and his family. They had left the palace for a secret place. More troubling were the reports that in a bloodless takeover, the entire west coast of Norway had been occupied by the Nazis as a barricade to the British.

A shipbuilding center, Førde was among the occupied towns.

"Hi, Mom, I'm home," Odny called as the screen door slammed behind her. "Did you hear anything today?" It had become her standard greeting.

Kristine was huddled in a chair in the living room near the window. Without a word, she held out a familiar thin blue "aerogram" letter.

She looked so stricken that Odny asked, "Did someone die?"

"I don't think so." Kristine began to weep.

Odny scanned the letter. Kristine was touched to see her hand shake. "Mama, I can't read this Norwegian. It looks like it is from Uncle Alfred, but what does it say?"

"*Ja*, it is. Look at the date, three weeks ago. It was written just before the invasion. I am surprised it came through. He writes about his business and Karl and the family, but at the very end, he says that there is a lot of tension between Oslo and the fjord districts and that if they side with Germans, his Rolf, your cousin, will join the Resistance."

"Which one is Rolf?"

"He's the oldest, only twenty." Kristine choked out the words. She had not considered what it meant to be the parents of four boys in an occupied country until she had read the postscript from her sister-in-law telling of her dread when the boys left the town to hike or hunt in the woods. She simply wrote of "uncertain times," a phrase that would haunt Kristine for years to come.

What news they got, as spring became summer, came via the exiled government of Norway in London. Their hope that the war would end quickly faded as Hitler marched through the continent.

The afternoon when Ruth came through the door looking confused, with Odny right behind her, Kristine knew something was different, something probably not good. She swallowed her concern and didn't stop kneading bread dough. She picked it up and slapped it on the floury board harder than usual before asking, "What has happened?"

"That stupid Mike LaPorte was calling Ruth names!" Odny shouted into the quiet kitchen.

"Mama, he called me a Nazi! He told me to go back to Germany where I belonged," Ruth cried.

"And then all his friends started singing, go home, go home, back to Germany where you belong." Odny interrupted Ruth.

"But Mama, aren't we already home? Where do they want us to go?" Ruth said.

Kristine felt dread drop to the pit of her stomach like a stone. She pushed the dough once more before summoning up the strength to give both girls a half smile.

"Normally I don't like you to call anyone stupid, but I agree. What Mike said was stupid. Worse, it was mean. But we do need to talk about what they said." Wiping flour from her hands, she waved at the kitchen table and sat down. "Odny, get me a glass of water, please."

"Ruth, what did you say back?" Kristine asked when they were settled.

"I told him I was an American." Ruth fidgeted, pushing against the edge of the table.

"I told him he was stupid for saying that," Odny said palms down in front of her, braced for a fight.

"Well, Ruth is right. We are Americans. We are all citizens and have worked hard to be Americans. But now we have to do even more to prove we belong."

"But, Mama, what if he keeps doing this?"

"Oh, he probably will, especially if you argue with him. He likes to get his friends' attention." Kristine wondered what Mike had heard at home to take after Ruth this way. "I know his mother. She is very afraid of war."

"He said they were going to lock up all the Germans, like they did before." Ruth's voice was rising. "Will they lock us up? I'm scared."

"America hasn't even joined the war, and we're not German." Odny sounded disgusted with the whole thing.

Kristine wanted to make sense of this for them, but she didn't know if she could. People were afraid, and they were looking for someone to blame for their fear. She thought of the years when so many had lost their jobs and homes. During those hard times, they had food and work, but others blamed them as dirty foreigners for taking it from them. She should have seen this coming.

"What did your friends do when Mike's friends started yelling at you?"

"They yelled back," Ruth said. "It was so embarrassing. And then Mr. McGinnis walked through the park, and we came home. But Shirley wanted to know if we were moving to Norway."

"Why would she ask that?"

"Because you and Dad are always talking about when we go back to Norway, as if it were tomorrow." Odny's sarcasm had become more evident. Distracted, Kristine wondered if all sixteen-year-olds were so bold.

"*Ja*, it makes us feel good to dream that, but if this war goes on very long, we are not moving anywhere. This is home now." Even as she said the words, Kristine knew their truth. It was sad that a mean, fearful high school boy had forced her to say this aloud. What would Fredrik think? He had already gone into one of his dark, gloomy moods. How would she talk to him about this? She would focus on the girls, what she and Fredrik needed to do for them to get through these terrible times.

"Girls, where did your father put that American flag he bought for the 4th of July?" Kristine was trying to find a visible way to claim their place in the United States.

"I think it's in the front hall closet, but Mama, it's not a holiday," Odny said.

"We are telling everyone who comes by whose side we are on." Kristine was adamant. She did not need a holiday to fly the flag she had given up a homeland for.

The next year when the United States entered the war, the Hjelmelands had already been public supporters of all things American, their immigrant backgrounds as muted as possible, even as their concern for their Norwegian families grew daily. With the declaration of war, Kristine knit and sewed for the troops, Ruth and her friends, accompanied by Odny, sang for the USO, Fredrik bought war bonds, and they scoured reports from the European theater for news of their homeland. The girls kissed their high school friends as they went off to war and grieved when news came of their injuries and death. They hosted

sailors stationed at nearby Great Lakes. They had become the
Hjelmelands of Waukegan who once lived in Norway.

* * * *

Odny Hjelmeland College Report, St. Olaf, 1943:

*Unfinished, this story is unfinished…Today my people
are rising with greater force to drive these power-thirsty
invaders out of Norway. Good will overcome evil, and the
Norwegian people will be set free to develop their own rich
culture…I am very proud to have an American flag flying
over me, for I know it was Norwegian Americans who along
with many others made the United States a land of freedom
and hope.*

I do homage to my ancestors!

Hjelmeland family: Ruth, Fredrik, Kristine,
and Odny, Waukegan, 1940.

Afterword

"All good writing is a blend of memory and imagination."
—Patty Dann, *The Butterfly Hours*

This book is Kristine's story of waiting and hoping and living each day to give meaning and purpose to the lives of those around her. Kristine's story becomes my mother's story and my story. The stories that form each chapter have been blended from the personal knowledge of the living descendants of Kristine and Fredrik, their eight grandchildren, many great-grandchildren, and the next generation who does not yet know these origin stories. Each of us descendants knows part of the story; some details differ, but none of us has a full understanding of what it was to come to the United States in 1925 with a baby in tow, or to make a home and a living in Waukegan, Illinois.

The stories in this book are a narrative of how it may have been. The facts, names, places, and events are all as accurate as memories, written records, and photographs allow. The conversations, motivations, and feelings form the arc of Kristine's transformation from naïve, bewildered newcomer to matriarch of her small family and leader in her church and community. An invaluable resource has been the hundreds of letters among my grandfather, grandmother, and family in Norway that my aunt Ruth Hjelmeland Monson was given access to and had translated. The original letters are with the family in Norway and form a bond that provides connections between twenty-first century descendants in Norway and the United States. Kristine and Fredrik had eleven living siblings between them. Odny and Ruth were among fifty-four first cousins. I was able to meet many of these people when my grandmother first took me to Norway as a teenager. There are many more stories that could not be included.

Another important document in these stories is the college report about her family that my mother, Odny Hjelmeland Reckling, wrote for Norwegian class at St. Olaf college in 1943. Excerpts from the letters and the report are incorporated in the story.

In 1962, I did not know how important visiting my mother's birthplace with Grandma was to me and my identity. To stand in the room where my mother was born, to walk the path from Kristine's girlhood home to the church, to have coffee with her friends, to hike in the mountains surrounding Førde, to listen to the waterfall, Huldfossen, was to experience my origin story rather than simply hear it. That first family visit, a semester later studying at Blindern in Oslo, and living in Førde with Margit and Daginn Reiakvam and their family and the many visits in the years since gave meaning and shape to who I was becoming then and who I am today.

Aleta Chossek, September 30, 2019

Norwegian-to-English Glossary

Ach — oh

bedehuset — parish hall, house of prayer

bestefar — grandfather

blåbær — blueberry

bløtkake — sponge cake with fruit filling and whipped cream frosting

boller — baked rolls, golden in color, often eaten for "kaffe"

deg — you

Du må reise, nå, Alt er ferdig. — You must leave now, everything is ready.

Er du sulten — Are you hungry

ekte Norsk Jul — authentic Norwegian Christmas

far — father

farvel — farewell

farina — cream of wheat

fiskekaker — fish cakes

flatbrød — a kind of cracker

frokost — breakfast

fryktlig — horrible

Fru — Mrs.

Gladelig Jul — Merry Christmas

god dag — a greeting, hello; literally, good day

god morgen — good morning

god tur — good trip, travel well

god kveld — good evening

Hardangersøm — Cut work embroidery originating in Hardanger, a region of Norway

Herr — Mr.

hjem, hjemmet — home

husmorskole — homemaker school

hvordan har du det — how are you

idag — today

ingenting — nothing

ja — yes; also used as an interjection, well or oh

jenter — girls

kaffe — coffee; also a kind of meal between a snack and lunch or a follow up to a dinner. Coffee is generally served, but tea or juice is also common as well as sweet and sometimes savory foods.

kjaere — Dear, a greeting on a letter to someone you know

kjærligst — beloved, dearest

knækebrød — thick cracker

kransekake — marzipan rings, stacked and decorated with flags

kveld — evening, *god kveld,* good evening

kveldsmat — literally evening food, light supper

kos deg — settle down, it's OK

koselig — comfortable, cozy

kyrke — church

kroner — Norwegian money

labskaus — lamb, potato and cabbage stew

lefse — soft, potato flatbread

lokken — onions

lyng — heather

mandelkake — almond cake

middag — dinner, main meal of the day

mor — mother

møltebær — cloudberries

nei da — certainly not, an exclamation

nei, neida — no, emphatically no

Norsk, Norwegian Ekte Norsk — truly or authentic Norwegian; "pure"

nå — now

Onkel — uncle

og — and

på — at or on

presten — minister, pastor. Until recently, Lutheranism was the state church of Norway.

rømmegrøt — sour cream porridge

rømmekolle — yogurt like peasant pudding

rugbrød — rye bread often with cardamom spice

rysngrøt — rice pudding

saft — fruit juice

seng — *bed*

saus — sauce

skikkelig — respectful

snakke — speak

sol side — sunny side

spekekjøtt — cured meat, often a lamb shank

stue — parlor or living room

sulten — hungry

sæter — summer passage for cows

takk — thank you, generally used with a modifier, e.g., *mange takk*, many thanks, or *tusen takk*, a thousand thanks, or *takk så meget,* thanks so much

takk for maten — thank you for the meal; literally, thank you for the food

takk for sist — greeting of respect; good to see you again; literally, thank you for the last time we were together

tante — aunt

Third Christmas Day — In devout homes, families numbered the days between December 25 and January 6, Twelfth Night.

tyttebær — Norwegian species similar to a cranberry

uff-da, also *uff a meg* — multi-purpose interjection; most commonly, oh, no or that's too bad.

vær så god — variously, dinner is ready, you are welcome, help yourself, please have some; literally, be so good as to…

velkommen — welcome

velkommen hjem — welcome home

CPSIA information can be obtained
at www.ICGtesting.com
Printed in the USA
LVHW051208300321
682936LV00019B/619

9 781645 380962